the

other
mother

also by matthew dicks

Memoirs of an Imaginary Friend

Something Missing

Unexpectedly Milo

The Perfect Comeback of Caroline Jacobs

Twenty-one Truths About Love

the

other
mother

matthew dicks

ST. MARTIN'S PRESS
NEW YORK

Published in the United States by St. Martin's Press, an imprint of St. Martin's Publishing Group

THE OTHER MOTHER. Copyright © 2019 by Matthew Dicks. All rights reserved. Printed in the United States of America. For information, address St. Martin's Publishing Group, 120 Broadway, New York, NY 10271.

www.stmartins.com

Designed by Devan Norman

Library of Congress Cataloging-in-Publication Data

Names: Dicks, Matthew, author.
Title: The other mother / Matthew Dicks.
Description: First U.S. Edition. | New York : St. Martin's Press, [2019] |
    "Originally published in Great Britain by Corsair, an imprint of Little,
    Brown Book Group, an Hachette UK company"—Title page verso. |
Identifiers: LCCN 2020024219 | ISBN 9781250103468 (hardcover) |
    ISBN 9781250103475 (ebook)
Subjects: LCSH: Psychological fiction. | GSAFD: Suspense fiction.
Classification: LCC PS3604.I323 O84 2019 | DDC 813/.6—dc23
LC record available at https://lccn.loc.gov/2020024219

Our books may be purchased in bulk for promotional, educational, or business use. Please contact your local bookseller or the Macmillan Corporate and Premium Sales Department at 1-800-221-7945, extension 5442, or by email at MacmillanSpecialMarkets@macmillan.com.

Originally published in Great Britain by Corsair, an imprint of Little, Brown Book Group, an Hachette UK company

First U.S. Edition: 2020

10 9 8 7 6 5 4 3 2 1

For Charlie

the

other
mother

one

This mother is not my mother. She looks like my mother. She looks exactly like my mother. Same curly brown hair with a little streak of gray on the side. Same pink slippers with a hole in the big toe. Same blotchy freckle on the back of her left hand. This woman is like my mother's twin. Her identical twin. But she is definitely not my mother.

"Hello?" My voice cracks, not because it's changing (though it is), but because I can't believe this is happening. It's impossible.

"Hi, honey," the woman says. She is standing over the stove, scrambling eggs. She stirs them the same way my mother does, by moving the pan and the spatula at the same time. The eggs dance in the pan. Just like my mother, she doesn't have to think about it. She makes them dance without even trying.

Still, this is not my mother.

"What's going on?" I ask. It's a dumb question, but I

don't know what else to say. I feel like I'm in a place where I don't belong. Like I've opened my eyes on some alternate universe.

"It's called breakfast, stupid."

Charlie says this. He's sitting at the table, drinking orange juice and reading a book. He's not wearing pants or shoes. Just underwear and the same blue shirt he had on yesterday.

Julia is sitting next to him with Mom's laptop on the table in front of her. She's staring at the screen. She's dressed already. T-shirt and jeans and sneakers. She's not a savage like Charlie.

I stare at Charlie and Julia. It's that wide-eyed stare I use when I don't want anyone else to hear me. Sort of like our own personal sign language. I'm yelling at them with my eyeballs. I'm practically screaming.

What the hell is going on here?

They don't even look at me. It's just a normal day for them. They must think this mother is our mother. She's tricked them, but I can't imagine how. Maybe it's because I'm fourteen and they're still in elementary school. Little kids are always easy to fool. It's why Charlie still thinks that a fairy flies into his room at night and steals his teeth from under his pillow in exchange for a quarter.

Honestly, I'm not sure if I ever believed that bullshit.

But how could they miss this? She looks exactly like our mother except *exactly not.*

I scan the kitchen. This can't be happening. This must be the wrong kitchen. It's a ridiculous thought, since Julia and Charlie are here, too, but it's all I can think of. I must be in the wrong place.

Still, everything seems right. The linoleum floor is cracked in the same patterns as our kitchen. The end of the counter is piled with the magazines that Mom says she'll read someday but never will. The drying rack is filled with glasses and plates that will go from table to sink to drying rack then back to table without ever making it back into a cabinet. The refrigerator is covered with the misshapen vegetable magnets that Charlie made in Cub Scouts last year. They're holding up one of Julia's spelling test (100 percent), expired appointment cards from doctors and dentists, coupons, a photo of Mom and Auntie Carole at some party last year, and a to-do list that I wrote about a year ago and haven't touched since.

It has just one item on it:

1. Don't

This was Mrs. Newfang's idea. She says that most of the time, the best thing for me to do is nothing. This doesn't apply to things like homework or chores, but I wish it would. It's a to-do list for when I'm feeling angry or sad or embarrassed. Whenever I get "emotionally charged," which is Mrs. Newfang's way of saying "pissed off." Instead of *do*, I should *don't*. Instead of acting *impulsively* (one of Mrs. Newfang's favorite words), I'm supposed to think first and do as little as possible.

Do nothing at all if possible.

I don't know if the to-do list has done any good, but I see it a dozen times a day, so maybe it's sunk in a little without me knowing it. Osmosis.

I look from the refrigerator to the pantry and then back

around to the table. It's all how it should be. I'm not in the wrong place. This is my kitchen. Everything is right except for the woman at the stove.

She is not my mother.

Anger fills me up. It fills me up *from my toes to my nose*, which is something my real mother would say. My hands ball into fists. I clench my teeth. My whole body gets tight. I don't think about doing these things. They just happen. It's like a switch is flipped inside me without my permission and I'm red, just like that. Just like all the times before. I don't want to be red, but it feels good to be red. It feels right to be red.

Why is this woman here?

Why am I the only one who can see that she isn't our mother?

What the hell is happening?

I say these words in my head, but they are still red words even if I don't say them out loud. I squeeze my fists even tighter.

I want my mother back.

These words surprise me.

I've wished my mother away a million times. I'm angry with her all the time. Nothing she does makes any sense to me. But I never wanted her to be replaced completely. I just wanted her to leave for a while. Get the hell out of my life. Take a vacation. Get her freakin' act together. That's all I really wanted. Go somewhere and learn how to be a real mother. And take Glen with her. This other mother is like the opposite of my wish. I wanted a better version of my own mother. The old version of my mother, really, before everything got ruined and she fell apart.

I don't want this new mother.

I stand still for a second, just being angry, *being full*, seeing all those red words, and wanting to hit something. Hit someone. Someone. I guess I was wrong. The to-do list isn't working. I don't want to *Don't*. I want to *Do*.

I count down from ten in my head and calm down a little.

I learned this counting thing from Mrs. Newfang, even though I knew the strategy from when I was little. Everyone knows this one. I went along and pretended to learn it because Mrs. Newfang likes to help me, and Mrs. Newfang and I have to spend three hours together every week—which is a long time—so I try to make it easy for her. And I like it when she smiles and says nice things to me like, "That's great, Michael. You are owning that strategy."

She actually says, "You're owning that strategy," but I do not like contractions. When I was little, I avoided them whenever possible. I use them a lot more now, mostly because people used to think I talked funny and made fun of me, which always made me angry, and I'm supposed to be trying to control my anger.

But I still do not like them.

Contractions are like fractions. They are messy. Not exact. Fractions like one-third are the worst. When you turn them into decimals, they never end. You have to draw a little line over the last three in 0.333 to tell people that the threes never stop. The little line is like a sign that says, "This number is crazy."

I am not crazy. I do not need a little line over me. I just do not like fractions or contractions. I like things to make sense. I just need to talk to Mrs. Newfang about stuff for three hours every week and take my medication and learn lots of strategies for when I get mad or sad or full.

No one in the kitchen has noticed that my hands are still balled into fists. Mom would've noticed. Mrs. Newfang taught her to notice, so she could help me *de-escalate* (another favorite word of Mrs. Newfang) before I do something stupid. This woman is definitely not my mother. Mom would be all over me.

Instead of hitting or throwing something or shouting at the woman stirring eggs (which I might have done three years ago and still want to do *right now*), I sit down beside Charlie. He is reading *The Zombie Survival Guide*. He has read this book a million times since he got it for Christmas last year. He doesn't really think that there will be a zombie invasion, but he likes to plan for all the ways that the world could come to an end. He's not a Boy Scout anymore, but he still believes in the Boy Scout motto—Be Prepared—more than anyone I know. He has canned food hidden on the top shelf of his closet that he thinks only he knows about, and a life jacket stuffed under his bed in case God decides to flood the world again. He got the life jacket from Santa last year, which really means that Mom bought it for him, which was kind of crazy. Just because a kid asks for a life jacket doesn't mean you should give him one.

I don't believe in God. I would like to believe in God and heaven and all that, but it just doesn't make any sense to me. It seems ridiculous. Babies die all the time. If there was a God, babies wouldn't die. Little kids, either.

Even so, I told Charlie that even God couldn't flood the world in one day. It would take a long time for all that rain to pile up, so a life jacket wouldn't help. He would need a boat like Noah, which is a bullshit story, too.

Even if Noah managed to squeeze every animal and every bug and every bird on his boat, which isn't possible, what about all the trees and the flowers? After forty days underwater, they'd all be dead.

"Maybe next time God won't give anyone a chance to build an ark," Charlie said. "Maybe it'll be quick. Like a flash flood. Then you'll wish you had a life jacket, too."

"Can't God just shoot lightning bolts at us if he wants?" I asked. "Wouldn't that be a lot easier than forty days of rain? And a lot more fun for him? Kind of like a giant video game."

"Don't be dumb," Charlie said. "Even if it's not another Noah's ark flood, I'm still ready for a regular flood. They happen all the time."

We have never had a flood in our town, but I let that one go. Sometimes you just have to stop fighting and move on.

Mrs. Newfang taught me this, too, and I think she's right. That doesn't mean it's easy, but with Charlie it's easier than most. I can't stand him most of the time, but I love him, too.

Julia is reading the box score from last night's Red Sox game on the ESPN website. They lost again. Even though Julia is a girl and a year younger than Charlie and five years younger than me, she pays more attention to sports than both of us combined. She can also throw and catch better than Charlie. The dumbass doesn't even care.

She throws and catches better than me, too, but at least I care.

"Did you talk to Mom this morning?" I whisper to Charlie.

Charlie keeps staring at his zombie book. He is reading a page about weapons. There is a cartoon drawing of a gun on the page.

I look back at the other mother. She's buttering toast now. She's left-handed, just like Mom. Or she's faking it. I wish I had a real gun right now. If I did, I could make her tell me where my real mother is.

I start to get angry again.

"Did you talk to Mom this morning?" I ask Charlie again, even softer this time.

"About what?" Charlie asks. He's still staring at his book.

"About anything. Did you talk to her?"

"Mom!" he calls out. "Did I talk to you this morning?"

"You're talking to me now." The other mother is using my real mother's voice, and she is saying what my real mother would say. It makes no sense. How could she so perfectly replace my mother? I feel like I'm trapped in some scary movie, but not a stupid one filled with blood and guts. A real one. The kind of scary that you secretly believe in even while you're trying not to. Like one of those old, black-and-white *Twilight Zone* shows.

I look at the other mother again. She is standing by the stove. Bacon is crackling and spitting in a pan. She's trying to flip it with metal tongs without getting burned. I look closely. Maybe this is my real mother. Maybe I'm just not all the way awake yet.

But I know this is not my mother. I know it deep down in my bones. I know it like I know that there was no ark filled with two of each animal and no Santa Claus delivering life jackets. I know it like I know that Charlie will not put his book down until someone takes it away or threatens to punish him. I know it like I know that even though Julia is the youngest of the three of us, she will have a boyfriend before Charlie has a girlfriend and maybe before I have a girlfriend.

I'm angrier now. I try counting back from ten again. It doesn't work. It's a stupid strategy. I want to ask this other mother where my real mother is. I want to know what she's done with her. But I'm too afraid to say anything. I'm afraid to know the answer, but I'm more afraid of what she might do if I ask. I'm afraid of what she might do if I stop pretending that she is my real mother.

I want to ask Julia if she noticed anything different about Mom, but thanks to my idiot brother, the other mother is listening now. I can't let her know that I know.

Asshole Glen walks into the kitchen. He is wearing his maroon bathrobe and probably nothing underneath it. I give him a hard look. I want to know if he has been replaced, too. If he is the other Glen.

He's not. He's still just Asshole Glen. Shaped like a walking baby, all pale and pudgy. He says he was a basketball player in high school, but I don't believe him. He's got squinty eyes and a mustache and beard. He's going bald. He combs his hair over the spot, but it only makes him look like more of an asshole.

I wish he had been replaced.

I watch to see if Glen can tell that this is the other mother. Except to Glen, she would be the other wife.

The other stepwife, really. That's what I call Mom sometimes. If I have to be a stepson, she has to be a stepwife.

I only call her that in my head, though. Never out loud.
I say a lot of things in my head. Mrs. Newfang says this is
a problem. I'm supposed to talk about my feelings more.
But I think I would have a lot more problems if I said what
I thought.

Asshole Glen doesn't realize that this is the other mother.
He grabs a slice of toast from the plate on the counter and
eats with one hand while he takes the other mother by the
waist and pulls her close. He's wearing brown slippers.

I hate this. It makes my stomach turn just thinking that
his hands are touching my mother, except now his hands
are on the other mother, so I don't care so much. I wish
Glen would run away with the other mother and leave me
and Charlie and Julia behind. Then all my problems would
be solved.

Not really, but at least it would be a start. Getting rid of
Asshole Glen would be a great start.

"What are you guys doing today?" Glen asks. He is eating eggs from the frying pan with a fork.

"Fishing!" Charlie says.

I say nothing.

Julia says nothing.

"All three of you?" Glen asks.

"Yup," Charlie says.

"I have a softball game tonight if you want to go," Glen
says. "You could be the batboy if you want, Michael."

*You haven't been to a single one of my Little League games
this year, and you think I'm going to go to your stupid-ass softball game?*

I say this in my head, too. More red words.

"No, thanks," Julia says. She is answering for me because

she knows how I feel. She does this for me a lot. Otherwise she would've said nothing, too.

"Breakfast is ready, guys and gals," the other mother says, just like my mother would. "Help yourself."

I will not be eating eggs today. Not from a pan where Asshole Glen has already stuck his fork. Not from a mother who is not my mother. My mother's eggs are good. These eggs only look good.

I eat toast instead. I stare at my feet. All of this is too strange. I should be calling the police and asking for help, except no one would believe me. If Julia and Charlie and Glen can't see the other mother, a policeman won't be able to see her either.

I'm suddenly glad that I'm still a kid. A teenager, really, but close enough. Stuff like this can happen to kids. Weird shit like moms being replaced by other mothers. If I were a grown-up, I'd have to be crazy right now. Mysteries and magic don't happen to old people unless they're losing their minds. If I was an adult, I'd probably call the police, and they would take me away to the funny farm, which isn't funny at all. Only kids and grown-ups in books and movies could believe that something like this could be happening without going crazy.

I see Mrs. Newfang for three hours every week, but it's not because I'm crazy (even though this asshole in my class named Luke said I was). I see her because I need to learn strategies. I need to learn "to see what people need from me." That's what Mrs. Newfang calls it. She says I need to learn to notice when someone is sad or angry or afraid so I'll know how to behave. Know how to treat them.

I'm not sure if she's right. I think I see all those things

just fine. I just make bad choices. I do dumb stuff and say dumb stuff.

Charlie fills his plate with eggs and toast as the other mother and Asshole Glen head upstairs. I hope they don't make loud sex like Mom and Asshole Glen do, because I'm not in the mood to hear it this morning. I have too many problems.

1. My mom is missing.
2. She has been replaced by this other mother.
3. I'm scared.
4. My brother is stupid.
5. Asshole Glen is still my stepfather.
6. Sarah Flaherty lives next door.
7. I have three detentions next week.
8. Brian Marcotte will be waiting for me to do the thing next week.
9. I don't have enough strategies to keep from getting full.
10. Today is payday.
11. The letter in the yellow envelope won't stop being real.

two

I tell Charlie to finish his eggs and meet us in the driveway. Julia and I pull the bikes from the garage and stuff fishing tackle into old pickle buckets.

I used to love the garage. It smells like oil and old books. The shelves are filled with camping and fishing gear and tools of all kinds, and there is a ladder to a small loft where I used to hide when I couldn't stand the world anymore. I would sit up there above my father's old cars and read books and eat potato chips. It was my place.

Not anymore. Ever since I found the letter in the yellow envelope, I can't stand being in the garage for a second longer than I need to be. The place feels like it's haunted. I can't even come in here at night. Even in the morning sunshine, I move as fast as I can to get our gear together.

"Hi, Sarah!" Julia shouts as I'm hanging buckets from the handlebars.

I turn. Sarah Flaherty is standing on the edge of her driveway. "Hi, Julia!" she shouts back.

Sarah Flaherty is the girl next door. She has long blond hair and brown eyes, but it's her face that makes her pretty. And her smile. It's friendly. It makes you think that she likes you even if she barely knows you. She has freckles, too, and I love freckles.

It isn't easy having a popular girl living next door. Instead of worrying about what I look like every second while I'm at school, now I need to worry about what I look like every second at home, too. Like right now. It's so early in the morning that I thought I'd be safe, but apparently not. I'm wearing dirt-stained jeans that are a little too short for me (*high waters*, a kid at school called them) and a stained white T-shirt.

I look terrible at the worst possible moment to look terrible.

My friend Jeff says I'm lucky to live next door to Sarah because he thinks I have a chance of seeing her half-naked someday when she runs outside to get the mail, thinking no one is looking. Jeff is a dumbass. Girls don't just walk out of their houses half-naked, and especially for something as stupid as the mail. And what does half-naked mean anyway? Topless? Bottomless? Underwear and a bra?

It makes a difference.

"Hi, Mike!" Sarah shouts.

Everyone calls me Michael except for Sarah. She's the only one in the world who calls me Mike. I always correct people who call me Mike or even worse Mikey (I find myself wanting to punch those people in the face), but I don't correct Sarah.

I wave back without really looking and turn around and go back inside to get Charlie. All I want to do is wait inside until Sarah is gone. Maybe she'll forget how stupid I looked by Monday.

Charlie is still sitting at the table reading his book. His plate and cup are empty. I can hear the sex sounds coming from upstairs, but this time it's the other mother and Glen, so it doesn't bother me much. It only bothers me because Charlie can hear it.

Except Charlie is reading, so he probably can't hear anything. A parade of elephants could march right through the kitchen and he wouldn't notice if his head was in a book.

Then it hits me. As long as the other mother and Glen are having sex, I can check the downstairs for my mother. I don't really think Mom is tied up in a closet or locked in the basement. I don't think she is anywhere in the house at all. I can't explain it, but it's the same way I know that the other mother is not my mother even though she looks exactly like my mother. I just know.

Still, I want to look. Better safe than sorry, especially when things are as fucked up as this. When your mother is missing, cover all the bases.

A new rule.

I don't say anything to Charlie. I let him read as I go through every room, opening closets and cupboards and looking underneath furniture.

Nothing.

There's no way Mom was jammed under the couch or stuffed behind the easy chair, but I look anyway. In the movies, it's always the place you don't look that holds the key to everything.

Then I go to the basement door. I hate the basement. It has three yellow bulbs that swing from cords in the ceiling and a dirt floor. It smells like worms and old leaves. I don't know if I will hear Glen and the other mother in the basement, but I hear them now and it usually doesn't last a long time. I need to check the basement. I know that Mom isn't down there, but I feel like should check anyway.

I open the door. I flip the switch. The yellow bulbs turn the black at the bottom of the stairs to a burned-yellow smudge. I walk down the thirteen steps to the bottom. I hate that there are thirteen steps. It's the worst number for basement stairs. I skip the last step to make it twelve, even though the universe still knows that it's thirteen.

The basement has a big room and a small room in the back. The big room is empty. The dirt floor gets wet sometimes, so we can't put boxes of old toys or winter clothes down here because they would end up getting wet and smelling like dirt. The walls are concrete, with pictures of hearts and smiley faces and little messages drawn in pink and white chalk.

MD + EG

BJ luvs GG

Red Sox Rule!

Yaz!

Don't Squeeze the Charmin! (I still don't know what that one means.)

The chalk drawings were here when Mom and Dad bought the house. I think of them as fossils of people who lived here before us. People who chose to spend time in this basement.

Clearly lunatics.

The small room in the back has a concrete floor. It has a furnace, a water heater, and an old furnace-like thing that is gigantic and reddish-brown. Dad once told me that it's an old coal furnace. It has an iron door on the front that looks like a mouth and two old dials that look like eyes. We call it Robo because it looks like the oldest, stupidest robot ever invented. Robo stares at me when I enter the small room. I feel a little bad for him even though he's not actually a robot, and even if he was a robot, robots don't need anyone feeling bad for them either because they're just machines.

Still, I can't help it. Sometimes fake things can feel as real as real things.

I look behind Robo and the furnace and the water heater. It's the only place down here where my mom could be. I find some copper pipes, a shovel and a screwdriver.

My mother would never fit inside Robo, but I decide to check anyway. I feel like I need to rule out all possibilities, just like the cops say on TV. I swing open his mouth. It screeches on its hinges. Robo is black inside. I lean forward and peek in. It smells like a rusty forest fire. A bloody forest fire. I exhale, and the sound of my breath echoes in his belly.

I lean in. I stick my whole head inside Robo's mouth. It's the bravest thing I've done in a while.

No Mom.

As I pull my head back out, I notice the shovel again. It looks new. The screwdriver, too. I've never seen either one before, but I don't come down here often. Only on dares from Charlie and Dad when Dad was not dead. I turn and look back into the big room. I look at the dirt floor. It looks just like it has always looked, but I've never really paid attention to the floor before. If the other mother did something terrible to Mom, she could've buried Mom here under the dirt floor.

That is what I am thinking now. Mom is buried under the basement floor. I don't believe it really happened, but I try to imagine it happening because it's possible.

Imagining the possible—especially when it's terrible—is something I do a lot.

When we flew to Florida three years ago, I imagined what it would be like if the plane crashed. I tried to picture all the different ways that the plane might hit the ground or break up in the sky. Belly first. Nose first. Water landing. Crashing into a mountain. I tried to envision those oxygen masks falling and the people screaming and praying just before impact. I didn't think it would happen, but I wanted to know what it would be like if it did.

I wanted to be prepared.

I guess I'm as much of a Boy Scout as Charlie.

I hate the unknown. I'd rather know all the terrible maybes than ignore them or pretend that they will never happen. I like to predict the possibilities. Also, I have a hard time not thinking of something. I can't put things out of my mind like Mom and Mrs. Newfang constantly tell me to do. I perseverate, which means getting stuck in a loop like that movie *Groundhog Day*. The same movie plays over and over again in my mind. Since I can't stop it from playing, I focus on it instead. I stare right at it. It's kind of like daring it to continue.

I do this with the good possibilities, too. Not just plane crashes and missing mothers. Like imagining having sex with Sarah Flaherty. It will never happen, but it's still nice to imagine.

I know what you're supposed to do in sex, but I don't know anything about the girl parts in real life. We saw pictures in health class, but no girl looks like a pencil drawing under her underwear.

Jeff's big brother says that girl parts are complicated, but the girl will help when you have sex, so you don't really need to know what's going on down there. "She'll guide you," he said. But I hate looking dumb and not knowing stuff, and I would really hate to look dumb while I'm naked. That seems like the worst part of sex: the nakedness. I wouldn't mind the girl being naked, but there's no way I want to be naked. I don't even like being naked by myself.

I don't have to worry about any of that, though, because it's impossible for someone like me to have sex with someone like Sarah Flaherty.

But this buried-in-the-basement idea is possible. If you can replace someone so perfectly and fool everyone in the house except me, you could probably bury a person in the basement.

I get the shivers. The basement is scarier than it has ever been. I walk to the stairs. I try to walk slowly and calmly, but the closer I get to the first step, the faster I walk. I am running by the time I start climbing the stairs. Something is going to reach between the wooden steps and grab my ankle so I lift my feet high and pump my elbows. I know that running is the worst thing you can do in a situation like this. People who walk up the basement stairs are never in danger of being dragged back down. Only scared people get caught by scary things. But I can't help it. It is a basement with yellow lights and a dirt floor and maybe my mom buried underneath.

I slam the door when I get to the top.

Sunlight. Just like that, it's another world. Like everything in the basement is a million miles away in an instant. There is no way my mom is buried in the basement. That would be crazy. This whole other mother thing is crazy. I'm imagining the whole thing. Kids might believe in magic, and believing in magic might not make them crazy, but that doesn't make the magic real.

I almost believe this. Then I find the other mother is in the kitchen, washing the pan that she used to make eggs. Still not Mom. Not even close.

"You all set?" she asks me.

"What?"

"You need anything?" she asks. "For fishing?"

"No," I say. "Thank you."

Charlie looks at me when I say "Thank you." It occurs to me that I would never say this to my real mother. I need to be careful. Act normal.

"Okay, then," she says. "Be safe."

My real mother would never say that, either. It's like we are dancing with words. Trying to see what fits with what.

"Thanks," I say.

Charlie looks again. Eyebrows scrunched. It's his way of saying, *What the fuck is going on here?*

I grab Charlie's book from his hand and walk to the door. Grabbing Charlie's book is the best way to get him moving. Like getting a dog to follow by waving a bone.

If we had a dog, I bet he would know that this is not my real mother. Dogs can sense those kinds of things. They can sniff out drugs in suitcases and dead people buried in basements.

When I get back to the driveway, Julia is standing beside Sarah Flaherty. The two are straddling their bikes. Sarah Flaherty is *in my driveway*. A pickle bucket is hanging off Sarah's handlebar.

"Sarah's coming with us!" Julia says.

"I hope it's okay?" Sarah says.

"Yuck!" Charlie shouts, running to catch up to me. "Fishing's supposed to be for boys!"

"Shut up," I say. I turn and throw *The Zombie Survival Guide* at him. It hits him on the chest.

"If it's going to be a problem . . ." Sarah says.

"No problem," I say. "Sounds good."

But it is a problem. The last thing I need is Sarah Flaherty fishing with me. Especially when my mom might be dead and maybe buried in the basement.

three

Sometimes I can want two opposite things at the same time. I don't know if that's normal, and I can't ask anyone if it's normal. I can ask Jeff about curveballs (which he says he can throw but can't) or the quadratic formula or cheat codes or even sex with girls, but I can't ask him if he ever wants something and the opposite thing at the same time. That's just not a question people ask.

I wish I could, though, because the whole time we were dragging the canoes down to the shore I was thinking about how nice it would be to ride in the canoe with Sarah. Amazing, even. But I knew I would have to ride with Charlie, and not just because he thinks girls have cooties. He and Julia are too young to go in the same boat, and I'm the big brother, so it's up to me to look after them (something Mom reminds me about a thousand times a week). But I was also happy to be going with Charlie because I was nervous about being alone in a canoe with Sarah. I was worried that I wouldn't know what to say and afraid that I wouldn't have anything to say at all.

At the same time, though, a part of me wished that it was just me and Sarah in the canoe.

When you want two opposite things at the same time, you're never happy no matter what you get.

The pond isn't like the ones I see in the movies. The water isn't clear. The sunlight doesn't twinkle on the ripples. There's no sandy beach or tire swing. The water is mostly green with lily pads and patches of gunk floating on the surface. I know the gunk is algae, but gunk is a much better word for it. Easier to spell, too.

This is not a swimming pond. It's not even a sit-by-the-shore pond. Glen calls it a good-for-nothing pond. He's wrong, but I know why he thinks this. It's mostly green and gross. It smells a little bit like dead things. It's the kind of place that adults avoid. All of this is great, though, because it makes the pond ours.

Sarah is sitting in the back of the canoe behind Julia. She's wearing a flowery bathing-suit top and jean shorts. When she pulled her T-shirt over her head before climbing into the canoe, I knew there would be a bathing-suit top underneath, but still. A girl took her shirt off in front of me. Not a sister. A real girl. It was one of those times when I felt like a secret corner of the world unfolded and made the universe ten times bigger.

I can hear the girls talking across the water. Sarah has never been fishing before, so Julia is explaining the difference between using worms and lures. "Boys like to use lures because it means you get to cast and reel constantly. They love that kind of stuff. Boys can never sit still." They laugh.

I catch a peek at Julia as she turns. She's beaming. She's made Sarah Flaherty laugh. I'd be beaming, too. "I use worms because I know how to sit still and be patient," Julia says. "And because you can catch more fish with worms."

Julia's not wrong, but I had never realized this until just now.

I don't know why Sarah is interested in any of this, but it looks like she's paying attention. She's probably just being nice. Girls understand how to be nice much better than boys. They understand how to be fake nice, too. And mean nice. The kind of nice that really hurts. The kind that kills you slowly but can't be seen and never be proven.

Boys are like rocks. Girls are like shark fins.

Charlie is sitting at the front of our boat. He's quiet. He has a paddle in his hand, but he's barely using it. He's stuck in his head. That's how Mom describes it. Charlie spends a lot of time stuck in his head. I don't mind. I get stuck in my head a lot, too. Charlie is a giant pain in the ass, but at times like this, we're good together. We can just sit and think without talking or annoying each other.

It's good because even though I know that the other mother is just some weird trick that my brain is playing on me, I can't stop thinking about her. I can't understand how I can be so sure that the other mother is really just my mother and at the same time be so sure that she is not. It's like my brain is divided into two parts. Like it wants two things at the same time. The part of my brain like everyone else's brain knows that mothers can't be replaced by identical other mothers, but the part of my brain that makes me different than everyone else knows that the woman making eggs in the kitchen this morning was not my mother.

There's a rock on the tip of the island where we go ashore. It's wide and flat and an easy place to beach the canoes. We call it Little Round Top. I have no idea how it got its name. It's not little, and it's definitely not round. My uncle called it Little Round Top when he brought me here for the first time five years ago.

It feels like five hundred years ago.

The canoes belong to my aunt and uncle, except that my uncle is dead and my aunt is losing her marbles. "Losing her marbles" is what Asshole Glen says, but I'm not sure if it's true. She just misses Uncle Norman all the time, and that makes her look a little lost. But missing a person is different than missing parts of your brain, even though it probably looks about the same.

I've heard Mom talk about moving Auntie Carole to something called assisted living, but Auntie says no. I don't blame her. Assisted living sounds like polite prison, but a prison is still a prison, even if it comes with a flower garden and bingo night. I think Auntie Carole knows it too, because she seems to have all her marbles every time Mom brings it up.

I'm glad. As long as she still lives in the big blue house on the pond, we can use the canoes and visit the island whenever we want.

Charlie and I reach the island first. I climb out of the canoe and pull it onto Little Round Top. Charlie is out of the boat fast and running through the forest before I've finished tying the boat to a tree. He reminds me of those boys in *Lord of the Flies*. He's a quiet kid in the real world, but when he gets to the island, he's a madman.

"Be careful!" I shout.

"I'm seizing my day!" he shouts back.

A minute later, Sarah and Julia arrive. I splash into the water to help them come ashore. I grab the bow of their canoe and pull. It's heavy. Heavier than I expected. I want to ask Sarah to climb out so I can drag the boat all the way up the rock, but I don't. I want to look strong in front of Sarah. It's ridiculous, because Sarah will never be my girlfriend, no matter how strong I am, but I still want to impress her. Mom would say that I'm "banging my head against a wall," and it's true, but I can't help it. Maybe it's a guy thing.

I've heard that expression lots of times before, too—"It's a guy thing"—but it's always said about things that I don't do. Like collecting baseball cards or making armpit fart noises, which I can't do even though I've practiced for hours.

When we were hiking in New Hampshire last summer, Asshole Glen refused to ask the other hikers where the blue trail started, so it took us over an hour just to get started up the mountain. Julia finally found the marker, though Charlie still claims to this day that he spotted it first. Mom said that not asking for directions is a guy thing.

I thought it was a stupid thing.

Maybe wanting to impress a pretty girl who will never like me is my first "guy thing" thing. And maybe a stupid thing, too.

Julia climbs out of the front of the boat as soon as it's clear of the water and sprints off into the trees, crashing through bushes and ducking under tree limbs. She wants to catch up to Charlie. She doesn't want him to steal her favorite spot.

Sarah and I are alone.

It's a small island. Tiny, really. Long and thin and pointy at the ends. Shaped kind of like a canoe. You can walk from tip to tip in about ten minutes, and that's only because it's overgrown with trees and bushes and prickers.

"Does this island have a name?" Sarah asks as I tie the canoe to a tree.

"We call it Barracuda Island."

"Why Barracuda?"

"I'm not sure," I say. "My uncle used to take me here when I was little, and he said the water around the island was filled with barracuda. I believed him until I learned about barracuda in a book. Maybe it's because the island is shaped kind of like a barracuda."

"Or maybe your uncle made the whole thing up," Sarah said. "Uncles like to terrorize their nieces and nephews."

"Maybe. He died, so I can't ask him."

"I'm sorry," Sarah says. Her voice changes when she says this. Her whole face changes. She shrinks. I'm so annoyed with myself. She was happy just a second ago. We were talking, and I wasn't even thinking about talking. I was just doing it, the same way I talk to Jeff. Then I had to mention a dead person and ruin everything.

"It's okay," I say. "He died a while ago." It takes me too long to say this, so now she's looking at me like I'm broken and stupid.

"Still," she says, "I'm sorry." She looks down at her feet. "Dying is the worst."

I nod. I nod slowly because that's the cool way to nod, but I want to nod fast enough to knock my head right off my shoulders. I want to nod in the way that screams, *Yes! I agree! You're right! My God! You're right!*

And just like that, I feel like I should tell Sarah about Dad. Like I *can* tell her. Like a door is open and I can step right through. It's the first time that door to my dad has ever felt open. I can already feel the weight slowing lifting off my chest.

I'm about to open my mouth, to say words I can't yet imagine, when Sarah speaks. "Should we follow Julia and Charlie?"

Just like that, the door slams shut, if it had ever been open in the first place.

"Let me get the gear first," I say. I turn away so she can't see my face. "We can't fish without poles and tackle."

"Do they always abandon you like this?"

"I don't mind." I pull the buckets from the bottom of my canoe. "They're excited, and they stink at lugging the gear."

"You're a good big brother."

"Or just a big, fat sucker," I say.

Sarah laughs. I've never made a pretty girl laugh before. It's fantastic. I want to do it again for the rest of my life.

I carry the pickle buckets full of tackle and worms. Sarah carries the poles. I lead the way through the trees.

"No path?"

"Nope," I say. "I mean, not really. It's not a real path. Just a way to get to the other side of the island without running into the big patches of prickers. No one comes here except us."

I push through the brush, making sure not to send any branches whipping back at Sarah. For a few moments, the sun disappears behind a canopy of leaves and branches overhead. The air seems warmer. More humid. It really is like *Lord of the Flies* for a minute.

"How much farther?" Sarah asks. She feels it, too. We've disappeared into another world.

"Just around this next bend," I say.

We step out of the trees on to a small patch of flattened grass and dirt. Near the water, the grass falls away to a muddy bank that drops off about three feet into the pond. Charlie and Julia are sitting on the edge of the bank, throwing stones into the water.

Julia is sitting on her favorite rock. I knew she would be. She always gets what she wants, at least when it comes to her and Charlie. It would be nice to think that Charlie lets her win, but he doesn't. She's just faster and smarter than he is.

"Hey, idiots," I say. "You want to scare away all the fish?"

"Told you," Julia says. She elbows Charlie in the ribs.

I'm worried again. We only have three fishing poles. If Julia offers to share her pole with Sarah, then the two of them will be stuck together like glue all day along. Part of me wouldn't mind this because sharing a fishing pole with Sarah scares the hell out of me, but a lot more of me thinks that sharing a fishing pole with Sarah Flaherty might be the greatest thing that has ever happened to me.

I'm in luck. Julia and Charlie have made a bet about who will catch the most fish today, so Julia can't afford to waste a second sharing her pole with anyone. In our family, every bet comes with a wager. It's Dad's rule. "A bet without a wager is just talk, and talk is cheap." Today's wager is dessert, which is one we use a lot. Within a minute, Charlie and Julia have hooks in the water, waiting for the first bite.

I teach Sarah how to fish. We have plenty of worms, but I decide to use lures. Julia's right. Casting and reeling is the best thing about fishing. Even better than catching fish. Plus I don't want Sarah to see me baiting a hook. Watching me slide worms on to hooks, watching them wriggle and smear black guts on my fingers, won't impress her one bit, so I take out a yellow and black lure instead. It's harder to catch fish with a lure, but if we do catch one, it won't be a kiver or a perch. It'll probably be a bass. A bigger fish. An impressive fish.

"We're going to use a lure that moves," I tell Sarah. "The sun is still too low for my shiners."

"What's a shiner?"

I take a lure out of my tackle box. It's silver with a metallic tail. "This is a shiner," I say. "My favorite one."

Sarah takes it in her hands. She turns it over.

"Shiners reflect the sun," I explain. "They attract fish with their reflections. When the sun is low, shiners are no good. That's the time to use movers. Movers are lures that jump around in the water. Some of them even make noise underwater. The trick is to find the right lure at the right time for the right fish."

"So you get them with either your looks or your moves?"

"Yeah," I say, smiling. "I guess. There are lures for different kinds of fish, too, and if we were fishing in the weeds, there are lures that won't get hung up in the gunk, but we won't worry about any of that for a while."

"There's a lot to know," Sarah says.

"I never thought of it that way, but I guess you're right. When you spend years learning something, it doesn't look so complicated, but for someone who's never held a rod before, it's a lot. But *looks* or *moves* is a good way to think about it for now."

"Sounds a lot like flirting," Sarah says. "Like you're flirt-ing with the fish."

I laugh, even as it occurs to me that I don't have any looks or moves.

I know that guys are supposed to have moves. Stuff that makes girls swoon, which is a word that Dad used to say when he was trying to impress Mom. "Am I making you swoon, honey?" he would say.

Mom would always smile and say, "Not one bit, my dear."

Guys in the movies always have moves to make girls swoon. Sometimes their moves make no sense, like when that guy held up a boom box in that movie that Julia watches whenever it comes on cable. He blasted a terrible song about eyes to get the girl, and somehow it worked. But I've never even seen a boom box in real life, and no girl is going to hear my phone blasting through its tiny speakers from the street. Besides, that move is already taken. It would be like some guy telling a girl, "You complete me."

You can only pull that shit off once.

I'm not exactly winning in the looks department. I'm not ugly, but I know that I'm nothing special to look at. I'm scrawny as hell and short compared with most of the boys in my grade. My head is way too big for my body. Mom says that I'll fill out eventually, but "eventually" is the kind of word that adults use to try to make you feel better. It never works. "Eventually" might as well be forever, because that's exactly how it feels to kids.

To everyone, really. No one in the history of the world has ever gotten excited over "eventually."

I show Sarah how to cast and reel. Our hands touch as

I teach her how to pinch the line to the pole. I show her how to make the lure move underwater. "Make it dance like the devil in the pale moonlight," my uncle used to say, but I don't. Some things sound good when they come out of an adult's mouth but stupid when they come out of a kid's mouth.

Sarah is about to cast for the first time when Julia shouts, "Got one!" Her red and white bobber disappears underwater.

"Big deal," Charlie shouts. "Every squirrel has lucky nuts."

Julia laughs. She may only be nine, but she understands all the balls jokes.

Sarah giggles, too.

"Even a blind squirrel can find a nut!" I shout. "You're such an idiot."

"Yeah. That's what I meant," Charlie says. He turns to Julia, who is pulling a small perch from the water. It flaps and twists at the end of the line. I love fishing, but there's always a moment when the fish first appears above the water line when I feel terrible about what I've done. I can't imagine being suddenly plucked from my universe into an entirely different one, and one without any air to breathe.

I told this to Dad once, and he said I shouldn't worry. Fish have tiny brains. They have no language, so they can't even think about what's happening to them. "They experience life one second at a time, and none of those seconds are connected. They don't even know how to be afraid."

I wasn't sure if I should believe him. I'm less sure today.

"We should've made perch worth two fish," Julia says. "Since all you ever catch is kivers."

"What's a kiver?" Sarah asks.

"A sunfish," I say. "A bluegill. They have a lot of names. But mostly they're trash fish. Worth nothing."

Dad called them trash fish. It feels weird using his words now.

"They're so dumb that you can catch the same one over and over again," Julia says. "And *some people* count that as a new fish every time."

"It *is* a new fish," Charlie says. "You can't tell two kivers apart."

"Yeah right," Julia says. "I've seen you release a kiver and then catch it again five seconds later."

"It's not my fault the fish like my hook better than yours."

"You're just a big, fat cheater. But I'm—"

"Hey! I got one!" Charlie's bobber disappears and his pole flexes slightly under the weight of the fish. He reels and grunts, pretending to fight with something that probably weighs less than a pound. A second later, the fish pops out of the water, flapping on the end of the line. It's about the size of my hand.

"Kiver!" Julia shouts.

"I don't care," Charlie says. "It's a fish. We're tied!"

By the time the score is six to six (with Charlie catching the same kiver at least three times according to Julia), Sarah and I have moved to a rock on the backside of the island. Not too far away. We can still hear Charlie and Julia yapping at each other, but it's a lot less annoying from this distance.

Sarah might be a stuck-in-your-head person, too. We sit for ten minutes, taking turns casting and reeling without saying a word. We fall into a routine, passing the pole back and forth like we've done this a million times before. I feel like I should pinch myself. Like today is an impossible day. Mom is replaced by another woman and Sarah Flaherty is fishing on Barracuda Island with me.

I'm not sure which one is less likely.

"Maybe we should switch to worms," I finally say after Julia catches her seventh fish and takes the lead. We haven't caught a single thing.

"No," Sarah says, casting the line. She's gotten good at it. She already has distance and aim. It's a little annoying. I liked the idea of being the expert. I wanted to impress her with my skills, but she's almost as good as me already. "I like this. It's fun just to cast. Better than sitting, waiting for one of those stupid bobbers to move."

"Okay," I say. "But let's switch lures. The sun is all the way up now. Something shiny might help."

I show her how to tie the new lure on to the end of a line. "The hardest part is getting the line though the loop," I explain. I hold the lure out in front of my face, close one eye, and slide the line through on the first try. "Here," I say, handing her a lure from the tackle box. "Careful for the hooks."

Her hands are small compared to mine. They don't have all the scratches and scabs that mine do. They look brand new, except for the nails. Bitten to the nubs, just like Julia's. It takes her a minute, but finally she gets the line to pass through the loop.

"Okay," she says. "Now what?"

I show her how to tie the knot. She follows along, step by step, matching me loop for loop. I have to start over once, but that's only because Sarah has to shoo away a bumble bee mid-knot.

"All right," I say. "Don't tighten anything yet. First, you need to wet the line before you pull it tight." I place the knot into my mouth, only realizing once it's beyond my lips how gross this probably seems.

"You can dip your line in the water," I say. "It just needs to be wet before you tighten the knot. It helps it to hold better."

Sarah opens her mouth and places her untightened knot inside. She smiles.

"You like this," I say, "don't you?"

"Yeah. I kind of do," she says. "I'm surprised. When Julia asked me to come, I got excited, but I wasn't sure why. I don't even like to eat fish. Maybe just something new? I don't know. And I can't believe we came out to this island by ourselves. No life jackets or anything. If my mother knew where I was and how I got here, she'd kill me."

"I can get away with stuff like this," I say. "My mom is like the opposite of a helicopter parent."

"Yeah? What's the opposite of a helicopter parent?"

"She's more like a Hubble space telescope parent. Positioned as far away as possible and always looking in the other direction."

Sarah smiles, but there is a sad look in her eyes, too. She gets it.

Just like that, the mention of Mom puts the other mother back in my head. Standing by the stove, stirring those goddamn eggs.

"Does your mom know you're here?" Sarah asks.

"She knows."

"And Charlie and Julia, too?"

"Yup," I say. "I guess she knows that I would never let anything happen to them." I smile. "Unless they deserved it."

"I think it's kind of sweet, trusting you to take care of Charlie and Julia. Your stepdad trusts you, too?"

I laugh. "I don't think my stepfather even notices me unless I forget to bring out the trash."

"Well, your mom trusts you, and mothers know that kind of stuff. They can feel it in their bones."

"She may trust me, but I sometimes wonder why. What the hell do I know?"

"You seem to be doing a good job," Sarah says. "Charlie and Julia listen to you. They look up to you."

"Not always. Sometimes it's like pulling teeth. And sometimes it would be nice to just be a kid again and not have to worry about them."

I feel like I said too much. I've accidentally said something I think but never say. Not even to Mrs. Newfang. But Sarah just stares at me, waiting for me to say more. "It sounds crazy," I say, speaking slowly. Trying on the words for size. "But sometimes I wish my mom had a little more helicopter in her. I don't feel all that responsible. I'm actually pretty irresponsible most of the time. And I want to be irresponsible. I don't want to have to worry all the time. I feel like I'm the last person who should be in charge of anyone."

"How come?"

She passes the pole back to me. It's my turn to cast. This gives me a second to think, which is good because I've fallen into a word trap. Mrs. Newfang sets these traps all the time. She gets me talking about one thing, and then, before I know it, I say something big and important. I give away a secret or tell her how I'm feeling even though I didn't want her to know. The only difference is that I can ignore Mrs. Newfang if I don't want to answer her questions. I can stare at the wall or my feet until she asks me something different. But here on this rock, I can't just ignore Sarah's question and say nothing. Sarah asked why I'm the last person who should be responsible for other people. There are a million answers to the question, and one really big answer, and they're all true, but I don't want to say any of them.

"I don't know," I say after I cast the line. "I guess I've got my own things to worry about."

"Like what?"

Another word trap. A question that requires a hard-to-say answer. I know she doesn't mean it, but it's frustrating. I decide to just say it. "I'm not exactly a good role model. I don't behave good at school all the time."

"I know," Sarah says.

"You do?"

"We're in the same school, remember?"

"Yeah," I say. "But not the same classes."

"Stuff gets around."

"What kind of stuff?"

Sarah smiles. "You punched your bus driver for starters."

"I didn't punch him," I say, a little too fast. "I shoved him."

I shoved his face, but I leave out that detail.

"You threw the cash register on to the floor. I was actually in the cafeteria for that one."

"They wouldn't give me lunch. I was hungry. I got angry. I got hangry."

Actually, I got *full*, which is a combination of angry and sad and embarrassed and sometimes other stuff, too. No one knows about me being full. It's my secret thing. Mrs. Newfang hasn't tricked me into telling her about that yet, but she probably knows a little bit about it already.

What I don't tell Sarah is that I was supposed to be a free lunch kid because Mom and Glen don't make enough money. But I didn't want to be a free lunch kid anymore, so I threw all the applications away and told Mom we didn't qualify anymore. Then she kept forgetting to send in the check because there was no money to send. So I got angry and pushed the cash register off the counter.

"And the office windows?" Sarah asks.

"One window. It was kind of an accident. I meant to scare the office ladies. Not actually break the window. I just threw my algebra book too hard."

"Okay," Sarah says. "But that kind of stuff gets around."

"I didn't know," I say. I really didn't.

"It's okay," Sarah says. "Everyone has something."

I wonder what Sarah's something is, but I don't ask. That would be a word trap, and I don't set word traps, even when I want to know something more than anything.

"Okay," I say. "So knowing all that and stuff you probably haven't even mentioned yet, would you put me in charge of these two little kids all day long? Let me take them to this island in canoes?"

"Before today, no way," Sarah says. "I kind of thought it was crazy right from the start. I wondered if I should even be with you." Then she smiles. "But now? Yes. I would. I see what your mother sees in you. She's a smart lady."

I think three things at the exact same time.

1. I love Sarah Flaherty.
2. Sarah Flaherty likes me. Not like likes me, but she thinks I'm okay, which only two or three people in the whole world think right now.
3. Sarah Flaherty only knows the tip of the iceberg about me, and that's a good thing. I want to keep it that way.

She casts the line. The lure plops in the water. She reels it in, slowly, just like I showed her. I've never wanted anyone to catch a fish as badly as I want Sarah to catch one now.

four

Julia wins the bet. She catches nine fish—two more than Charlie—including a largemouth bass that was probably a foot long. It is the biggest thing she has ever caught. Bigger than anything Charlie has ever caught, too. I tell her that it should count for at least ten fish, though she doesn't need any extra credit to win.

Her victory means three things:

1. Charlie is going to act like an asshole for at least an hour and probably all afternoon.
2. Julia will eventually feel bad about beating him and give back at least half of his dessert.
3. Charlie will act like an even bigger asshole while eating his dessert.

It's an annoying routine, but it's nice to know what to expect.

Sarah and I don't catch anything, but as we pack the tackle into the pickle buckets, she asks if she can come fishing again.

Before I can say yes, Julia does.

"Sure thing," I add. I want Sarah to know that I want her to come back, too. I wish I had said it first.

The fear that I felt this morning returns as soon as I climb out of the canoe and back on to my aunt's dock. For the three hours that we spent fishing on the island, I only thought about the other mother a couple times. For a little while, I forgot about her completely. But now that we are back in the real world of sad aunts and after-school detentions, the other mother is sitting in the front of my mind again.

I know it's impossible to replace a person with an exact duplicate, so I tell myself not to worry. This can't be a real thing, especially because I was the only one who saw it. I must have been doing some version of sleepwalking this morning. Some half-awake dream. Maybe it's a puberty thing. Hormones and stuff messing with my brain.

Still, I'm afraid to go home. As long as I don't see her again, I can tell myself that the other mother is not real. I can pretend to believe that I was sleepwalking or it was something I ate or maybe I hit my head in the middle of the night. As soon as I see her again, I won't be able to fool myself anymore. It will be real again.

Auntie Carole is waiting on the dock. She's tall and thin. Her gray hair is tied up in a bun. She's wearing a dark blue dress. She always wears a dress. She calls to us as we get close. "Hello, my little ones!"

"Auntie Carole!" Julia shouts. "I caught more fish than Charlie!"

"Good for you," she shouts back.

"She cheated!" Charlie says.

"Did not!" Julia fires back. She splashes at Charlie with her oar. "Besides, how do you cheat at fishing anyway?" She splashes again, and this time, she hits him with a spray of water.

"All right, knock it off," Auntie Carole says. "And don't go tipping over. I see that no one bothered to wear life jackets again."

"You heard Auntie!" Charlie says, sticking his tongue out in Julia's direction. "No play horses!"

"What?" Sarah says to me from her boat, mouthing the word. "Play horses?"

"He means no horseplay," I say. I can't blame him for that one. Horseplay makes no sense.

As the girls maneuver their canoe, Julia tosses a line to Auntie Carole and climbs out onto the dock. Sarah follows, exiting the canoe like she's been doing it all her life. "Hi," she says. "I'm Sarah."

"Hello, Sarah," Auntie Carole says. "Did my little ones take you to the island today?"

"They did. It's beautiful."

Auntie Carole laughs. "I've been to the island, my dear. It's certainly not beautiful, and even if it was, it's not mine. No one owns it, really. The town, I guess, since they own the pond, too. My husband loved to tell people that it was his island. That he planned on retiring to it some day, but no one was ever dumb enough to believe him."

"He died," Charlie says, climbing out of the boat. "Uncle Norman, I mean."

"Yes, he did," Auntie Carole says.

Just like that, her sunniness is gone. It's nothing specific. I can't pick out any one thing that has changed about her. It's a combination of everything. It's like every tiny bit of her body—every cell—instantly flipped from happy to sad. Except it's not exactly sad. It's worse than sad. It's what Glen sees as crazy, but it's not crazy. It's lostness. I know that's not a word, but I'll bet that's exactly how Auntie Carole feels. She's lost without Uncle Norman. It's like all the roads and streets and sidewalks have been wiped away, and Auntie Carole is walking through the world without any idea where she should go.

"I'm so sorry," Sarah says. It's the second time today that she's had to say this to someone about Uncle Norman.

"Thank you, dear," Auntie Carole says, but she's not really with us anymore. This is what happens. She's somewhere else now. I can see it in her eyes. She will still chat with us and offer lemonade and help pull the canoes onto the shore, but her mind has gone to another place.

This is what worries Mom. It's what makes Glen think she's lost her marbles.

I think she's just trying to get back to Uncle Norman. In her mind, at least.

As we turn on to our street half an hour later, I see that Mom's car isn't in the driveway. She probably went to work already. She gets called in early a lot, and when they call, she always says yes because we need the money. We always need the money.

It gives me hope. I don't think the other mother could fake being a nurse. Being a nurse is way too complicated. Mom says that nurses need to know more than doctors, because doctors can go back to their offices and look stuff up on the internet. Nurses don't have offices. They have desks in the middle of hallways where everyone can see them all the time, and they need to be "on" all the time. Mom once told me that she got a wedgie when she was working at one of those hallway desks but couldn't pick it for like an hour because she never had even a second of privacy. Patients and doctors and other nurses were around her the whole time. I didn't want to take my meds that day, so she might've just made the whole thing up to make me laugh and be more agreeable (which it did), but I don't think so. It sounded like a Mom thing. And a nurse thing.

Only a real nurse could be a nurse, so the other mother must be Mom.

I pretend to believe this. In a tiny (*huge*) part of my brain I know it's not true, but that doesn't mean I can't pretend until it's impossible to pretend again.

We stop at the bottom of the driveway and Sarah hands me the pickle bucket hanging on her handlebars. "I need to get going," she says. "My cousin's birthday party is this afternoon." She's wearing her T-shirt again. I miss her bathing-suit top, but I feel like I know a secret now. I know what Sarah Flaherty looks like in a bathing suit, which means I practically know what she looks like in a bra. It's not my biggest secret. Not by a long shot. Still, it's a pretty good one.

"Thanks for fishing with us," Julia says. "You're the first girl who ever went fishing with me."

"I had fun," Sarah says.

"Michael had fun, too. I think he liked having a girl with us, too," Charlie says. He's grinning. He thinks he's funny. He's trying to embarrass me, and it's working. I feel my cheeks turning red. I want to punch him in the face, except I've never punched Charlie and Julia before. I've punched plenty of other kids, and I punched an adult once, and I shoved my bus driver's face, and I've wanted to punch Glen a million times, and I even wanted to punch the other mother this morning, but I've never hit Charlie or Julia, though they sometimes deserve it more than anyone.

Charlie especially.

Julia shoves Charlie for me. It's a hard, two-handed shove that almost knocks him off his bike. "Of course Michael liked having Sarah with us," she says. "Fishing with anyone is better than fishing with you, stupid."

Julia is in fourth grade. She can't ride in a canoe alone and is still afraid of the dark and secretly watches little kid shows like *The Wonder Pets* in her bedroom with the door closed, but sometimes she is more like my older sister. She knows just what to say when I need something said.

"I had fun with you, too, Charlie," Sarah says. She bends over when she says this, making way too much eye contact with him, the same way some adults do when they talk to little kids. She's not being sweet, though. She's treating him like a baby on purpose. She's *patronizing* him. Patronizing is pretending to be so nice that it becomes insulting. It's an amazing trick. Kind of like poisoning someone with chocolate or bacon. Mrs. Newfang said that I can be patronizing when I agree with people like the principal just to make them shut up. Sarah is patronizing Charlie because she didn't like him trying to embarrass me. She's trying to let him know it without telling him that he's a jerk.

Brilliant.

"Thanks," Charlie says. He's so stupid. He thinks she likes him.

Then I think: Maybe she's patronizing him for me. For my benefit. Maybe she wants me to know that she didn't like him embarrassing me. I hope it's that. I kind of love that thought.

Sarah turns her bike around. "Bye," she says and waves.

I wave back. I walk my bike up the driveway slowly while watching Sarah out of the corner of my eye. She rides up her driveway and into her garage. A second later the garage door closes.

I miss her already.

We're putting the tackle back on the shelf in the garage when Glen opens the door to the house. "Did you forget it's payday?"

"I didn't forget," I say.

"You were gone awhile."

"Yeah," I say. I hate questions that aren't questions. Glen asks these kinds of questions all the time. Plain old sentences that demand an answer. "The fishing was good, so we stayed awhile."

"It was really good for me!" Julia says.

"Michael didn't catch anything," Charlie says. "Not even a kiver."

"Nothing?" Glen asks. "Fish didn't like your hook today?"

"No," I say. "Sarah from next door went with us. I spent most of the time teaching her."

Glen laughs. "That explains a lot."

"What?" I say. I say it *defiantly*. Mrs. Newfang taught me this one, too. *Defiantly* is something I'm supposed to

avoid no matter what. The world could be on fire and earth-
quakes could be shaking us to bits, and I still shouldn't be
defiant, at least according to Mrs. Newfang. I tell her that
it's hard for me not to be defiant when people are stupid or
rude or saying things to hurt me.

"Easy, buddy," Glen says. He puts his hands up like I'm
going to charge him. "No need to be so defensive."

I clench my jaw. I ball my hands into fists. These things
happen automatically. I want to tell him that I know exactly what he meant by it, and that he's a fucking coward to
deny it. I want to tell him that I can already see the script
that I'm trapped inside. The fake words. The pretend feelings. He knows what he meant, and he knows I know what
he meant, but I still need to pretend and play act this stupid
scene, even though our audience—Charlie and Julia—have
seen this show a million times. I want to tell him that there
is nothing wrong with being defensive when you need to
defend yourself. I want to tell him to go to hell.

I want to punch him.

Instead of all those things, I turn away and pretend to
organize the tackle on the shelf. I take a deep breath that
doesn't help me calm down. Then I say the only word that I
can live with that won't get me in trouble. "Whatever."

Glen just stands in the doorway. He knows I am trapped.
He knows I can't organize the tackle forever, that eventually I will have to turn and face him again. He knows that
my "Whatever" will be defeated by his patience. We are
in a battle to see who can outlast the other, and I know I
can't win. Glen is patient. Assholes are always patient. They
would rather waste a lifetime and win than lose a battle

or even tie. But that doesn't mean I won't try. People fight when there is no hope of winning all the time. I do it all the time.

"Guess what I caught today?" Julia says.

"What did you catch?" Glen asks. It's not a real question. He asks it in a flat voice that's almost like a robot. He's saying it because he can't just ignore Julia even though he's fighting with me.

"A bass," Julia says. "Michael says it was at least a foot long."

"Not *at least* a foot long," Charlie says. "One foot long exactly."

"Maybe longer than that," I say, turning and facing Charlie. Avoiding eye contact with Glen. "It was a monster."

"Good for you, Julia," Glen says. "Next time you catch one that size, bring it home. I'll teach you how to bone it, and we'll have it for dinner."

"Okay," she says. "I will."

I know she won't. Julia is good at saying things that aren't true to keep people happy.

I'm not good at that at all.

"You're going to collect now?" Glen asks. This question is for me.

"After I wash up," I say. Not a yes, which is a small win for me. And I'm still not looking at him. I stare down at a pickle bucket like it's full of gold and jewels. I still can't win, but I don't have to lose everything.

"Good," Glen says. "Hurry up. You're already late." He turns and closes the door.

I feel my teeth unclench as soon as the door clicks shut.

My hands relax. I take a deep breath, and this time, it helps a little. I take another. "Thanks," I say to Julia.

She nods.

"Thanks for what?" Charlie asks.

"Nothing," I say. "Finish putting this stuff away. It's payday. You heard Glen. I can't be late."

five

I hate payday for a lot of reasons.

1. It's not *my* payday.
2. I'm doing work for Asshole Glen.
3. No one wants to pay me.
4. The customers are all old, annoying people who can't use computers.
5. Glen keeps adding customers.

My first stop is the yellow house on the corner of Connecticut Avenue and Farm Street.

The person who lives here is one of my favorite customers because he-or-maybe-she-but-probably-he always leaves an envelope in his-or-maybe-her mailbox. It's probably a man. The handwriting on the envelope looks like it was written by a man. All capital letters.

Girls love lower-case letters. All those dots over the i's and j's that they can turn into hearts and smiley faces.

If everyone was like Yellow House, my job would be easy. I still wouldn't make any money, but I wouldn't hate it as much. Just ride my bike around, collecting money in mailboxes. Piece of cake.

Glen says that when he was my age, he was a paperboy. He delivered *The Woonsocket Call* every day after school, tossing the papers onto doorsteps until people started putting up those plastic newspaper mailboxes. He collected the money on Fridays because Fridays were payday back then.

Glen is still a paperboy, which is pretty pathetic, but if I said that to his face, he would be mad. He drives around in the morning before anyone else is awake and throws newspapers rolled in plastic bags onto porches and stoops, just like when he was a kid. That's his job. Drive around and throw.

He was working for Home Depot on the weekends for a while, but he got laid off, which means he either quit or got fired. I heard Mom arguing with him about it one night after dinner, but I couldn't tell if she was mad at him for being lazy or stupid, because he's both things. I think he quit, though, because if he got fired, he would be looking for another job.

Instead of trying to find another job, he does something called *investments* on the computer all day, which doesn't make any money and might be costing us money. As far as I can tell, he's doing the same thing that Steve Zimmer in my algebra class does with comic books. Steve buys tons of comics but never reads a single one. Instead, he puts them in plastic sleeves that cost more than the comic books themselves and seals them like he's a cop on a TV show handling a DNA sample. He says that someday they'll be worth thousands. "With inflation," he says, "maybe millions."

Steve's a little crazy, but at least he isn't responsible for feeding a family. Steve doesn't have a wife who works double shifts at the hospital to pay the electric bill. Besides, Steve gets dressed every day and actually leaves the house. Glen sits in front of his computer in his bathrobe and slippers like a pasty human toadstool and buys stocks for one price in the morning and then mostly sells them for the same or less in the afternoon. Sometimes he has a "big day," but those days don't happen often, even though in his head I bet they happen a lot.

It's weird, because I think most people remember the bad days more than the good ones. They remember the morning when the dog died but forget all the mornings before that when the dog was perfectly fine. It's a good way to live, I suppose. It keeps you alive. Keeps you safe. Better to remember the time you ran into traffic to chase the ball and got hit by the car (which Charlie did two years ago) rather than the hundreds of times you did the same thing without getting hit.

But Glen remembers the "big days" and somehow forgets the days when he loses all the money Mom made at work that day.

Probably because he's an asshole.

He also loves to say that he'd be making a fortune if it weren't for all the commissions. I don't know what commissions are, but I'm pretty sure it's another word for bullshit excuses.

"Then just stop paying commissions," Julia said once at dinner after he told us about some should've-been-great trade he made that day.

"You can't just stop paying commissions," Glen said. "It doesn't work that way."

"Then maybe you should stop trading altogether," Mom said in that way when she speaks quietly but somehow makes it sound like thunder.

Glen didn't say a word for the rest of the meal.

Before investments, Glen played poker on the internet. He loved to tell people that he was a professional gambler, which made men ask lots of questions and made ladies frown and leave the room. But then online poker became illegal and "all the fish went away," whatever the hell that means.

He wasn't making a lot of money with poker, either, but I think he had more good days back then.

So now he's just a paperboy with bad investments.

People pay for their newspapers on the internet now, but Glen says the trick is to find the people who still want a newspaper but can't or won't pay online. Mainly old people who don't know how to use computers or don't trust technology and one weirdo who says that he's living off the grid even though he has a TV and works for the electric company driving one of those bucket trucks. Old people are also the only people who want to read newspapers anymore, so Glen's plan kind of makes sense. He goes to places like the VFW and coffee shops and leaves his business card with the old people who sit there and drink beer or coffee all day. His card says:

𝔗𝔥𝔢 𝔅𝔬𝔰𝔱𝔬𝔫 𝔊𝔩𝔬𝔟𝔢

On your stoop by sunrise. GUARANTEED.

I'm like the pony express. Nothing stops me.

Checks and cash accepted.

Tips not accepted. No arguments.

Glen isn't making a fortune, but for an idiot, it's a good idea. That "Tips not accepted" line may suck for me, but it helps him find customers. The old people are constantly reminding me about the policy when they pay me for the newspapers. "Gee, I'd love to tip you, but you know the policy!" They love to tell me about how hard it is to live on a fixed income.

I want to tell them to try to live on the income from a nurse and a paperboy who loses money on the internet every day.

That one business card idea added about fifty new customers in the first month and has been adding about half a dozen every month since. I couldn't believe it. I still can't. I don't think Glen can, either. Now he makes me collect from everyone who I could reach by bike. He says that people are more likely to pay if a kid is collecting the money, but that's bullshit. Collecting money by hand instead of just getting paid on the internet is a pain in the ass, and he knows it.

People hate seeing me at their door. I see the look on

their faces when they peek through the curtains to see who's ringing their bell. They can't stand handing over their checks, and giving me cash is worse. It's like they're cutting their wrists and dripping blood into my palm. I guess it's because they already read their newspapers by the time I show up, so they don't feel like they're buying anything anymore when they pay me. It's like I'm making them pay for something they already got for free, so it pisses them off.

I told Mom that I shouldn't be knocking on strangers' doors. I told her it was dangerous. Who knows what could happen to me? Every mother in the world would agree except my mother. Glen said that he did the same thing when he was a kid, and even though the media wants us to think that the world is full of murderers and child molesters, it's actually safer than ever before.

I didn't believe him, so I looked it up. He was right. It really is safer today.

Every squirrel has lucky nuts, as Charlie would say.

Even though none of these old people are murderers or child molesters, they really are a pain in the ass. Mrs. Dubois can never find her checkbook. Mr. and Mrs. Dunn bicker as they pile their coins and dollar bills on the table. The old lady in the blue house with the yappy dog offered me a bowl of Cinnamon Toast Crunch last week because she thought I looked hungry.

Who does that?

She was probably just lonely and wanted someone to talk to (and it was true that I was hungry), but there was no way I was hanging around to eat a bowl of cereal, even if I do love Cinnamon Toast Crunch. I actually felt a little sorry for the old lady, but I'm not going to sit at her kitchen table, eating cereal while she complains about the way her daughter is raising her kids.

Old people hate giving me money, but they love telling me about all their shit, especially if they live alone. Jeff said that trying to serve a paperboy a bowl of sugary cereal so he'll listen to your shit is fucked up. I agreed.

I never want to get old.

It used to take me less than an hour to make my collections, but with all the stops I have now, it's almost 5:00 by the time I pull into the driveway for my last stop of the day. Mom might be home from her shift at the hospital by now, unless she's working a double. I want to get home and see her. It was crazy for me to think that the other mother was real, but I need to see Mom to know for sure. I'll see her and laugh at myself for being so stupid this morning. It'll be just like the time Mom drove for an hour in the direction of New York City, got off the highway to get a coffee, and then got back on going the wrong way. She didn't realize it until almost an hour later when she was two exits from home.

"How is that even possible?" I asked. "You drove in the wrong direction *for an hour?*"

"I know," Mom said. "I guess I got lost in my thoughts and didn't notice."

"You realize that's insane," I said. "Right? You drove past all that stuff. The baseball stadium. That big power plant. The exit with the huge McDonald's arches. *The tunnel?* You didn't notice any of it?"

"I know," she said. "I guess I can't help being me."

That's how it will be for me when I realize that there is no other mother. It'll be a good laugh. A save-my-life kind of laugh.

My last stop of the afternoon is a new customer. Mrs. Foley. Glen met her at a yard sale last week and signed her up. He goes to yard sales on the weekends, hoping to find things that he can sell for a profit on eBay. Old toys. Electronics. Baseball cards. Part of his "investment strategy," he says. "Like mining for gold," he said. "It's out there. You just got to find it."

Mrs. Foley lives in the big, yellow house with the blue door on the corner of Elm and Summer Streets. It's way too big for an old lady. I can't imagine how she manages to keep the grass cut and the gutters clear of sticks and leaves. She probably has a son or daughter who helps out. In my experience, the bigger the house, the more annoyed the people are about paying me, and the more places they have to lose their checkbooks.

Big-house people suck.

Mrs. Foley, I'm sure, is going to suck.

I ring the bell. The door opens so fast that it scares me. It was like she was standing on the other side, just waiting for me to press the button. I jump back a couple steps.

"Hello," she says. "You must be Michael."

"I am," I say. "Are you Mrs. Foley?"

I ask because this woman isn't as old as I thought she'd be. Maybe this is Mrs. Foley's daughter. Or a housekeeper. She doesn't look much older than my mother.

Or the other mother, a voice in my head says. I recognize the voice. It's mine, but it's also a part of my voice that sometimes speaks on its own. Says things I don't want to hear. I push it away. Shove it into the back of my brain.

"Yes," Mrs. Foley says. "That's me. But you can call me Louise."

Mrs. Foley (there's no freakin' way I'm calling her Louise) is wearing a T-shirt and jeans. Her black hair is pulled back into a ponytail. She's smiling. This doesn't look like a woman who can't use the internet.

"I'm here to collect the money for the *Globe*," I say. "For my stepfather."

She sighs. Puts her hands on her hips. "You look just like your father."

The words hit me like a punch in the gut. I've heard them before, but not for a long time. Not since he died. I actually take another step back until I'm standing at the edge of the stoop.

"Oh God," Mrs. Foley says. "I'm so sorry. That was stupid."

"No, it's fine," I say. But it's not. I still can't catch my breath.

"Look at you," she says. "I'm so sorry. That was so inconsiderate of me. It just came out because you do. You look just like him when he was your age."

"What?" I'm still trying to catch my breath.

"You and your dad . . . you look just like him when he was a boy."

"You knew my dad?" I can barely get the words out.

"I did. I thought your stepfather would've told you. We talked about it last week."

Now this makes sense. "He didn't say anything to me about it," I say. I want to tell her that he doesn't tell me much about anything. I want to tell her that she was dealing with an idiot at that yard sale. An asshole and an idiot. But I don't.

"I went to school with your father," Mrs. Foley says. She

smiles. Laughs a little. "I wasn't a Foley back then. I was a Perkins. Louise Perkins. My husband's name was Foley. He passed away a few years ago."

Louise Perkins. The name rings a bell. Not a big one, but I've heard it before, which is saying a lot. Dad wasn't exactly a fountain of information.

"I'm so sorry for your loss, Michael. I know it's terribly late in coming. I didn't hear about his heart attack until well after it happened. But still, I'm so sorry. Your father was such a good man."

"Thank you," I say. This is what I say when people offer me condolences. When it first happened, I didn't know what to say—and people said things like "I'm sorry for your loss" all the time—so Mrs. Newfang helped me find a strategy. "Just say thank you," she said. "Then you can stop talking."

I know that thanking a person and saying nothing more is kind of like setting a word trap. I say thank you and then I wait. That forces the other person to talk, and the silence before they figure out what to say can be super awkward. But at least the person can talk about anything they want—usually a story about my dad—and all I need to do is pretend to be interested and nod a lot. It's not like I'm asking them a hard question.

It's actually a good strategy. One of Mrs. Newfang's best.

Mrs. Foley is stuck in one of those awkward silences now. She doesn't know what to say, so she just stares at me for a second. Blinks. Then she says, "Sorry. You have places to be, I'm sure. Let me get my checkbook."

As Mrs. Foley disappears into her house, she leaves the door open. I can see down a hallway into a kitchen. Most people either invite me inside, which I hate, or close the door as they go for their money, which I hate even more. It makes me feel like a criminal. Like I can't be trusted to stand on their front stoop with the front door wide open.

Mrs. Foley has left her front door wide open. There aren't too many people like her. I like her for that.

She also knew my dad. I've never met anyone who knew my dad when he was young. Mom met Dad in the hospital after he fell out of a tree and broke his arm and nose, but he was in his twenties when that happened.

This lady knew my dad when he was my age.

Suddenly I'm mad at myself for putting Mrs. Foley into that word trap. I wish I had asked her a question.

There are a billion terrible things about your dad dying, and every day you find a new one. It's like an endless list that just keeps getting more and more endless, which I know doesn't make mathematical sense but makes real-life sense. I remember the minister telling me that things would get easier with time. "Time heals all wounds," he said.

I knew it was a lie on the day the minister first said it to me, and I know it even more now. He was either a liar or a fucking idiot. Time doesn't heal any wounds. It infects them. Poisons them. I feel worse today and will feel even worse tomorrow.

When Dad died, he took all his memories with him. Everything that I didn't know about him—every question never asked and every story never told—can never be known now that he's dead. It's like losing your only copy of a book before you finish reading the story, except it's the only copy of the book *ever*. There's no way to get those pages back.

When I was a little boy, I watched Dad fall into some water. I can't remember where we were, but I remember that there was a Mello Yello can floating in the water. I don't even know what exactly Mello Yello is, but I remember that aluminum can as clear as day, reflecting the sun off its shiny top. Dad fell off a dock, maybe, or out of a canoe. Maybe off a rock. I'm not sure. I'm not even sure why we were near the water. I don't know if it was a river or a pond or the ocean. Probably not the ocean. But I'm really not sure.

Maybe he even dove into the water on purpose.

But I remember he was wearing a hat that day. A straw hat, I think, which makes no sense, but that's how I remember it. A big-ass straw hat. And when Dad fell in, he disappeared beneath the water, but his hat remained floating on the surface. It just sat there, bobbing in the water, waiting for him to come back up and claim it.

It felt like he was underwater forever. I remember staring at that straw hat and thinking that Dad wasn't coming back. I was so afraid. More afraid than almost any other time in my life. In my mind, he was dead. I was already mourning his loss. Then, at last, he burst through the surface of the water with a smile on his face, and a second later, he was laughing. I felt so happy. So relieved to have my father back.

But I don't remember anything else about the day. All I really remember is the Mello Yello can, the straw hat, and the feeling that I'd lost Dad forever.

And now I have. I've lost him forever, and with him, all the details of that day are gone, too. Every bit of that day is gone except for those few details in my brain. Erased from the universe forever. That day by the water and hundreds of other days that I can't remember or can't quite remember or never knew. Days that Dad was supposed to tell me about when I was older. His first kiss. His first driving lesson. The time he threw his first punch. The first time he fell in love. Every single one of those moments is lost forever. I can never know anything more about that day by the water or anything else about my father ever again.

Except that Mrs. Foley knew my father. She knew him before I knew him. Before Mom knew him. It's like finding a few pages of that long-lost book behind a blue door.

She returns with a check in her hand. "I made it out to cash. I hope that's okay."

"It's fine," I say. "Thanks."

"Okay, then. I'll see you next week."

"See you next week," I say. I turn. I climb down the four steps and start down the cobblestone walk, and then I stop, and turn back. Mrs. Foley hasn't moved. It's like she was waiting for me. Like she knew something else was coming.

"Did you go to middle school with my dad?" I ask.

She nods. "Grade school, too. We were in the same kindergarten class. I remember him from the very first day of school because of his name."

I laugh. I can't remember the last time I laughed about anything to do with my father, but imagining this woman as a little girl, hearing my father's name for the first time, is hilarious.

"It was actually the first time our teacher called the roll," she says, climbing down the porch steps and joining me on the cobblestones. "We were all sitting in neat little rows, hands folded on the desk. I was so nervous. I didn't go to preschool, so it was my first time in a classroom. My first time with a teacher. Your dad's, too, I think. We sat alphabetically, so your father was sitting in front of me. Parsons and then Perkins. It was like that all the way through grade school. Then I heard Mrs. Avicolli call out his name. Does anyone ever forget their kindergarten teacher's name?"

She pauses for a moment and looks up, like she's waiting for the clouds or the sky to answer her question. I'm about to tell her that my kindergarten teacher's name was Ms. Owen, and no, I don't think anyone forgets their kindergarten teacher's name, when she starts speaking again.

"Sorry," she says. She smiles. "When I heard Mrs. Avicolli call out 'Venus Parsons' it was all I could do to not laugh. I didn't know about how his name rhymed with . . . well, you know. I just thought how silly it was for a boy to be named after a planet."

I nod. "Venus is almost always the first star you see in the sky at night. Not really a star, but it looks like one. My grandmother named him Venus because she thought of my father as her very first star."

"I never knew that," Mrs. Foley says. "He never told me." She speaks softly, like she's just heard something important. Like she's just been given another page in the book of my father.

"Yeah," I say. "But I bet that didn't help him when the kids started calling him Penis Parsons all day."

"No, it did not," Mrs. Foley says. She takes a couple steps back and sits on the steps of the porch. Put her hands in her lap.

I wait a moment, then I move forward and join her. It's

different now. We're not paperboy and customer anymore. I'm not sure what we are, but it's definitely more.

"And I bet it didn't help that Venus is a woman's name, too," I say.

"No, that didn't help either," she says, smiling again. "But I'll tell you this: it didn't take long for your father to put an end to the teasing."

"What did he do?" I ask. I feel myself lean forward, like Mrs. Foley suddenly has a gravitational pull. I'm interested in what she will say next. I'm more interested in this than anything else in my life right now, and Mrs. Foley seems to know it.

She looks up again, but this time she looks like she's caught in a memory of my father from way back when. She can see him. I know it. I wish I could see through her eyes. See my dad when he was still young and happy and brave. She stares into the sky for another moment, and then she smiles. Looks right at me. "It was so simple, really. He just acknowledged how funny his name was and moved on. 'Yes, my name is Venus, and yes, it rhymes with penis,' he would say. And that would usually be the end of it. Sometimes he would even crack jokes at his own expense. That's when I knew I liked him."

"Because he was funny?"

"He was funny, all right. Even as a little boy. But it was mostly because he was confident. He didn't give a hoot about what other people thought. That's a pretty attractive thing at any age."

This does not sound like my father.

"You thought he was cute?" I ask.

She smiles. "We were sweethearts for a while. He took

me to the freshman-senior dance. I loved your father in that way that only a teenage girl can."

I'm staring at my father's high school girlfriend. I can't believe it. It's like meeting a part of my father that I thought was lost forever.

"I miss him," she says. "I'm so sorry that he's gone."

"Me too."

There's a silence between us, but this time it's not awkward. It feels like we're standing in the same silent space.

"Next week, then?" she asks.

"Yes," I say. "Next week. You can put the money in the mailbox if you want."

"That's okay. I'll be here. Just knock on the door."

"I will," I say.

I can't wait.

six

Mom's car is parked in the driveway. I'm happy. At least that's what I tell myself. I can finally stop being a dumbass. I'm going to walk inside the house, take one look at Mom, and see that she's real. That she's been here all along.

But then my other voice speaks. It surprises me. I almost fall off my bike. I need to plant my feet to keep myself from toppling over. *You can lie to yourself if you want, but that won't make it true.*

The other voice might be right this time, but it's not like it's God's voice inside my head. It's just me, saying the things that I don't want to hear. My other voice has just as much of a chance of being wrong as I do.

Mrs. Newfang says it's normal for people to have another voice in their head that speaks to them from time to time. Especially creative people. I'm not creative, but she thinks I am, so I just nod when she talks about it.

But she doesn't like how my other voice can sometimes

surprise me. I guess that with most people, it's sort of expected. It doesn't almost knock them off their bikes. She
asks me about it a lot, and she asks in that no-big-deal way
that makes it seem like a very big deal.

Mrs. Newfang would be a terrible poker player.

So I tell her that the voice hasn't surprised me in a long
time, even though it still does. It's kind of sweet that she
worries about me so much, but it's annoying, too. She can't
let go of certain things, and they're always the things I want
her to let go. The things I don't ever want to talk about. Or
can't talk about.

I park my bike on the side of the garage. I'd like to put it
in the garage, but I don't go in there alone, and I never go
in at night.

Not anymore, at least.

I walk up the brick path. I hear her voice before I see her.
I hear it through the open window in the kitchen. I hear it
as clear as day.

It's not my mother's voice.

Even though I'm still outside the house, with walls and
glass between us, I can tell just by listening. She's in the
living room with Glen, and they're fighting. Glen is almost-
yelling. He's not so loud that he's shouting, but he's angry
enough to make it feel like he's shouting. He's a master of
almost-yelling.

The other mother is speaking in Mom's way-too-calm
voice because she's trying to stop Glen from almost-yelling,
even though I know this voice makes him angrier. It's as if
Mom thinks that Glen's almost-yelling knocks the world
out of balance, so she tries to rebalance it by doing the
opposite. I had a third-grade teacher named Mrs. Ganci

who used to do the same thing. She would speak so softly that the whole class would have to get quiet so we could hear her. And we did. It works with Charlie, too. When he's having a tantrum, the best thing to do is act as calm and disinterested as possible.

But this never works with Glen, even though Mom (and apparently the other mother) thinks it does. Glen can see right through it. It makes him crazy. It's making him crazy right now.

It makes me crazy, too. It makes me crazy when she does it to me, but it makes me even crazier when I hear her using it on Glen. I wish Mom would stand up and fight instead of running away and hiding. Just let the asshole have it for once. Fire back. She's like a solider asking the enemy to put his gun down while he's shooting her in the chest.

It's the same old fight, too. Glen is telling the other mother about how hard he works. How he needs her support. How she needs to be patient. She's telling him that she works hard, too. She's saying how she worked a double today and would like to come home and have stuff done around the house for once. Dishes. Laundry. Anything.

I'll never understand how adults can have the same arguments again and again and not realize it. Only this time it's not the same argument because it's the other mother who's arguing. It's the same argument for Asshole Glen, but it's the first time for the other mother.

But maybe the other mother doesn't know that this is her first fight with Glen. I guess it's possible that she doesn't know that she's the other mother. Maybe she really thinks that she's my mother. Maybe my mother and the other mother have been switched somehow, but neither one knows it.

This is crazy.

How could my mother be switched for this other woman? How can Glen almost-yell at this other person and not know that it's not the same woman he almost-yells at all the time? It's not possible. I'm starting to wish that Luke was right. I wish I was crazy. Not just angry crazy but really crazy. Loony-bin crazy. Crazy would be so much easier than this. Crazy would at least be possible. People go crazy all the time. It's almost normal. This is not normal. This is like *Invasion of the Body Snatchers* except in real life, but pod people don't exist in real life.

Maybe they don't exist in real life until they do. Maybe this is like astronauts walking on the moon and the self-driving cars and Labradoodles. One day none of those things existed, and the next day they did. Maybe this is the moment when everything changes. Maybe this is when pod people become real.

This is ridiculous. I'm going inside. I'm going to find out what the hell is going on. Glen may be an asshole, but if the other mother tries to hurt me, he'll stop her. Unless she has a gun or some creepy pod people technology, he'll be able to protect me. Glen might not like me, but there's a part of him that loves me, even if it's a tiny part. I know this. He wouldn't let her hurt me. I'm going to go stand in front of the other mother and say, "I know you're not my mother!" I'm going to watch her face as I say it, just like Hamlet did to his scumbag uncle. If she's not my mother, I'll see it in her expression. She won't be able to hide it. She thinks she has everyone fooled, and she does.

Everybody except for me.

I listen and wait. I want to walk in just as their fight is ending. I want to confront her at the moment when she thinks she's in the clear. If this were a movie, I wouldn't be doing any of this. I'd be investigating first. I'd hide in the back seat of her car under a blanket when she leaves for work tomorrow to see where she's really going and what she's really doing. I'd follow her to her hideout. Discover what her master plan is, because there must be some plan. You don't just replace a person for no reason. A lot of work had to go into this insanity. If this were a movie, I'd listen in as she talks to her accomplice or I'd hack into her computer. Do lots of stuff to stretch the suspense out for a couple hours before the climactic battle at the end. Movies need to be dragged out because people pay twelve bucks to see them. They need action and suspense. But in real life, I think it's fine to skip all that nonsense and just get to the end. Pod person or no pod person, this is real life, and I need to know what the hell is going on.

"Do they fight a lot?"

The voice startles me so badly that I scream. It's Sarah's voice, but for some reason my first thought is that it's my father's voice. Then I think it must be the voice inside my head. Those two thoughts crash into each other as I scream, even though I know at the same time that it's Sarah's voice.

I spin around and see Sarah's face. My scream has frightened her, too. Her hands are covering her mouth. Her eyes are wide. They're beautiful. It's the first time I notice that a girl's eyes can be beautiful. Brown and perfect.

"I'm so sorry," she says. She reaches out and puts her hand on my shoulder. She squeezes. "Geez, are you okay?"

"I'm fine," I say. "You just startled me."

She doesn't say anything. She just stares. Her hand is still squeezing my shoulder. She's the same age as me and almost as tall as me, but her hand feels so small on my shoulder. She still doesn't say anything. Just stares at me wide-eyed.

"Okay," I say, finally filling the silence. "You've heard me scream like a little girl. That makes us best friends now. It's a rule."

I hate the words as they come out of my mouth. They sound so stupid. I sound so stupid. But then Sarah smiles. Then she laughs.

I feel like a genius.

"It was a good scream," she says. "Good enough for the movies."

"Yeah, it really was," I say. "And I don't practice screaming all that much. I guess I'm a natural."

Sarah motions over my shoulder to the house. "So? Do they fight a lot?"

The yelling inside the house had disappeared for a moment. Everything in the world became my scream and Sarah's eyes and her laugh. Nothing more. But now it's back. Glen is almost-yelling something about respect, and the other mother is telling Glen about how proud she is of him, which means that she's probably made him feel exactly the opposite. This is what Mom does all the time. Says things—true things—that make Glen feel bad about himself, and then takes it all back once he starts believing her. Back and forth like a tug-of-war.

I don't know about the other mother, but it's hard to imagine anyone being proud of Glen. Deep down, I think

Glen knows this. I don't think he's very proud of himself, either. It's probably why he's an asshole.

"Yeah," I say. "They fight a lot." This is technically a lie, since as far as I know, this is the first time the other mother and Glen have fought, but I'm not going to tell Sarah that my mother is actually a pod person, so maybe the lie is okay. "And they always fight about the same stuff. It's so stupid."

"My parents don't fight at all," Sarah says. "But that might be just as bad. Maybe worse. They walk around the house not talking to each other until they aren't mad anymore. Sometimes it can take a day or two. Do you know how silence can sometimes be so loud?"

I nod. I do. I know exactly what she means.

"That's what it sounds like in my house." She bites her lip. "But they don't fight a lot. And don't all parents fight at least a little?"

"I think so."

From inside, I hear Asshole Glen shout, "Goddamn it!" Then there's a bang.

Sarah jumps.

"It's okay," I say. "He loves to hit things in frustration. Walls. Tables. Countertops. But never people. He just likes to scare them."

"Your poor mom."

I want to tell Sarah that Mom didn't have to marry this asshole. I want to tell her that Glen was so clearly an asshole long before their stupid backyard wedding with more musicians playing "Here Comes the Bride" than there were guests. I want to tell her that Mom knew exactly what she was getting into. Knew what she was getting us all into.

"Are Charlie and Julia okay?" Sarah asks. "Are they inside?"

"They're fine. Upstairs, I'm sure. Charlie wouldn't notice if the house was burning down, and if it gets real bad, Julia will put on her headphones and listen to music. But this isn't so bad, and it sounds like it'll be done soon. I just hate walking into it."

Sarah nods. It's one of those tiny little motions—just a quick bobbing of the head—that says so much. She understands what it's like to walk into a parental war zone. "You want to go over to my place for a while?" she asks. "Wait for things to cool down?"

"What do you mean?"

She smiles. "I mean . . . do you want to hang out at my house for a while?"

I don't say anything. It's probably just a second or two, but it feels like the longest pause ever. Big enough to march armies through.

Sarah laughs. Shakes her head. Grabs me by the wrist, which is almost like holding my hand. So close to holding my hand. "C'mon," she says. She pulls. We walk away from the shouting and toward her house.

I look ahead. I peer an hour into the future. There are so many opportunities for me to make a fool of myself.

seven

My sister read somewhere that only two people in the whole world know the secret recipe for Coke. The company says that two people know in case one of them dies, but I believe it's because the recipe is too big a secret for just one person. Having to carry around something like that all alone could kill a person. It's killing me. I just want to tell *someone*. It's kind of like wanting to write my secrets down on a piece of paper, stuff them into a bottle, and throw them into the ocean, except I want that ocean to be a human being.

What I really want to do is just walk into some restaurant in some faraway town, sit down at a booth with some stranger, and tell that person all my secrets. I just want the chance to say my secrets out loud to someone so I won't feel like the only person in the world carrying them. It's hard to be alone with secrets. I know it sounds weird, but secrets are heavy. They have real weight.

And I'm good at keeping secrets. I might be the best

secret keeper ever, because mine are really starting to pile up, and I haven't told a single person. And they're big secrets, too. Serious ones. Life and death kinds of secrets. Not just "Johnny likes Jane" kind of stuff.

My list of secrets:
1. My mother disappeared and another mother has taken her place.
2. Brian Marcotte has a very not good plan that scares me.
3. I have a letter in a yellow envelope that would change the world if I showed anyone.

I thought for a second that Sarah could be my stranger. She could be the person in the restaurant booth who I tell everything to. She's the closest I've got to someone I know but don't know, and I wouldn't have to travel to some far-away town to find her.

But now I know I can't tell Sarah any of my secrets. Sarah isn't a secret keeper. She's a problem solver. A fixer. She worries a lot about other people. You can't be a person who wants to save the world and keep secrets at the same time. I had an asshole science teacher last year who said he liked to watch the world burn. He would stand in front of the class like he was on some stage and say, "Study for the test or don't. Your choice. If you don't pass, that's on you. I love to watch the world burn."

He was a jerk, but I bet he was a good secret keeper, too. Guys like him—they're almost always guys—have no problem watching people suffer and fail. They say stuff like, "Struggle builds character" or "Everyone needs to experience failure." But most of them didn't grow up poor or hungry or with an asshole stepfather. They like to watch the world burn because their world has never burned.

Sarah isn't like that. I know this already. I knew it from the moment we sat on that rock on Barracuda Island. If I told Sarah my secrets, she would spring into action like some superhero. She would try to save me, when all I really want is for someone to listen to me.

This is what I am thinking as I sit in a chair in the corner of Sarah's bedroom, waiting for her to come back with soda. It's a small chair made of wood and wicker. I had to move her teddy bear aside to sit down. It seems like a chair made for a teddy bear. I feel awkward sitting on it, stuffed into the corner of the room, but I can't sit on Sarah's bed, and there's no other place in the room to sit.

Sitting on Sarah's bed would be presumptuous, which means thinking you belong somewhere before anyone says you do. That's not how Mrs. Newfang explained it, but she likes to use nine hundred words when just a few will do.

While I wait, I stare at the bed that Sarah Flaherty sleeps in every night. Maybe in a nightgown, or maybe, on summer nights, in just her underwear. I've seen porn before on the internet, accidentally at first and then on purpose sometimes, but somehow staring at Sarah Flaherty's empty bed seems more like sex than all the sex I've ever seen on my computer screen.

"Why are you sitting in the corner?" Sarah asks. She's back. She's carrying two cans of soda and a bag of popcorn.

"I don't know," I say. "I like chairs." This may be the stupidest thing I have ever said. It might be the stupidest thing that any human being has ever said.

"You like chairs?" she asks.

"Yes. I do."

She smiles. It's one of those smiles that's meant to say something, but I have no idea what it says. I feel like I'm on an alien planet. I'm surrounded by stuffed animals and books and pillows and pink. There's an overhead light and a lamp by the door and a smaller lamp on her desk, and they're all turned on. The room is practically bursting with light. Everything is so organized and neat. The pens and markers have separate cups on her desk. A half-dozen trophies are lined up on a shelf. Dancing. Or maybe gymnastics. Her schoolbooks are stacked on a little table like a pyramid, with the biggest books on the bottom and the smallest on top. I can't imagine taking the time to sort my schoolbooks by size. This place looks nothing like my bedroom. Like no bedroom I've ever seen.

"Here," she says. She hands me a can and sits down on the edge of her bed. There's too much space between us. She's on one side of the room, and I'm on the other. It's like we're sitting on opposite sides of the Grand Canyon. There's a round, blue rug between us, and it feels like an ocean separating us. I feel stupid for choosing this seat. I should've just stayed standing while I waited. I could've pretended to be looking at the books on her shelf or the drawings taped on the walls. Old crayon drawings of unicorns and mermaids and castles. Now I'm trapped in this stupid corner on this stupid chair feeling stupid.

"Are you sure Julia and Charlie are okay?" she asks. "We could call and invite them over, too."

"No. They're fine. Honestly, I'd be fine, too, if I was home. They fight like this a lot."

"Do you ever worry they might get divorced?"

I laugh. "I wish they'd get divorced. I hate that fucking asshole." As the words come out, they feel wrong. I don't think I've ever sworn like that in front of a girl before. And in her bedroom it somehow feels even worse. I take a sip of soda. "Sorry. Didn't mean to . . . you know. Use that language."

Sarah laughs. "Don't be ridiculous. Actually, I take that back. Don't be *fucking* ridiculous. You can swear all the fuck you want." She laughs again. Then she lowers her voice. "But not in front of my parents. Okay?"

"Don't worry," I say. "I'm not that stupid."

"I know."

She says those two words like they're made of cotton. Her voice is soft. Warm. She means them as a compliment. She thinks I'm smart. Or at least not stupid, which is almost as good. It's a tiny compliment, but it might also be the best compliment I've ever received.

The prettiest girl in the world thinks I'm not stupid.

"Isn't it weird," I say. "Adults can swear right in front of us—right at us sometimes—but we can't drop the occasional F-bomb without them going ballistic?"

"Hypocrisy at its best."

I'm not entirely sure what hypocrisy means, so I nod and take a longer sip of soda. I can probably guess based upon the context clues, but this is not the time to take any chances. She doesn't think I'm stupid. I want to keep it that way.

"I don't think they mean to be hypocrites," Sarah says. "I think they're afraid of us growing up. Anything that makes us look or sound or act older is bad. It starts with swearing, but before they know it, their little girl is drinking beer and smoking pot and having sex and she's not so little anymore. They're just trying to hold back the future as long as possible."

"I never thought of it like that," I say. I also want to say that this is the first time I've ever heard a girl say the word *sex* in my presence, and it was *in her bedroom*.

But I'm not stupid enough to say any of this aloud.

"Maybe that's just my parents," Sarah says. She pulls at the popcorn bag, trying to tear it open. When she can't, she uses her teeth, tearing away the corner of the bag and spitting it into her hand. "They're always telling me to stop growing up."

"I don't think my parents are trying to stop me from growing up. If anything, they're pushing me to grow up faster than I want. Giving me stuff to do that none of my friends ever have to do. I guess I have the opposite problem. I wish my parents would grow up."

"What do you mean?" She quickly adds, "You don't have to tell me if you don't want."

"No, it's okay. It's mostly my mom. Glen's a loser. He'll never grow up. I knew that the second I met him. He's one of these guys who thinks he's going to make it big, but he doesn't do anything to make it happen. He's like the kid in class who doesn't study for a test and fails and is pissed at the teacher for it. Like he deserves more than he gets."

"What does your mother see in him?"

"No clue," I say. It's a question I've been asking myself ever since Glen moved into our house. It feels good to hear someone else say it. "I honestly can't imagine what she was thinking."

"Do you think she loves him?"

I open my mouth to answer and realize I don't know the answer. I've never asked myself this question.

"I'm sorry," Sarah says. "I shouldn't be asking questions like that."

"No, it's fine. I just don't know the answer. I assume she loves him. Right? Why else would she marry him?"

"People get married for lots of reasons," Sarah says. "Love is a good one. Probably the best one. But people get married because they're lonely or in trouble or are afraid that they won't ever find someone better. Lots of reasons."

"Yeah?"

"I think so."

"How would you know?" I ask. "You been married before?"

"Call it female intuition. And a lot of Jane Austen." She shakes the popcorn bag at me. "You want some?"

"Sure." I stand up and walk across the room, each step feeling more ridiculous than the last. It's like we're sitting a mile away. Once I've crossed the blue-carpet chasm between us, I reach into the bag and pull out a handful of popcorn. I turn around to begin the return trip back to the chair when Sarah grabs my wrist again.

"Just sit on my bed, dummy. It's okay."

"Oh," I say. "Okay."

I sit. The two or three inches of space between our legs evaporate as the mattress sags under my weight, pulling the two of us together. I look down. Our thighs are touching. Pressed up against each other. Denim against denim. I stare for a second. A long second. I'm sitting on Sarah Flaherty's bed, our bodies joined at the thigh.

It feels almost more impossible than the other mother.

I look up. Sarah's looking at me. She was looking at me looking at our thighs. She giggles. Every minute spent in this bedroom is the best and worst moment of my life at the same time.

"If you really want to know if your mom loves him, you could ask her when she fell in love with him for the first time. Maybe ask when she first knew that he was the one."

"My dad was the one," I say, a little angrier than I intend. "Asshole Glen isn't even close. Not even on the same planet."

"Sorry," Sarah says.

"It's okay. And it's not a bad idea. Better than me asking her what the hell she was thinking when she married the guy. Right?"

"Exactly."

Except my mother is gone. She's been replaced by a pod person or a genetic duplicate or something else I can't even imagine. I suddenly feel the urge to tell Sarah about the other mother. Trust her with my secret. Maybe even ask her for help. Let her be the superhero I know she wants to be. But I know I can't. She wouldn't believe me, and even if she did, there's nothing she could do. Still, I want to tell her so badly.

I reach for more popcorn instead. I'd like a sip of soda, but my can is on the other side of the room, on the dresser beside the chair, and I don't want to risk losing my spot on the bed. Only a lunatic would give up this spot.

Sarah's mom calls from the bottom of the stairs to ask if we need anything.

"No!" Sarah yells back. "All set!" She doesn't move from our spot, either.

"Should I go?" I ask. "I can go if you think your mom wants me to go. The fight's probably over by now." Glen and the other mother are probably having sex now, which is what Glen and my mother usually do after a fight. I don't tell this to Sarah. She may be ready to say the word *sex* to me, but I'm not ready to say it to her.

"She's just making sure we know that she's downstairs. Like I could forget."

"Do you know when your parents fell in love?"

"Mom says it was love at first sight," Sarah says. "She was in college, working at a roller-skating rink. She handed Dad a pair of rental skates. Their fingers touched. That was it."

"For your dad, too?"

"No," she says. "He doesn't even remember seeing my mom that night. He says Mom wore him down. 'Love's version of erosion,' he likes to say. Not exactly romantic."

"They're still together today," I say. "That doesn't happen a lot anymore."

"I'm lucky, I guess."

Something about the way Sarah says this makes me not believe her. I want to ask more. Find out what might be wrong. I've only known Sarah for a day—this impossible day of the other mother and Mrs. Foley and Sarah Flaherty—but I already want to save her from the sadness I can see hiding behind her eyes.

I eat more popcorn instead. I wish I had remembered to bring my soda across the chasm. I try to avoid saying any more stupid things while keeping our thighs pressing together as long as possible. We talk about school. I tell her about Charlie's need to be prepared. She tells me about her old school and the best friend she left behind. We talk for about fifteen minutes before her mother calls again, asking if we need anything. We decide it's time for me to leave.

I feel like I should kiss Sarah as I say goodbye. I could. We're standing alone at her front door. I'm almost sure I could lean in and kiss her on the cheek, and she wouldn't mind.

I don't, of course. I say thank you and goodbye and walk away.

I may not be crazy like Luke thinks and Mrs. Newfang might think, but I can recognize when I'm acting delusional.

eight

Brian's plan is a bad one. That's why I agreed to help. When it comes to Mr. Morin, he deserves all the bad that he can get.

I'm just not so sure if his bad plan is good anymore. It's so strange. Two days ago I couldn't wait to get started. It was all I could think about. But now all of my thoughts are focused on getting my mother back. Figuring out what the hell is going on.

It's hard to imagine caring at all about Brian's plan tomorrow.

I guess it makes sense. In all those movies with asteroids and aliens about to destroy the world, no one is ever worried about homework or a busted washing machine or paying the bills. Big problems make little problems go away. The other mother isn't an asteroid, but she's still a big problem. An asteroid-sized problem.

Quite possibly an alien.

Maybe she is an alien. I know it sounds ridiculous, and

I don't really believe it, but the explanation for where my mother went and how she's been replaced has to be ridiculous. Nothing not ridiculous makes sense. An alien is just as likely as anything else, as stupid as that idea may sound.

But there's something else. Another reason for maybe not helping Brian. After spending today with Sarah Flaherty, I feel like I should try to be a better person. The same kind of person I am when I'm taking care of Charlie and Julia. That might not be possible, but I feel like I should at least give it a shot. Not to impress Sarah but just because of Sarah. It's like my orbit has changed since yesterday, and now I revolve around Sarah instead of me. A little bit, at least.

But Brian is counting on me. And Mr. Morin is a real asshole.

Mr. Morin is my science teacher. He's also a dictator. His nickname would be Hitler except he's only about five feet tall, so we call him Little Napoleon instead. We should drop the *Little* from his name, since Napoleon was short. Just calling him Napoleon would cover his height, too. But someone who isn't me decided to call him Little Napoleon—probably someone who had never seen a picture of Napoleon and didn't know what a shrimp he was— and it stuck. It kind of annoys me. It's not as clever a name as it should be.

Mr. Morin has favorites. Kids who can do no wrong. Kids who get away with murder and get all the stupid privileges that kids want for doing nothing. Just because he likes them. He knows their parents or taught their brothers or sisters or just heard good things from other teachers. So they get stuff like friends for lab partners. First in line for lab equipment. Hall passes without the third degree.

But it's mostly the way he speaks to the kids he favors that annoys me. He talks to them like they're human beings. He says hello as they walk into the classroom. Asks about their weekends. Knows the sports they play. Remembers details about their lives that he never even bothers to ask the kids who aren't his favorites.

Kids like Brian and me are not his favorites.

My best school year ever was fifth grade. My last year of elementary school. My teacher's name was Mr. Maroney. On the first day of school, Mr. Maroney called me over to his desk and asked me to sit down. "I have to talk to you," he said. I thought I was in trouble, because back then I was always in trouble.

I guess I'm still always in trouble. It's just harder to see it when you're in the middle of it. Maybe that's what teachers mean when they say you can't see the forest through the trees. That always sounded so stupid to me, but maybe it makes a little more sense now.

Still, if you can see a ton of trees, you can pretty much assume you're in a forest.

Mr. Maroney said that he had heard about all my problems in fourth grade. All the trouble I got in. The fights. Yelling at teachers. The time I flipped my desk. The other time I flipped my desk. The rock I threw at the bus. But as far as he was concerned, I had a clean slate. "You're starting from scratch," he said. He told me that I was a model student in his mind, and I would remain a model student unless I did something to ruin it.

I know it sounds small, but it changed my whole year. When you're the kid who punched Trevor Dalton in the back of the head and ripped the door off the bathroom stall and smashed your violin into Aspen Rosner's science fair project, teachers look at you differently. They never relax when you're around. They stare at you like you're a walking talking time bomb, just waiting to detonate. Eventually you can't stand the pressure anymore and you blow.

Mrs. Newfang calls it a "self-fulfilling prophecy."

Asshole Glen says, "If you're going to be blamed for it, you might as well do it."

I think they're both right.

But Mr. Maroney gave me a chance that year. He treated me like a regular kid. *A model student.* I'd never been a model student in my whole life. Even in kindergarten, I was in trouble all the time. Standing in the corner. Losing recess. Phone calls home. But Mr. Maroney looked at me just like everyone else. He wasn't waiting for me to explode. I wasn't perfect that year. I still got into a lot of trouble, but I got in a lot less trouble than the year before, and less serious trouble, too. Little things instead of big things like rocks and punches. That was good.

I miss Mr. Maroney. I loved Mr. Maroney.

Little Napoleon is nothing like Mr. Maroney. He hated me on the first day of class. I could tell just by the way he called my name when he was doing attendance. He said my name like it was a history lesson, full of every bad thing I'd ever done. He made it sound like a shadow, and I knew he was going to hold everything against me all year long, no matter what I did.

Most teachers are like that. They hear about you from another teacher, and they just assume that everything is true. They never bother to ask if the teacher was a jerk. Or if your mom and stepdad fight all the time. Or if you're always stuck taking care of your little brother and sister before school and after school and on the weekends. They don't care if your dad died in your garage or if your mother married an asshole. All they want to know is how many office referrals you had and how many detentions you served and if you do your homework.

That's Little Napoleon. I never had a chance with him. He doesn't understand that sometimes kids get into trouble because the world around them sucks. That it's hard not to lose your temper when everything in your life is hard.

That's why I agreed to help Brian. Not because I like Brian. He's okay, but he's the kind of kid who scares me a little. I may get into a lot of trouble at school, but I don't plan my trouble. Dad used to say that trouble finds me. He was kind of right.

Trouble doesn't find Brian. Brian finds trouble. He organizes trouble.

But I like Brian's plan. Or I did, until I spent today with Sarah Flaherty. Now I'm not so sure.

nine

The house is quiet.

It's been almost two hours since the other mother and Asshole Glen were fighting. I spent an hour in Sarah's bedroom—I can't believe that combination of words exists in the world now—and an hour in the backyard behind the woodpile, waiting, making sure that the fight was over. Killing time. Thinking about Brian and his plan. Thinking of a way to get out of it.

But the house is too quiet. Standing in the middle of the kitchen, I don't hear Charlie or Julia. I don't hear sounds from a TV or video game. I don't hear Charlie stomping around. Nothing.

"Hello?" I say. "Is anyone home?"

I move the curtains aside and peek out toward the driveway. Glen's truck is gone. He's probably taken Julia and Charlie out to pick up a pizza. They love to go to the pizza place. Ideal Pizza lets you pick out your toppings, a little bit of this and a little bit of that, so they put all kinds of stuff on their pizza. It's like a salad bar full of toppings that you toss on to the pie.

"Franken-pizza," Julia calls it.

It's awful.

I check my phone. No messages.

It's weird that they left without me. It's not like I need a babysitter, but they don't just leave without telling me. I hate Ideal Pizza, but still. Just leave me behind?

Maybe they've disappeared, too. Maybe they're being re-placed right now just like Mom. Being duplicated or cloned or whatever. That thought only lasts a second. I push it away. It's crazy and not true, but it sends a shiver down my spine anyway.

I'm home alone, which almost never happens. This is good. I can go back to the basement and see if I can find a place where a body might be buried. I know that Mom isn't really buried in the basement, but I feel like I should make sure. Otherwise I won't stop thinking about it, even though I know she's not down there.

I didn't check upstairs yet, either. I don't think I'll find Mom in one of our bedrooms, but maybe I'll find a clue.

This is starting to feel a lot like one of those episodes of *Scooby-Doo*. The Scooby Gang ends up in some hotel where all the guests are leaving because they've seen a ghost. Then the Scooby Gang sees the ghost, too, and it looks real. This is different than something like *Encyclopedia Brown* because there's a serious creep factor in *Scooby-Doo*. *Scooby-Doo* wants you to believe in the ghost until the gang discov-ers that the ghost isn't real.

Of course, Fred and Velma know that the ghost is bullshit

right from the start, but they don't tell anyone because they're a couple of smart-asses who think that no one else could possibly understand what they already know. Why bother telling your friends—who are scared out of their minds—that there is a rational explanation to the mystery? So the gang splits up instead. Starts looking for clues, and somehow Shaggy and Scooby fall ass-backward into the most important clue of all and discover that it wasn't a ghost after all. Just some angry old groundskeeper who was trying to scare away customers so he could buy the hotel cheap and knock it down to put a concrete factory in its place.

That's the situation I'm in now. Something impossible like a ghost haunting a hotel. It would be as exciting as a *Scooby-Doo* mystery except Mom is missing and something bad has maybe happened to her. Something worse than all the *Scooby-Doo* episodes combined.

I'll skip the basement for now. I'm going to look for clues upstairs. Maybe I'll fall ass-backward into an important one.

I climb the stairs to the second floor. I hear her crying before I reach the top step. I can hear her sniffling and sobbing.

Her door is open.

I try to be quiet as I walk down the hallway. There's a board about halfway down the hallway that squeaks. I've made it squeak a million times, but this time I step over it. I want to sneak up on her, but I don't want her to think I'm sneaking up on her if she catches me. If she knows that I know she's the other mother, she might do something bad. Try to hurt me or Charlie or Julia or even Mom if Mom is still alive.

Mom is alive. I'm an asshole for even thinking that she might not be.

I stay close to the right-hand side of the hallway. I pass by Charlie's and my bedroom. The door is closed. We always keep it closed because if it's open, Glen sees the mess and yells at us. I pass by Julia's bedroom. Her door is open. I look inside. Her bed is made. Not a single thing on the floor. Everything has a place. I don't know how she does it.

When I reach the end of the hallway, I peek my head around the doorway to see her.

The other mother is sitting on the edge of the bed. Part of me was hoping that I would see Mom and all this craziness would be over, but I knew it wouldn't be her. The woman on the bed who isn't my mother is wearing my mother's clothing and has a pillow in her lap. My mother's pillow. She's staring down at it. She looks so sad.

I've looked long enough to know everything I can know, but I can't stop looking. I've never seen my mom cry like this before. She gets mad and cries, but that's not like this. Her mad cry is like when firefighters lose control of their hose and it flaps around and sprays out of control. This is different. This is sad crying. If she wasn't the other mother, I would feel bad for her.

"Michael?"

The woman on the bed with my mother's face and my mother's voice is staring at me. She's stopped crying. Just like that. She still has tears in her eyes, but she's staring up at me like nothing happened. Like she's some kind of robot who can turn crying off and on with the flip of a switch.

"Michael?" she says again.

"Sorry," I say. "I heard you. I was worried."

"I'm fine," she says. "I was just feeling a little over-whelmed."

"Overwhelmed?"

"Yeah." She sighs.

"With what?"

She takes a second to answer, so I know that what is com-ing is a lie. People who tell the truth don't need to think. "You know," she says. "Work. Laundry. Your brother. Lots of stuff."

I'm right. This is bullshit. I don't know this other mother, but I know that she's not crying over work or laundry or even pain-in-the-ass Charlie. These are not those kinds of tears. I've cried tears like this before, and I know damn well what it takes to feel this sad.

Then it comes out. Unplanned and unexpected. "Do you miss Dad?"

I've never asked Mom this question before. I have no idea why I'm asking this woman. The words just fly out.

The other mother is just as surprised by my question as I am. Her eyes go wide for a moment. "Of course I do," she says. Her words sound so real and honest.

I wish this were my real mother saying these words. I wish my real mother felt this way.

"Me, too," I say. "I really miss him."

I know.

"I know?" These two words make me so angry. Who is this woman who is pretending to be my mother and pre-tending to know me? Saying things that I wish my mother would say to me?

I know?

My hand closes into a fist.

"Do you want to go to the cemetery tomorrow?" she asks. "To visit him?"

I take a step forward. It's not planned. It's the kind of thing that happens at school. Somebody says something and before I even realize it I'm moving, fists closed, ready to punch him in the ear or the nose.

I stop. I'm able to stop. Not because I'm using one of Mrs. Newfang's strategies. This isn't just some asshole kid in the cafeteria or a bully in the locker room. This is someone who probably knows where my mother is. Someone who can explain what the hell is going on. This is an impossible person. And even if I wanted to hit her, I don't think I could. If she's as strong as my mother, I might not win. And she looks like my mother. So much like my mother. Too much like my mother to hit her.

"The cemetery?" I say. "Maybe." But the real answer is no. No way I'm going to the cemetery tomorrow.

"We can go together," she says.

"Maybe," I say again.

"You can't stay away forever."

"Jesus! I said maybe."

"Okay," she says in her too-calm voice. "Just think about it."

There's nothing to think about. I loved my dad. I still love him, if you can love a dead person. Maybe I love the memory of him. The way he used to be before he died in the garage.

But I hate him, too. I might hate him more than I love him.

How am I supposed to stand over the grave of a man who I hate more than I love? A man who I want to forget more than anything else in the world? A man whose secret only I know?

"Where'd everyone go?" I ask, trying to change the subject. "Pizza?"

"Yeah," she says. "They should be back soon."

"Okay." I turn to leave. I stop. It's the perfect moment and maybe the worst moment to ask my question. I turn. "When did you fall in love with Dad?" I ask. "Was it the day you met him in the hospital?" The question is ridiculous. This isn't Mom. I'm asking an impostor or a pod person or a robot, but maybe this woman has the same memories as Mom, which is also ridiculous but feels true. Maybe what she tells me—even though she's not Mom—will be true.

Maybe knowing this isn't Mom makes it easier to ask, too.

"No," the other mother says. She laughs a little and shakes her head as if she's remembering something. "He asked me out that day. While I was finishing off his cast. But I almost said no. He was so ornery that day. Not much to like about him."

"Ornery?"

"Angry," she says. "Annoyed. His arm was broken. It hurt like hell. But even worse, he knew he was going to be out of work for at least a month, which was hard for your father even back then. I sometimes think that's why he asked me out. He knew he was going to have a lot of free time on his hands."

"So when did you know, then?" I ask. "When did you fall for him?"

"Our first date," she says. "We went to the Dairy Queen over in Milford. The waitress dropped my ice-cream cone right into my lap as she was handing it to me. She was

young. A teenager, I think. Super embarrassed. Her boss—
who wasn't much older than she was—saw the whole thing,
and he came running over, all huffing and puffing. I didn't
care about the ice cream. I thought it was funny. No big
deal. But this manager let her have it. He was about ten seconds into this ridiculous speech about treating customers
with respect when your father stood up and sort of wedged
himself between the manager and the waitress. Then he
said, 'Decent people don't do this kind of thing. Knock it
off.' I'll never forget it. You should've seen that manager. He
folded like a paper doll."

"That was it?" I ask. "That's when you knew?"

"That's when I knew. Nothing better in this world than
a man who stands up to tyranny."

I wish I knew if this story was true. I wish I knew if this
woman was telling me the truth or just telling me something I need to hear so she can keep pretending to be my
mother.

"What about Glen?" I ask. "When did you know about
him?" I can't bring myself to say, "When did you fall in love
with him?" The idea that my mother loved my father and now
loves Glen makes no sense to me, even if this isn't my mother.

"I'm afraid that wasn't quite as dramatic," she says. "It
was mostly the way he didn't care that I was a single mother
with three kids. The way he took you guys on like you were
his own. Not a lot of guys his age are willing to take on a
family like that, especially later in life. It's a lot of baggage
to assume."

"You're right," I say flatly. "Not nearly as dramatic."

"Love can't always be a fairy tale," she says. "Sometimes
it's gritty and practical and sweet. But it's still love."

"Sure," I say, but this sounds like bullshit. It sounds nothing like what my mother would say to justify bringing Asshole Glen into our lives.

"You don't have to visit the cemetery to talk to your father." The words startle me. Anytime someone mentions my father unexpectedly, it's like getting punched in the gut.

"Yeah?"

"He's always listening," she says. "He's always with you."

"Except there's no heaven," I say.

"You really believe that?"

"Yes. Don't you?"

She doesn't answer for a second. I wonder if she's somehow calculating probabilities. Analyzing possibilities. Deciding what my real mother would likely say.

Or just getting ready to lie again.

"I don't know," she says. "But I hope you're wrong. I want to believe."

It's a good answer. I don't know if it's Mom's answer, but it's one of those parent answers that lets them say something and nothing at the same time.

I turn and head back down the hallway. I leave the other mother sitting on the edge of the bed.

There is no heaven. I don't know who she is, but we at least agree on that.

ten

No one should have to eat a pizza with a dozen toppings un-evenly spread out. Toppings that don't even go together, like pineapple and anchovies and barbecue chicken. *Eggplant.* No one in our house even likes eggplant. It's ridiculous.

Charlie is so stupid.

I assume it was Charlie. Julia would never do something so stupid.

It's not even good pizza. The crust is lousy. The sauce is too sweet. It's like they know their pizza sucks, so they trick you into buying it by letting you touch the toppings your-self. And it works. We go back again and again.

Julia and Charlie and I are eating alone at the table. Glen said that he and Mom would eat some "real food" later, after his softball game, but then he grabbed a slice and left the room while shoveling it into his mouth.

Charlie is reading again. This time it's one of his end-of-the-world prepper guides. He's lost in the book. His head is practically hanging in his paper plate. I could set his feet on fire and it would take him ten minutes to notice. The boy is terrified about the world ending and has "In case of fire" and "In case of flood" escape plans taped in every room of the house, but if his head is in a book, the whole house could be in flames and he might not notice. He's chewing with his mouth open. He's got sauce all over his face and shirt. There's even a little in his hair.

Was I so stupid when I was his age?

"I like Sarah," Julia says. Her words startle me. She's been quiet since she got home with the pizza. Really quiet. I've been wondering why she's so quiet. Hoping that maybe she had finally seen the other mother, too.

"Yeah," I say, "I like her, too." Charlie doesn't even hear us. He's too concerned with a list of emergency medical supplies and the expected lifespan of rechargeable solar batteries. Still, I speak in a whisper. This feels like something for me and Julia but not for him.

"She *really* likes you." Julia says this as she pulls another slice of Franken-pizza from the box. She's looking down at the pizza as she says it. She's trying to make it seem like no big deal. *Nonchalant*, it's called, which means that you pretend that something gigantic is tiny. It's a perfect way to tell me that Julia likes me. No big deal except it's a huge deal. Nonchalant is like an invisible exclamation point.

Sometimes I think she's the smartest fourth grader in the world.

"I don't know if she likes me," I say. "But she doesn't hate me, and that's pretty good for me."

Julia laughs.

"But next year we go to high school. She'll make new friends and forget all about me."

"I can't wait to go to high school," Julia says.

"Don't be in a rush," I say. I sound like Sarah's parents, trying to hold back Julia from growing up, but in truth, I can't wait, either. Anything for a fresh start. "Elementary school is a pretty good gig," I tell Julia. "Recess every day. A lot less homework. Less drama. No detentions. Be careful what you wish for."

This is advice that Dad gave us all the time.

"Be careful what you wish for" is something I've been thinking about a lot since I found the other mother standing in our kitchen. I wished a million times that my mother would stop fucking up our family, and now she's gone. Gone and replaced. It's like my worst wish came true. Like some asshole genie found a way to make my wish come true in the worst way.

"I don't know what will happen next year," Julia says. "But Sarah likes you now. She likes you today. Who cares about next year?"

"Maybe," I say, "but it won't last. She'll figure out that I'm a weirdo soon enough."

"You're not a weirdo."

"And she's older than me. Almost a whole year apart. And a lot smarter."

"Smarter? Maybe," Julia says, but I can tell she doesn't mean it. "But who cares? Maybe she'll stop you from doing something stupid."

"I don't think anyone can do that."

Julia smiles. "And the year apart is nothing. You're in the same grade. That's all that counts. Mom and Dad were *seven years apart.* Just think. When Dad was your age, Mom was seven or eight years old. Younger than me and Charlie."

"Yeah, but they were in their twenties when they met. Age isn't as big a deal when both people can drive a car and eat ice cream for dinner and stay up as late as they want."

"You know what I mean," Julia says.

"I know."

"I wish I could've been there when they met," Julia says. "You know?"

I nod. I've seen old photos of Mom and Dad, but they are like tiny windows into a time that seems just out of reach. Right around the corner but forever around the corner. It's hard to imagine that those young, smiling people were ever real.

Julia's eyes return to her pizza. She's thinking again. She's finished with this conversation. I can tell. I start to get up from the table when she surprises me.

"Do you think—" She bites her lip. She has something important to say.

"What?" I ask, sitting back down. Something about the look on her face tells me that I don't want her to finish her question. She looks worried. Maybe even scared.

"Do you think that Dad can see us? Do you think he's watching us?"

I can't believe she's asking this. Less than an hour ago, the other mother and I talked about the same thing. This is *Matrix* shit. A glitch in the system. Proof that this is all some kind of computer simulation, which would be great if it was. That would at least explain the other mother. Maybe

Mom's programming got buggy and the machine over-
lords had to replace her with a new version of herself. An
update.

That actually makes the most sense so far.

The answer to Julia's question is no, of course. No. Dad
doesn't watch us because there is no God. No heaven. The
whole idea is ridiculous. It's nothing but a bunch of old stories that people who thought the Earth was the center of
the universe turned into religion because they were afraid of
death. No, Dad isn't watching. He's gone. Disappeared forever. It's just us living people and the dead people buried under our feet.

Dad didn't believe in heaven, either. He used to say,
"There are only two things a person can do: breathe the air
or sleep with the worms. There ain't no before, no after or
no in between. It's just one or the other."

Mom hated when he said that.

"No," I say to Julia. "I don't think Dad's watching. Not
all the time, at least. Heaven is probably full of things he
loved. Right? Old cars. Springsteen songs. *MacGyver.* I bet
he stays busy. He's probably fixing an engine and listening
to 'Born to Run' right now. Besides, when he was alive, he
didn't watch us all the time, so why would he now? But
he probably checks in on us. Looks at our report cards.
Watches your dance recital. Makes sure Charlie isn't playing in traffic. That kind of thing."

"I don't play in traffic," Charlie says, still staring at his
book.

"You're right," I say. "You're more like a human speed
bump."

"That happened once!" Charlie says.

"Heaven's not full of *everything* he loves," Julia says. "Maybe he watches us more than you think."

My heart breaks for her. I'm sadder about Julia's loss than my own, which seems impossible. I can't imagine anyone missing their father more than I do or feeling sadder about his death more than me, and yet, I look at Julia and feel like I would do anything to take away her pain. I got to know Dad for five years longer than she did. Practically a lifetime.

"You're right," I say. "He's definitely missing some of the things he loves up there. But you'll get to heaven for sure someday. I'm a maybe at best. And Charlie? No chance. God's not interested in pains-in-the-butt."

"Don't joke about that stuff," Julia says. "It's not funny." She sounds like Mom.

"Sorry," I say. I wish I believed like Julia believes. It must make everything else so much easier.

"Do you think that Dad likes Glen?" Julia asks.

I stare at her. It's like she's chosen this moment to ask me all the biggest questions in the world. One after another. I open my mouth to say something, but nothing comes out.

"What?" she asks.

"How am I supposed to know?" I ask. "I can't imagine he loves the guy."

"Don't you think he'd want Mom to be happy?"

"I guess," I say. "But if it was me, I might want my wife spending the rest of her life missing me. Dreaming about me."

"Dreaming about you?" Julia says. "For the rest of her life?"

"Yeah," I say. "Why not?"

"Seems kind of selfish to me."

"Me, too," Charlie chimes in.

"Maybe," I say. "But she didn't need to move on so fast. She could've waited a few years before getting married again. And of all the guys in the world, she chose Glen? If Dad was still alive, I don't think he and Glen would be friends."

"Why not?" Julia asks.

"Why not?" I ask. I can't believe I need to answer this question. "The two are like total opposites. Dad owned his own business. He worked hard. He made money. He was tough. Glen . . . he's none of those things."

"Not exactly two peas and a pod," Charlie says.

I open my mouth to correct him, but the word *pod* hits me like another punch in the gut. Two peas—Mom and Glen—and a pod—the other mother. Pod. A pod person. It seems too perfect to be a coincidence. Too creepy. More *Matrix* shit.

"I guess," Julia says, sounding disappointed with my answer.

"What?" I ask. "What'd you want me to say?"

"I don't know," Julia says, her eyes returning to the pizza. "I just wish I knew if Dad likes Glen."

"Why?"

"If I knew for sure that Dad was okay with Mom and Glen, maybe it would be easier to like him. I feel like being nice to Glen is somehow turning my back on Dad, and I hate that."

"You want to be nice to Glen?"

"It's not like he's going anywhere," she says. "And he loves us. I know he's sometimes not the nicest person, but he loves Mom, and he loves us."

I raise my eyebrows in disbelief.

"It's true," she says. "And you know it. He loves us. No one is perfect, and finding someone who would love a woman and her three kids wasn't easy. We're not easy. Anyone who's willing to jump into this family can't be that bad."

Julia is a negotiator. She compromises. Tries to make things work. Tries to get along with people. Tries to make friends. And she usually does, no matter who it is. Given enough time, she can make friends with almost anyone. It's kind of amazing.

I get stuck with my ideas. I don't bend. I don't care if my mother is going to be married to Glen for the rest of my life. Glen is an asshole. Even if it would make my life easier to find a way to get along with him, I can't. I don't want to.

I'm not sure who I'd rather be. Julia's way seems like a better way to live, but my way feels right. Julia is like a rubber hose. She can bend and weave. Her opinions are flexible. I'm like an iron pole. I only point in one direction. I stand by what I believe, even when it causes me problems or hurts someone's feelings. Mom says I'm stubborn, but I tell her that I'm only stubborn because I know I'm right. And I'm right about Glen. He's an asshole.

"Have you noticed anything different about Mom lately?" Julia asks.

My heart leaps. "Yes," I say, holding back my excitement. Trying to stay calm. "Why? What did you see?"

"She seems sad. Sadder than usual."

"We're all sad," Charlie says, looking up from his book for the first time.

"What do you mean?" Julia asks.

"I don't know about you, but I'll probably be sad for the rest of my life. Isn't that how you're supposed to feel when your dad dies? She's probably just thinking about him a lot lately. Their birthdays are coming up in a couple weeks. It makes sense."

Mom and Dad shared a birthday, and they got married on that same day, too. It was like a super holiday in our family. Annibirthdaypalooza, we called it, which was great before Dad died. It made it feel like they would be together forever. It was just too perfect and too special for the world to ever ruin it. But now it's like a giant black hole in the calendar.

"Is that all you noticed?" I ask. "That she's sad?"

"Not just sad," Julia says. "Like *really sad*. When Dad died, she was the least sad of all of us. Or at least that's what it seemed like. I barely saw her cry at all. But now she cries all the time. Yesterday she was crying in the bathroom. She had the water running, but I could still hear her."

"She's crying all the time?" I ask.

"Maybe not all the time, but a lot. But it's more than just crying. She seems depressed. You don't see it?"

"You think Mom's depressed?" Charlie asks. Charlie is now worried. *Depressed* is very different than *sad*. Depressed is a medical condition. I know this because Charlie has explained it to me many times. When Dad died, Charlie was worried that he might become depressed, and if he became depressed, he might kill himself. He talked about it for months. He actually asked Mom for antidepressants. "Just in case I get depressed," he said. He wanted the pills ready to go—just like his life jacket and canned food—in case of an emergency.

"I don't know if she's depressed or just sad," Julia says. "But I'm worried about her."

We sit in silence, eating the last of the pizza. I consider what Julia has just said. How I found the other mother crying in her bedroom. Maybe the other mother really doesn't know that she's the other mother. Maybe she thinks she's Mom.

Charlie's attention has returned to his prepper's guide. I look across the empty pizza box at Julia. I smile. She nods and smiles back, but it's not a real smile.

Julia is worried about the wrong person, and I want to tell her that. I want to tell her about the other mother and our missing mother. She's seen a difference, so maybe she'd believe me. Maybe if I told her, she would see the other mother as clearly as I do.

I can't, of course. Even if she believes me, it wouldn't change anything. Two kids claiming that their mother isn't their mother wouldn't be any better than one kid. I have to solve this on my own.

I need a plan.

eleven

My Problems
**(in no specific order except the first one is
the biggest one):**

1. My mom is still missing.
2. The other mother has replaced her.
3. I'm scared.
4. I didn't sleep last night.
5. There's a shovel in my basement that I can't stop thinking about.
6. Asshole Glen is still my stepfather.
7. Sarah Flaherty knows I exist.
8. I have three detentions this week.
9. Brian and I start our plan tomorrow.
10. I don't have enough strategies to keep from getting full.

11. I'm afraid that when I see Mrs. Newfang today she'll see what I'm thinking or trick me into telling the truth.
12. The letter in the yellow envelope under my mattress won't stop being real.

twelve

I open my eyes. Julia is standing over my bed, looking down at me. "What?"

Julia holds her finger to her lips to silence me. She motions to Charlie, who is fast asleep in the bed next to me. She leans down. Brings her mouth close to my ear. Whispers. "Get dressed. Meet me in the kitchen. Don't wake Charlie."

I look at the red digits of the alarm clock on the table beside my bed.

12:37 a.m.

"Why?" I whisper.

She shushes me with her finger again. She turns to leave, and I see that she's still wearing her pajamas. The pink footy ones with the little flying princesses.

"Hey," I whisper. "Why do I have to get dressed?"

She ignores the question and leaves the room.

Then I realize what this is about.

Julia knows. She's figured it out.

I pick a pair of jeans and a T-shirt off the floor and put them on. I stuff my feet into sneakers. I head downstairs, wondering when she realized that our mother had been replaced. Did she know all along like me? Has she been keeping it from me like I kept it from her? This suddenly seems more than possible. It seems probable. Did she catch the other mother doing something? I'm not sure if I'm happy that Julia knows. It feels good not to be alone anymore, but now I'll have to worry about Julia, too. I'll need to keep her safe.

The first floor is dark save a smudge of yellow light coming from the kitchen. Probably the bulb over the sink. As I step onto the linoleum and look over the counter toward the sink, I freeze. I stifle a scream.

Julia isn't alone. Standing in the shadows beside her is Sarah.

"Quiet," Julia whispers. "What is wrong with you? You'll wake up the whole house."

"What are you doing here?" I ask.

"Are you incapable of whispering?" Julia asks.

"All right. But you two scared me half to death," I whisper. I walk across the kitchen so only the counter separates us. "What's going on?"

"I'm sorry," Sarah says. "This is my fault. I didn't know what window was yours, so I guessed wrong. But it turns out it was a good thing I did. I didn't know you shared a bedroom with Charlie. That would've been a disaster."

"What are you talking about?" I feel like I've started reading a book somewhere in the middle.

Julia sighs. Even in the partial light, I can see her roll

her eyes. "Sarah threw pebbles at my window thinking it was your bedroom. She woke me up, so I went and got you."

I turn to Sarah. "Why were you trying to throw pebbles at my bedroom window?"

Julia shakes her head. "She was trying to wake you up, dummy. She wanted to see you."

Sarah shrugs her shoulders and smiles.

"You get it now?" Julia asks.

"Yes," I say. "I get it." I want to tell her that it's perfectly reasonable for me to be confused when the situation involves the most beautiful girl in school tossing pebbles at my window to get my attention in the middle of the night. It's not exactly an everyday occurrence.

"Good," Julia says. "Then I'm going back to bed. I'm beat." As she turns her back to Sarah and walks around the counter and past me in the direction of the staircase, she smiles and flashes me a wink.

"Goodnight," she whispers. "Don't you two stay up all night. We all have school in the morning."

Sarah and I say nothing until Julia disappears around the corner and up the stairs.

"It's hard to believe that she's only in fourth grade," Sarah says.

"Tell me about it," I say. "She walks around in footy pajamas and is still afraid of the dark, but she talks like someone who could be running for president."

"It must be neat to have her for a sister."

"Sometimes it feels like a blessing," I say. "But other times it can be a damn curse."

Sarah laughs. I will never get tired of making her laugh.

"I wish I had a sister," she says. "It can get lonely as an only child."

"I dream of loneliness. A little peace and quiet would be nice."

"Oh, I'm sorry to wake you. It's so late."

"I wasn't talking about you," I say, feeling stupid. "It's no problem. I'm happy to see you."

As I say the words, I regret them immediately. I'm happy to see you? Why don't I just tell Sarah that I love to listen to her laugh. Or that I'm falling in love with her. Why is it that the worst thing you can say to a girl who you like is anything that would make her think that you like her? It's so stupid.

"Good," she says. "I'm glad, too."

"Is everything okay?"

"I couldn't sleep, and I was hoping that you might still be awake, too. But if you want to go back to bed, this can wait until tomorrow."

"No," I say, maybe a little too fast. "I'm fine. I just went to bed a little bit ago. But maybe we should go outside. My mother's a nurse. She gets called in at all hours, and lately she's been taking every shift she can get. She could come downstairs at any time."

I don't tell her that the other mother is upstairs, and I don't trust her. It sounds ridiculous, but she might be some kind of android that doesn't sleep. That's a stupid thing to think, but unless I'm trapped in the Matrix, I can't think of anything else to think. And if she is an android or a pod person or anything else, I can't let her catch us in the kitchen, even if we're just talking. I feel like it might be the worst thing that could happen.

"Sure," Julia says. "We can sit in the gazebo behind my house." As she turns to head to the door, I remember that I'm wearing jeans that have been on the floor for days and a T-shirt with an enormous brown stain on the front from who-knows-where. And my hair. There's no telling what it might look like.

"I'm sorry I'm such a mess," I say.

"Shut up," she says, grabbing my wrist and pulling. "Don't be dumb."

It's warm outside, but a breeze blows through the slats of the gazebo, bringing a chill to the air. Sarah sits beside me, close enough for our shoulders to touch. Her arms are crossed over her chest, trying to stay warm. She's wearing a white T-shirt, plaid pajama pants and sneakers.

She didn't dress for the occasion either.

"I hate nights when the moon isn't out," she says, craning her neck to search the night sky. "It's so depressing. A sky without a moon, I mean. There should be a rule that the moon is required to come out every night no matter what. The sun never takes a day off. Why should the moon?"

"It might be hard to get a big, dead rock to obey your rule."

"Yeah, I know. I just like it when things make sense. Sun in the daytime. Moon in the nighttime. That makes sense to me. You know?"

"Sure," I say. "But maybe you appreciate the moon more because it's not always waiting for you. And it's always changing. Never the same two nights in a row."

"Too much of a good thing?"

"Exactly."

"So what happened?" I ask. I know she's beating around

the bush, trying to find a way to get started. I do this kind of thing with Mrs. Newfang all the time. It feels strange to just say the thing that's on your mind. It's like you need to find the right stones in the river to step on before you can get across. You can't just dive in and start swimming for the other side.

"What do you mean?" Sarah asks.

"What's wrong?" I ask. "Did something happen? I assume you didn't wake me to complain about the moon."

"Oh. Yeah. Nothing new happened. Nothing that didn't happen before." She looks up again. Staring at the moon that isn't there. "I guess the only new thing is you."

"Did I do something wrong?"

"No," she says. "Nothing at all."

I wait for her to say something else, which is easy because I have no idea what to say. I'm sitting in a gazebo after midnight with Sarah Flaherty. Close enough that I can feel the heat of her body on mine. The impossibilities are piling up.

"Maybe you did," she says after a beat. "You asked me about my parents. Earlier. When we were in my bedroom."

"I'm sorry. I didn't mean to pry." A phrase Mrs. Newfang says to me a lot but never means. Her job is to pry. Even I know that.

"No, don't be sorry," Sarah says. "I haven't had anyone to talk to since we moved. Before that, even. No one I could trust, at least. Do you know why we moved?"

"You were desperate to live next door to Charlie?"

Sarah smiles a little but doesn't laugh. Something in my gut tells me that nothing could make her laugh at this moment.

"We moved here . . ." She stops speaking for a moment. She looks down at her hands. She has something to say. Something she wants to say, but saying the words will be hard. I know this feeling. I can spot it a mile away. I'm actually made of this feeling. Boil me down in a test tube and you'll have a bunch of atoms that all want to scream something important but can't.

I wait. I'm patient. Another Mrs. Newfang strategy. Don't speak. Let the other person do the talking that you know they want to do.

Sarah takes a deep breath. "We moved here because my dad cheated on my mom with someone at his office. A paralegal named Gail. A married woman. Can you believe it?"

"It happens a lot, I think."

"I know," she says, suddenly sounding energized. Like I have said the perfect thing in response. "That's the thing. I used to think my dad was special. The best dad in the whole world, but even more than that. I thought he was a unique human being. You know what I mean? Then he goes and does this awful, average thing. If he had robbed a bank or hijacked a plane, at least that would've been interesting. Something special. But no. He had sex with the woman named Gail who worked down the hall. And in some sleazy motel a couple miles from our house. It's so ordinary. So . . . ? I don't know."

"Mundane?"

"Yes," she says. "That's really it. Mundane. My dad wasn't supposed to be mundane. He was supposed to be someone other people wanted to be."

"How do you know about it?"

"I heard them arguing," she says. "I heard Mom, really. Dad was silent. He had nothing to say."

"So you moved here to get away from the other woman?"

"Yeah," Sarah says, craning her head again at a moonless sky. I wish I could make the moon appear. Like the presence of the moon might make it better for her. "Mom made him quit, so he had to find a new job. I guess he screwed everyone in the deal, me included. I had to leave all my friends behind because he needed to fuck some other woman. Some stupid married woman named Gail down the hall who he didn't even love." She sniffles a little. A tear slides down her cheek.

"I'm so sorry." It's all I can say. I don't know what else to say.

"There's so much about the situation that sucks, but mostly, I just hate how my dad isn't who I thought he was. He used to be my hero. I wanted to grow up and be just like him. Now he's someone I don't even recognize. Someone I don't trust anymore. He's just some stupid man who couldn't be faithful to his wife and daughter. I feel like I don't know him anymore. You know what I mean? I feel like I'll never really know him ever again."

That door opens again. I can feel it swing smoothly on its hinges. Her words are the key that opens it. If I want to, I can step right through and tell Sarah my secret. One of them at least. I'm frozen, caught on the threshold. I want to tell her. I know that this is the right moment. Sarah has all but invited me to speak. It's almost as if she wants me to tell her the secret that she doesn't know exists. But the tricky thing about secrets is that once you tell them, they can never be untold. Telling a secret is like changing the world forever.

"What's wrong?" Sarah asks. She sees me trapped on the threshold, wanting to step through. She reaches out and takes my hand. As she squeezes it, she pulls me through.

"My mother," I say. Two words that say it all to me but mean nothing to her. Two words so hard to say that they feel like I'm trying to roll a boulder. I haven't really said anything yet. Not even close. I'm not sure if I can. Those two words were hard enough to say already. I mark the seconds as they pass, waiting for a sign. Waiting for something that will tell me to finish the impossible sentence.

"Your mother?" Sarah asks.

"Yes," I say. "My mother." I take a deep breath. I step all the way through the door. "My mother," I repeat. "She's missing."

"She's missing? What do you mean?"

The boulder is rolling now. Down a hill, I think. I just need to run to keep up. The words begin tumbling out of my mouth. "This is going to sound crazy, but my mother is missing. There's a woman inside my house who looks just like her, but it's not my mother. It's someone else. Some other mother."

The corners of Sarah's mouth begin to turn up into a smile, but then she sees me. Really sees me. I'm shaking. My hands and arms are trembling. Tears are welling in my eyes.

"You're serious," she says. This isn't spoken as a question. It's a statement of impossible fact, though the impossibility makes it feel like a question, too.

I nod slightly. I'm afraid to do more. I feel like I might

fall apart at any moment. Like I'm being held together by some powerful magnet at my core that's losing its attraction by the second. At any moment, I feel like I could collapse into spare parts on the floor.

"Mike," she whispers, even though there's no longer a need to whisper. "That's not possible."

"I know. But it's true. It's impossible but real."

"How do you know?" she asks.

"I can see it. No one else can, but I can. I took one look at her this morning and knew it wasn't Mom. She looks like Mom except everything is a tiny bit off."

"Maybe you were overtired. Or sleepwalking. Do you sleepwalk?"

"I saw her a few times today. It's not her. Believe me, I want it to be her. It's just not."

She reaches out for my other hand. She holds them both in hers. She squeezes. "Mike, that can't be. Maybe your eyes are playing tricks on you. Maybe you need glasses."

"It's not my eyes," I say. My voice sounds weak, like I'm about to cry. "Everything about her is wrong. Her voice. The way she moves. The way she's speaking to me. What she says. Everything. It's all just a tiny bit off."

"But Julia and Charlie don't see it?"

I shake my head.

"Your stepfather?"

"Nope."

"Mike." She says my name but somehow behind the single word is so much. It's worry and disbelief and confusion and caring and maybe even love. I think I hear love in her voice. Not the kind of love that will have us making out any second, but the kind of love that lasts longer. I think she might love me. She might only love me in this moment, but it feels as real as the other mother does not.

"I know," I say. "It's crazy, except I'm not crazy. I promise that I'm not crazy."

"I don't think you're crazy, but how can it be?"

"Every crazy thing in this world once started out as impossible. Right? Dinosaurs seemed impossible at first when people started finding their bones. The creatures that live at the bottom of the sea and get their food from the chemicals around vents in the ocean floor. It was science fiction until someone actually found them. Charlie told me about that one. And can you imagine telling someone two hundred years ago that we would be walking around with an encyclopedia in our pocket? Even a telephone in our pockets would've seemed impossible. Maybe this is just another one of those things. Impossible and crazy until it's real."

"Mike, I promise you. It's your mom."

"You don't know that," I say. There's unexpected anger in my voice. "You don't know my mother. I've known Mom longer than anyone. If anyone would know, I would."

"If that's not your mother, where is she?"

"I don't know," I say. This question breaks me open. I start to cry. Tears roll down my cheeks. I've tried so hard to not think about my mother. Tried not to think about where she could be and what might have happened to her. Now the question is standing right in front of me like a marble statue. I can't look away. "I don't know," I repeat. "But I'm worried. I'm afraid that something happened to her. That something will still happen to her."

"Oh, Mike." Sarah pulls me into her arms. "I don't know

what's happening, but I'm here for you. Okay? We can fig-ure this out together."

"Okay," I manage between sobs.

"I promise. We'll get to the bottom of this."

"All right," I say.

I'm supposed to feel better now, but I don't. Somehow the burden feels even heavier. Like I have even more to worry about.

And I might.

thirteen

I was hoping that I would wake up this morning and find everything as it should be. One crazy, impossible, ridiculous day over at last. Sarah was hoping for the same, too. "Sleep has a way of washing the dirt away," she said last night. "You'll probably wake up feeling like today was just a bad dream." But as I step into the kitchen, there she is, pouring coffee into Mom's travel mug and watching *Good Morning America* on the little TV on the counter.

For a moment, I can barely move. I've heard people say that they've felt gutted when something terrible happens, but I never understood what that really meant. I always thought it sounded a little too dramatic, the same way people like to make a big deal out of a cheeseburger or a slice of pie at some new restaurant around the corner from their house. But I understand it now. For the first time in my life, I feel gutted. A tiny part of me—maybe the best part of me—was sure that this would be over. Mom would be back. Life would be normal again. Seeing the other mother standing there in my mother's clothes, pouring coffee into my mother's coffee cup makes all of this feel so real. So permanent. No matter what happens after this moment, I know that my life will never be normal again.

"Hi," I say. I try to sound normal even as I feel like I'm falling apart inside.

She turns. "Oh, hey, kiddo." She smiles before turning back to finish with her coffee. It looks like a real smile; but it's not my mother's smile. It's a little off, like everything else.

I take a second to look at her closely as she rinses the empty coffeepot in the sink. I want to be sure. Sarah's words are still ringing in my ears. The way she kept saying, "It can't be." She sounded so certain, and I can't blame her. An impossible thing is happening to me. I can barely believe it myself. How could I expect someone who has known me for exactly one day to believe me?

But I don't need the closer look. It's not Mom. No question. The differences are microscopic, but they all add up to someone who is so clearly not my mother. Her eyes aren't as blue as Mom's or nearly as bright. Her hair is a little shorter and curlier in the back. She's heavier. Just a little bit bigger around her waist and thighs, but I can see it clear as day. And she looks tired. More tired than Mom has ever been. Dark splotches under her eyes. More lines in the crow's feet at the corners of her eyes. Everything about her is just a tiny bit wrong, but it makes her completely wrong. She looks like the hand-me-down version of my mother. A thrift-store version of the woman she replaced.

My hands ball into fists. My jaw clenches. I don't count to ten. I don't use any of my strategies. Mrs. Newfang would probably disagree, but there are times when it's okay to be angry. Times when it's right to be red. This is one of those times. In my gutted gut, I'm sure that this woman knows where my mother is. She must. You can't step into someone's life like this and fool the world without knowing exactly what you're doing.

She puts the coffeepot into the dishwasher and closes the door. She sighs. Rubs the back of her neck with her hand.

"What happened?" I ask. "To your neck, I mean?"

"Just slept on it funny," she says. "Did a lot of tossing and turning last night." She takes a sip of coffee and smiles. "Thanks for asking."

"Sure," I say. She sounds sincere but I know she's not. Whatever is happening, the last thing she wants is for me to be asking questions. Bad guys hate answering questions. Questions are like traps to them. "Why were you tossing and turning last night?"

"It's just something mothers do," she says. "We look for things to worry about. We can never have enough worry. Sometimes I think that all I do is worry."

"What are you worried about?" I ask.

"It's nothing, honey. Don't you worry."

"If it's keeping you up at night, it can't be nothing," I say. It's one of those questions that isn't a question.

She stares at me for a moment. Sort of squints like she's trying to get a better look at me. For a second, she looks just like Charlie when he stares into the tropical fish in the tank at the doctor's office. It's like Charlie's face is overlapping her face, and for a split second, the two faces become one. Then she smiles. Still not Mom's smile, but a real one.

Unplanned. "It's mostly work stuff," she says. "My supervisor's been riding us a lot this week, and I can't figure out why. He's usually such a good guy. He's never been difficult before, so it makes things stressful for everyone, and our job is stressful enough already." She sighs again. I can see her looking back into her memory on something that happened before. Yesterday, maybe. Something between her and her supervisor. Her lips pinch into a straight line. The space between her eyes wrinkles. "But don't worry," she says, her face relaxing again. "Okay? Lots of people have annoying bosses. I guess I'm just one of those people now."

"Maybe he has something going on at home." I say this quietly. I almost don't say it at all. It feels important and wrong at the same time.

She stares at me again for a second before speaking. Less than a second, really, but I see it just the same. I feel it. It's one of those enormous less-than-a-second moments. She's surprised by what I said. Maybe as surprised as I am about saying it. "What do you mean?" she asks. She sounds like Charlie now. Full of curiosity.

"Sometimes it's hard to keep things together when your life is screwed up somewhere else. It's like when the lion in that story gets a thorn in his paw. He's king of the jungle, but one tiny thorn can make everything else impossible. He goes from king of the jungle to king of nothing, all because of a little bit of dead plant in his foot."

"You think my supervisor has a thorn in his paw?"

"Maybe," I say. "It doesn't take much to turn a good person into a real asshole."

She nods a little. Smiles. "Sometimes just a thorn will do it. Huh?"

"Maybe," I say. "Yeah."

She stares at me as she takes another sip of coffee. "Okay," she says. "What would you suggest then?"

"Me?"

"Yeah," she says. "What should I do?"

"I don't know."

"Well, what would you do? If you were in my shoes?"

It's my turn to pause now, not because I don't know what to say but because I feel like I'm in uncharted territory. I'm worried that I might say something that I shouldn't, and I'm mad at myself for being so nice to her. This woman has probably done something with my mother, but somehow she has me worried about her at the same time. It's like she's hypnotized me into forgetting what she's done, and now I'm stuck in this giant word trap, forced to give an answer. "If I were you," I finally say, "I'd just give him a little time. In the lion story, a mouse pulls the thorn out, but in real life, most thorns don't come out that easily. Sometimes they never come out. But people can figure out how to live with thorns. They learn to limp or hop or grit their teeth and move on. Most of the time they just need time."

"Did you come up with that yourself?" she asks.

"What do you mean?"

"That advice," she says. "Is it yours?"

"I wouldn't call it advice," I say. "It's just a thing that's true. At least, I think it's true."

"Okay," she says. Her smile is the widest it's been all morning. It makes me feel good even though I don't want it to. "I'll give him some time. Maybe bring him a donut."

"Make it a cupcake," I say.

"Yeah? How come?"

"Cupcakes are better," I say. "That's a true thing, too. Everyone knows that."

"Okay. I'll do that. A cupcake."

"Good," I say.

She laughs a little. Shakes her head. "Anything else?"

"Mrs. Newfang says to listen. She says that if you listen carefully, people will tell you what they need. Even if they don't know they're doing it."

"Really?"

"That's what she says," I say, shrugging my shoulders. "I don't know if it's true, but she's right a lot more than she's wrong, so it's worth a try."

"Okay," she says, scooping her keys off the counter and looking over her shoulder at the clock on the microwave. "Maybe I should spend some time with Mrs. Newfang."

"Maybe," I say. The words sound like a joke, but I wish she would spend some time with Mrs. Newfang. If anyone in the world could see that this woman is not my mother, it's Mrs. Newfang. It's her job to figure people out. And she would at least have an open mind going into it. That's part of her job. Kind of like a curse. She has to believe kids until she has a reason to stop believing them.

The other mother turns to the sink to wash her hands. On the television, the *Good Morning America* people start talking about tornados touching down in Georgia. "Dozens killed," the man says. "Hundreds left homeless."

I hate the news people. They sit behind big desks that they don't need and talk as though they've lived through the terrible things that they read about on their teleprompters. All serious and sad. Then they switch from being all serious and sad about dead people to laughing about some recipe for squash soup in the span of one commercial break.

Mrs. Newfang would call this disingenuous. I think it just makes them awful people.

I step forward to turn off the TV, but the other mother turns and flips it off first. "Let's try to keep that news away from Charlie," she says.

"I was thinking the same thing," I say. And I was. Charlie wants us to build a tornado shelter in the backyard, even though there has never been a tornado in our town and probably our state. Apparently the basement isn't safe enough because the house can fall on your head. He even went online and found a company that would build it for about $4,000.

"All set for school?" she asks.

I nod. "I hate Mondays."

"Me, too," she says. "If only every day could be a Friday."

"But you work on the weekends," I say. "Why do you care if it's Monday?"

"It's nice to have you guys home, even if I'm not always here. You know?"

I don't. This is not something my mother would ever say to me.

She takes another sip of coffee. Slurps it just like Mom does. "Thanks, honey."

"For what?" I ask.

"For stopping to talk," she says. "You're usually stuffing cereal into your mouth and staring at your phone. This was nice. And I like your advice. I like it a lot."

"No problem," I say. But now I'm wondering: Did I make

a mistake? Did my change in routine make her suspicious? Does she know that I know that she's not my mother?

If *she* even knows that herself. I'm starting to wonder again.

"You'll get breakfast for the brats?" she asks as she puts her jacket on. Mom's jacket.

"Sure."

I still can't believe that she's going to the hospital. There's so many more people there who she needs to fool. It seems so risky.

Of course she might not be going to the hospital at all. She could be going someplace entirely different. Maybe she's wearing Mom's uniform but going somewhere else. That must be it. You can't just pretend to be a nurse. Being a nurse isn't something you can fake. Mom says that every shift is life or death.

But if she isn't going to the hospital, wouldn't her boss call to check on her? That stuff about her supervisor acting like a jerk was probably real. Maybe she really is a nurse. If you go to the trouble of replacing a person so perfectly that no one except for me can tell, it would only make sense to teach her replacement how to be a nurse, too. I just can't figure out how all those people at the hospital who she works with can't see what I see.

Maybe it's because I've known Mom longer than anyone. I've known her fourteen years. I've known her longer than everyone in the world except Grandma and Auntie Carole, and Grandma lives in Dallas, so we barely see her, and Auntie Carole hasn't seen the other mother yet. Maybe she would see it, too, if I could get them together.

And I guess some of her friends have known her longer, too. Lorraine and Jane. Josie, too. But she doesn't even see them much anymore. Not since Dad died. Not since she started working so much. Maybe that's why I can see the other mother and other people can't. Maybe I know Mom the best.

"Have a good day!" she says as she walks past me toward the door.

I nod. Smile. I'm afraid to say anything else. I'm afraid that these breaks in my routine are going to tip her off. Put me in danger. Put all of us in danger.

fourteen

Asshole Glen still hasn't come downstairs yet. Probably still sleeping. Julia's getting dressed again. She's changed her outfit three times already. She may be smart for a fourth grader, but she still worries a lot about fourth-grade bullshit.

Charlie is sitting on the floor under the coat hooks by the door, reading. His usual spot in the morning. He'll be there until I open the door to leave. Even then I'll probably have to take his book away to get him to move.

He reads more now that Dad is gone.

The bus will be here soon. I want to finish my chart before we need to leave. If I'm going to have a plan, I need to know all that I can know. I need to be organized.

Other Mother Possibilities

Who is she?	Where is Mom?	How much does the other mother know?	Reason/Intent	Probability
Duplicate	Unknown	Everything	Evil	3%
Android (Stepford wife?)	Unknown	Everything? Or nothing?	Evil (Glen?)	1%
Alien	Unknown (alien abduction?)	Everything	Evil? Experimental?	2%
Slippage from a parallel universe	Alternate universe maybe?	Possibly nothing	Accidental	5%
Weird religious shit	Unknown	Everything or nothing	Part of a bigger plan	Less than 1%
This is all just a dream	Same place she's always been	N/A		

I can't decide what to put in the last two empty boxes. "This is all just a dream" would be the best explanation for the other mother. Nothing happened to Mom. The other mother doesn't exist. I'm just stuck in a long, crazy-ass dream that will eventually end.

Except if it really was all just a dream, then fishing with Sarah Flaherty was part of the dream. Later on in her bedroom and last night, too. As much as I want my mom back, I'd hate for it all to have been a dream.

Actually, that might be the best evidence that this is all a dream. What are the chances that Sarah Flaherty would invite me into her bedroom and let our thighs touch like that?

"Ready?" Julia asks. She's practically skipping as she enters the kitchen. She loves school so much. I'll never understand it.

"Are *you* ready?" I ask.

She spins in the center of the kitchen floor. "Don't I look ready?"

She's wearing the same pair of jeans that she had on two outfits ago, but she's wearing a new shirt now. One I've never seen before. She probably borrowed it from Katie or Jen. Julia and her friends swap clothes all the time. I could see Katie owning this one. It's flowery with short, puffy sleeves. Katie's like a fourth-grade hippy. She listens to the Grateful Dead and eats seaweed. She's already cooler than I'll ever be.

"I like it," I say.

"The top?" Julia asks. She calls shirts "tops," which makes sense because she wears it on the top part of her body, but why not just say shirt?

She's also started calling pants and shirts "separates," which I guess means that I've been wearing separates all my life, except that I've never used that word, and I've never heard any of my friends use that word, and I think it's kind of stupid.

Isn't everything that isn't connected to something else a separate?

"You look great. Top and bottom and everything in between." I'd say this even if she looked ridiculous, which she sometimes does. Everyone can use one less asshole in their life.

Julia smiles. She grabs a banana and heads for the door. I save my Other Mother Possibilities chart into my ELA homework folder on my desktop. I name it "Reading response 133" in case the other mother searches my laptop at some point.

I choose 133 because it's Sarah Flaherty's house number.

I grab Charlie's book from his hands as I open the door. He whines. I throw it into the middle of the driveway. "Fetch!" I shout.

Charlie stands and shoves me hard. Almost topples me over.

I don't mind. I get it. Sometimes you just need to give someone a good shove and tell them to go to hell. It just feels good and right. A release of pressure.

Sometimes you want to throw your desk through a window or punch someone in the face, too, but that's a lot harder to get away with. I can't give Charlie a hard time like I do and not expect him to get a little revenge every now and then.

A little revenge every now and then is a lot better than a lot of revenge all at once. I've learned this the hard way.

Charlie shouts, "Hey, Sarah! Are you riding the bus today?"

I look out the doorway. Sarah is standing at the end of the driveway. She's never ridden the bus in her life. Her mother drives her to school every morning. She's not even standing at the bottom of her own driveway. She's standing at the bottom of *our* driveway.

What is she doing?

Then I realize: she's waiting for me.

The door slams. Julia appears beside me. She nudges me with her elbow and giggles. "I think Sarah Flaherty likes you."

Sarah high-fives Charlie at the bottom of our driveway. He's so excited to see her. She takes the book from his hands and turns it over. She holds it in hands that grabbed my wrist yesterday. Hands that touched mine as we cast our fishing line on Barracuda Island. Hands that held mine as I told her my secret last night.

"You should get moving," Julia says. "You look stupid just standing here."

I wish we had mouthwash. I have deodorant on, and I'm wearing clean clothes, but I can't even remember if I brushed my teeth this morning.

Worse, I have absolutely nothing to say.

Still, this has the potential of being the best bus ride of my life. I've never liked the bus. When I was little, the bus scared me. It was loud and bumpy and I couldn't see above the seats, so I never knew where we were going. I couldn't stop imagining us driving into walls or over cliffs.

Then the bus went from scary to torture. An older kid—two grades older than me—named Eddie Raymond teased me every day. He'd call me a pussy and a faggot before I even knew what those words meant. He'd trip me as I walked down the aisle looking for a seat. He'd throw balled-up paper and pennies at me. And he'd laugh at me, which was the worst. Somehow being laughed at is worse than all the other terrible things a person can do.

Even worse, Eddie didn't pick on everyone. Just me. For some reason, he singled me out. Maybe he thought that I wouldn't fight back, and he was right. Back then I wouldn't. I'd just sit there and take it. I'd listen to his bullshit and say nothing. I don't know how he knew that he could pick on me. Maybe that was his talent. Seeing the cracks in people. Finding their broken parts. Knowing who he could hurt and how to hurt them.

Eddie bullied me for three years. He never missed a day. Never let up. There was nothing I could do about it. The bus is a bad place for kids. There's only one adult on the bus, and all he does is drive. He doesn't pay attention to anything going on behind him, and it's always so loud that even if he did have the time to listen, he would've never heard it. Eddie was an asshole, but he wasn't stupid. He kept his voice low. He smiled a lot. He was sneaky. Eddie was like a soft, constant hum of cruelty, day after day, year after year, to and from school.

This went on until last year. October. Eddie was in eighth grade by then. One more year and he'd be off to high school. Gone from my life forever. I couldn't wait. And he looked like he was ready for high school. He already had a shadow of a mustache and some whiskers on his chin. He had bulked up, too. Big arms. Thick neck. A real meathead.

Then one morning—without any warning—Eddie decided to go after Charlie. One day Charlie was a nobody to Eddie. The next day he was a target. It was like some switch had flipped, and suddenly Charlie was someone who he needed to hurt.

Maybe he saw the cracks in Charlie, too.

Charlie was in his seat, reading. That's what he does on the bus. He reads. He barely looks up from his book. Never bothers anybody. But on this particular day, for no reason at all, Eddie reached over and slapped the book out of Charlie's hands. He waved it in the air. Refused to give it back. Called him a "loser nerd," "teacher's pet," and "little butt licker."

Before I even knew what was happening, I was screaming. Telling Eddie Raymond that he was a fucking coward who picked on kids half his size. Calling him a lowlife with no balls. I was screaming at the top of my lungs. Standing.

Hands balled into fists. Spitting as I shouted. I don't remember deciding to do any of it. I just did. I saw Charlie's book in Eddie's hands and heard him call Charlie those names, and I exploded. Everything that I had bottled inside of me for years came out.

I had no idea how angry I was until that moment.

The bus driver shouted at me to knock it off. Told me to sit down. Stared at me through his rearview mirror. He looked at me the same way teachers look at me in school, like I was a time bomb waiting to explode. But I couldn't stop. I just kept screaming. I saw Charlie sitting there, staring at his book still in Eddie's hands, tears filling his eyes, and I couldn't stop.

Then bus driver slammed on the brakes hard enough to knock me back into my seat. That stopped me. It sort of knocked the fight out of me. I could barely breathe. I was shaking. "Sit down and be quiet!" the bus driver yelled. He was turned around in his seat now, pointing his finger at me. He was an older guy with bushy eyebrows and a backward baseball cap. He yelled about all the little kids on the bus who had heard my foul language. Told me how much trouble I was going to be in when we got to school.

Eddie was looking at me, now. He was smiling, knowing how much trouble I was in, but he was scared, too. I could see it in his eyes. He was afraid of me. I stared him down while the bus driver was still shouting, and then—and I still can't believe it—I leaned close and whispered to him, "Give him back the book right now before I kick your ass."

Eddie didn't move, so I stood up and walked toward him. That scared Eddie. It scared me, too. The bus driver shouted for me to sit back down, but I ignored him. Barely heard him. I took three steps toward Eddie and had two more to go before I would be on top of him when he threw the book back at Charlie. I stayed there for another second, staring at him, *staring him down*, and then I sat back down. Eddie turned to the front of the bus. Didn't look back at me again for the rest of the ride. He never looked my way again.

When we got to school, my plan was to walk right past the driver and into school. I knew the principal would eventually come for me, but I didn't want to give the driver the chance to say a single word to me. As I walked past him, he said, "Hey! Where do you think you're going?"

I just kept walking. I grabbed the handrail and started to go down the first step when the driver reached out and grabbed my arm and tried to pull me back. That's when I went after him. I didn't punch him, no matter what he said later on. I just reached out with my open hand and pushed his face away. So he squeezed my arm even tighter. Twisted a little. He was pissed. "Who the hell do you think you are?"

It just came out. "I did your fucking job today! Now let go of me before I call the cops!"

I pushed his face again, and he let go. He looked more surprised than Eddie.

I got in a shit ton of trouble. The only thing that kept me from getting kicked off the bus completely and expelled from school was my arm. The bus driver squeezed it so hard it bruised. And Dad had just died a couple months before. Mrs. Newfang helped me with that. She told the principal and the principal's boss and a bunch of other people that a kid whose dad died a month or two ago isn't entirely responsible for his actions.

I'm glad she helped, but I know that I was plenty responsible.

Eddie didn't say a word to Charlie or me for the rest of the year. The bus driver got moved to a new bus, and now we have Sandra, who knows everyone's name and says hi and bye to me every day.

All of that—the years of Eddie's bullying and the day I shoved the driver and told Eddie that I would kick his ass—it all seemed easier than this, though. Sitting on the bus with Sarah. Sitting in the same seat with Sarah with absolutely nothing to say and knowing that she's going to ask me about the other mother.

"Are you going to ride the bus every day?" Julia asks. She's sitting in the seat across from us with her friend, Penny.

"I don't know," Sarah says. "But my mom was happy to be able to stay in bed a little later today instead of driving. If she had her way, I would."

"You should!" Julia says. "The bus is fun."

"It is?" Sarah asks.

"No. Not really," Julia says, smiling. "I'm just glad you're here."

"Me too," Sarah says.

Julia and Penny pull their lunchboxes from their backpacks and pop them open on their laps. A second later they're swapping food. You're not allowed to trade food at school because of food allergies. The teachers don't want some kid allergic to peanut butter accidentally trading for something with peanuts in it, so they swap on the bus every morning. Serious negotiations. Sometimes it takes the whole ride to school before they can agree.

Julia usually wins. She gets exactly what she wants. When she doesn't, she's just being nice.

"You want to swap lunches, too?" Sarah asks, turning to me.

"I don't think you'd want my lunch. I make my own. It's not . . . I don't know. I just don't think you'd like it. I like it, but I don't think anyone else would. No offense."

Sarah laughs. "I was kidding. I'm buying lunch today. Do you make Julia and Charlie's lunches, too?"

"Yup."

Sarah motions over to Julia and Penny. "Does it hurt your feelings that she's trading away the food you packed for her?"

"No," I say, looking over at Julia. She's offering up a pear for a bag of Cheetos. "I don't care as long as she gets what she wants."

"You're a good brother."

I want to tell Sarah that I wish I was a good brother. Instead, I feel like a terrible parent. Someone who's trying to take care of kids when he can barely take care of himself.

"So how do you feel this morning?" Sarah asks.

"What do you mean?"

She rolls her eyes. Leans in close. "You know what I mean."

"I'm fine," I say, as if these two words are going to stop her from asking more questions. I shouldn't have told Sarah about the other mother. It was a mistake. Sarah is too much of a superhero. Too much of a fixer. She's not going to let it go with a simple, "I'm fine." It's like trying to stop a run-away train by throwing pebbles at it.

"Don't bullshit me," she says.

"I'm not."

"I can see by the look on your face that you're not fine." She says *fine* like it's a dirty dishcloth jammed in her mouth.

Mrs. Newfang says that I wear my emotions on my sleeve, which is a stupid expression because it just means that I wear my emotions on my face. Why even mention a sleeve? But she's right, even with her stupid expression. Some people can hide their feelings and keep them secret from everyone, but I can't. It's kind of like my emotions are more in charge of me than I am of them. Julia's an expert at hiding her emotions. She can be so angry at Glen and still smile. I don't know how she does it.

"It's Monday," I say. "I've got homework and tests to look forward to all week. What do you expect? I'd rather be fishing."

I love this last sentence. *I'd rather be fishing.* It's perfect. It says that I love fishing or that I loved fishing with Sarah. She can take it either way. Except Sarah doesn't look happy with my sentence at all. Her face shifts. She looks annoyed. Now she's wearing her emotions on her sleeve.

"What?" I ask.

"Nothing." It's a two-syllable word, but she somehow says it with just one syllable.

"No," I say, adamant now. "What's wrong?"

"We don't have to talk about it if you don't want to," she says, "but don't tell me that nothing's bothering you."

I want to tell Sarah that this school bus ride is too damn short to solve all my problems, and even though she knows the first problem on the list, there are others that she can't begin to imagine. I want to tell her that it's not as easy as she thinks. My problems aren't regular kid problems. Even without the other mother, I've still got Brian Marcotte and Asshole Glen and a yellow envelope, and each one of these things is too big for me by itself. Bigger than anything that any kid in our school is dealing with.

"Sorry," I say. "I'm fine, though. Seriously."

"And your mom?" she asks. "How is she?"

I consider lying but can't. Not to Sarah. "You said we don't have to talk about it."

"I lied."

I smile. I can't help it. I wish she wasn't asking, but I'm also so happy that she is.

"I'm undecided," I say, which is a lie but somehow feels okay. It's not a big lie. Sort of a half-hearted one.

"Undecided?"

"Yeah," I say. "I'm not going to say that she's my mom, but I'm also not so sure anymore. Maybe it's Mom after all." The lie feels like a boulder now. One that is rolling down a hill. Picking up speed. "Maybe I was wrong. Like you said."

"Did you see her this morning?"

"Just for a second," I say. "I didn't have time to take a good look. But you were right. I felt different this morning. A little better. Maybe it's nothing. Hormones or something making me think like a crazy person."

"Are you sure?"

"Definitely," I say. The boulder is unstoppable now. One lie leads to another and another. Before you know it, you've left the truth somewhere at the top of the mountain. Easy as pie. "I have problems worse than some crazy idea that Mom isn't Mom."

"Yeah?" she says. She stares at me. I'm not sure if she believes me. "Tell me one of them."

"Why?"

"Because I want to know."

"Fine," I say. "I have detention today. Tuesday and Wednesday, too."

"What for?"

I smile at the memory. "I didn't do my homework last week, and when Mrs. Bennett asked me why, I told her that her stupid assignment was stealing my childhood."

Sarah shakes her head. "That was kind of stupid."

"I know. Sometimes I can't help it. And it felt so good to say it, too. It's actually not as stupid as you might think."

"No?"

"I'm serious. It's like a trade. I get to say something perfect and right that makes me feel amazing, and she gets to steal three hours of my life. It doesn't sound like a fair trade, but it's not bad. It's hard to feel that good. Also, the assignment was stupid. Diagramming sentences? Give me a break."

"Okay," she says. "But that's not a problem. That's just detention."

"Have you ever had detention?"

"No."

"Okay, then."

"Fine," she says. "You have detention. What else?"

"You said I only had to tell you one problem."

"If we're going to be friends, you're going to have to actually talk to me."

If we're going to be friends?

I force myself not to smile, but it's almost impossible. In my whole life, I've had exactly one real friend. Now I might have two. And that possible second friend is Sarah Flaherty. It's one of those dreams that are so impossible and so ridiculous that you never bother dreaming it.

But it's even better than having Sarah Flaherty as a friend, because Sarah isn't just the prettiest girl in school and maybe the world anymore. Sarah likes fishing. She's not afraid of silence. She loves Julia in that way that older girls love younger girls who are in trouble or who remind them of themselves. She's easy to talk to. She thinks I'm a good brother. She doesn't think I'm crazy.

I thought she was just pretty, but it turns out that she's perfect. And now she's my friend.

"Okay," I say. "I'll talk, but you'll have to talk, too. Tell me one of your problems."

"I don't have any problems."

The bus comes to a screeching halt just as she finishes her sentence. I reach out to brace myself on the seat in front of me. Sarah grabs my arm.

"I think she tried to beat the light," Sarah says, looking over the seat at the front of the bus.

"Don't change the subject," I say. "Tell me one of your problems."

"Fine," she says. She lets go of my arm and thinks for a second. "My friend Tricia is a pain."

"How so?"

"She's a drama queen. Everything is something with her. It's making me a little crazy."

"Why not ditch her?"

"I can't," Sarah says. "We've been friends since kinder-garten."

"Okay," I say doubtfully.

"What?" She sounds a little angry. "Would you just ditch one of your friends if he was annoying you?"

I want to tell her that Jeff is my only real friend, so no. I wouldn't ditch him no matter what he did. When you only have one friend in the whole world, you hold on to that person like your life depends on it. You cling to him in the same way Charlie clings to his life vest and his canned food and all the other things that make him feel safe. But Sarah has lots of friends. She could lose one and still be fine. She wouldn't understand.

"No," I say. "I guess I wouldn't just ditch my friend. But if he was being a dick, I hope I'd tell him."

"It's not that easy," she says. "Girls are more complicated than boys. And people don't change just because you point out their flaws. Sometimes it's not worth the trouble."

"I guess," I say. "But sometimes just saying the thing you're thinking is important. It will make you feel better. I got assigned three detentions for telling Mrs. Bennett how I felt about her homework assignment, but it was worth it. I said the thing I wanted to say, even if it cost me three hours of my life."

"Maybe I'll mention it to Tricia," she says. "If she ever lets me talk about something other than her. Okay, your turn."

"What?"

"A problem," she says. "Tell me another one."

"I thought we weren't swapping?" I say, motioning over to Julia and Penny. It looks like negotiations have ended. Both lunchboxes are put away.

"Very funny," Sarah says. "Stop changing the subject."

"Fine. My stepfather is an asshole."

"How so?"

"In every possible way," I say. "He's stupid and lazy and a prick. I call him Asshole Glen. But never to his face."

"What's one thing that he does that you hate? Give me an example."

"He doesn't work hard enough, so my mom has to work twice as hard to support the family. That's the worst thing he does. By a lot."

"Maybe your mother should say something," Sarah says. "Take your advice."

"I don't think she'd listen," I say. "And honestly, I think she already knows. But even if she took my advice, it's too late."

"What do you mean?"

"Mom's been working double shifts for more than a year now. Maybe two. Even if she won the lottery tomorrow, she's already lost a year of her life. Instead of being at home with her kids, taking care of them and spending time with them, she's been at the hospital, working her ass off. She can never get that time back. It's like Glen stole a year of her life away because he's so fucking lazy. Instead of getting a real job with a real salary, he's running scams that don't require him to work hard. It's as if he thinks there's some winning lottery ticket in the world, just waiting for him."

"Winning the lottery might make it all worth it," Sarah says, smiling.

"No," I say. "Don't say that. Money's good, but time is more important. There's lots of money in the world and a million ways to get it, but you have no control over how much time you have. You can't save it or work hard to earn more. When your time's up, that's it. Losing a year is a terrible thing."

"Why did your mom marry him?"

"Good question," I say. "I have no fucking idea."

"Maybe she sees something in him that you don't."

"No," I say. "There's nothing there to see. She just fucked up. Dad died and she grabbed the first loser she could find."

"But why?"

"No idea."

"How did your dad die?" she asks.

It takes me a moment to speak. A fraction of a second, one of those less-than-a-second seconds, which is so much better than it used to be. I used to be silent for what felt like hours after a question like that. Still, I feel it. The pause. Sarah does, too. I see it in her eyes. "Heart attack," I say. "In the garage. He was home alone."

"I'm so sorry, Mike."

"Thanks."

We sit in silence for a moment as the voices of the other kids and the rumble of the bus fill the space between us. The sun is rising over the trees, shooting slants of yellow light through the windows. We are silent, but Sarah keeps looking at me. Most people stare at their feet or pretend to notice something in the distance. Sarah's eyes don't move. It's such a small thing but also incredible. After a moment, she speaks. "It must've been horrible for your mom, too."

"Yeah," I say. "But that doesn't mean you marry an ass-hole less than two years after your husband dies."

"No. Of course not. But adults have stuff going on that we don't understand."

"I know an asshole when I see one."

"I know," she says. "I just think it's hard to be a parent."

"Are we supposed to be sharing our problems or explain-ing why my problems aren't really problems?" The words come out angry. Unexpectedly so. I also want to tell her that she's right. It's hard to be a parent, especially when you're a fourteen-year-old kid with a million problems of your own already, but I hold that back.

"You're right," she says. "Sorry."

"It's okay. I'm sorry, too. I didn't mean to jump down your throat. I don't usually get to tell people about this stuff. It's nice to have someone else know. It's good to say it, even if it doesn't change anything."

Sarah smiles. Then she reaches out and takes my hand. She pulls it into her lap and squeezes. My heart starts beat-ing quickly. I can hear the pounding in my ears. I want to look around and see if anyone has noticed, but I'm afraid to look away for even a second. "Now tell me the truth," she says. "What are you thinking about your mother?"

"I told you. I'm undecided."

She moves her hand in mine. Her fingers pry my fingers apart and fill the spaces. They're warm and soft. She leans in toward me. I think she's going to kiss me. "I don't believe you," she whispers.

"What?"

"Mike, you should talk to someone."

I pull away. Part of me can't believe I'm doing it. Sarah

Flaherty is holding my hand. Her face is inches from mine. I'm in a place that I could only dream of a day before, and now I'm pulling away. Yanking my hand back. It feels like I'm ejecting from a spaceship without a spacesuit. It's insanity.

But a larger part of me flashes red. She doesn't believe me, and though she's right not to believe me, I don't care. I don't need anyone telling me that I should talk to someone. She should just believe me. I trusted her last night in the gazebo, and I knew it was a bad idea. "I don't care if you believe me," I say. "I'm fine."

"There's nothing wrong with needing to talk to someone," she says.

"Do you think I'm crazy?"

"No, Mike. Not crazy. But sometimes we need help."

"You need help," I say. I hate saying it. I hate saying what I say next. What I already see coming. But the boulder is rolling again, and I can't stop it now. "I'm not the one with the cheating father."

Sarah stares at me for a second. I'm sure she can't believe what she has just heard. I can't, either. She stands. She throws her backpack over her shoulder and walks toward the front of the bus. Sandra shouts for her to sit down, but she ignores the request. She keeps moving forward until she finds an empty seat near the front. She sits.

I turn. Julia is staring at me, shaking her head.

"What?"

"Go talk to her," Julia says.

"What are you talking about?"

"I don't know what you did, but there's still time to fix it."

There will be no fixing this. I have ejected from the

spaceship and crashed into an asteroid. There are lots of terrible things that you can say to a person and eventually be okay, but I managed to find the one thing that will never make me and Sarah okay again.

"Too late," I tell Julia.

fifteen

I check in with Mrs. Newfang every morning when I arrive at school. It's something kids with behavior plans are required to do. Anyone who flips their desk when they get angry or steals from the cafeteria or generally behaves like a criminal has a behavior plan. I stop in the cafeteria every morning to talk with her about my day, and then I check out at the end of the day. Basically we set some goals in the morning, and then she checks to see if I met the goals in the afternoon. In elementary school I had a chart that teachers would fill out every hour, but now she just takes my word for it. I could lie and tell her that every day went perfectly, but she never punishes me no matter how bad my day was, so I don't bother lying unless I'm in a hurry.

It's easier to be honest.

I wouldn't mind checking in with Mrs. Newfang every morning if it wasn't for all the other kids checking in alongside me. It's like a line of losers that stretches halfway down

the hallway. Everyone in the school knows why we're standing there, and not because they know about the Check-In
Check-Out system. It's because they know what it means
when you gather all the misfits and monsters in one place
in the school.

This is the thing that teachers don't understand: if you
want to help someone like me, you can't announce what
you're doing to the world. You need to find a way to keep
it private. I'm sure that adults who go to therapy don't line
up on sidewalks under big, red signs that read *Therapist's
Office*. I've never been to a therapist, so I don't know what
their offices are like, but I guarantee that there isn't a line of
depressed people waiting in some hallway to check in.

Teachers do this all the time with normal kids, too. A
kid might not do his homework for three days straight or
get caught throwing a paper airplane across the room, and
instead of just telling the kid to knock it off or assigning him
a detention, the teacher will pull the kid into the hallway,
thinking that this is a better way to handle the behavior.

You'd think this is more private, but it's not. As soon as
you drag a kid into the hallway, you stick a giant neon sign
over his head. Anyone walking by knows the kid is in trouble. Those teachers take something that could've been small
and ordinary and turn it into something big and mysterious.

If you've ever had to walk back into the classroom after
getting lectured in the hallway, you know it's the worst. The
looks that the other kids give you. The questions they ask.
The whispers. Better for teachers to just say, "Joey, do your
goddamn homework. Two days detention, dumbass" than
make some private spectacle of him.

Normal kids get in trouble. Normal kids get detention.

No one thinks anything of it. Misfits and monsters get their asses dragged into the hallway for lectures.

I avoid standing in the morning check-in line by entering the school just as the bell rings. I wait outside by the doors until the last second, pretending to read something on my phone or text, and then I head inside just before the bell so by the time I get to the cafeteria, there's only one or two kids left in line at most. And no kids a lot of the time, like today.

"Hey," Mrs. Newfang says. "Ready for the day?" Mrs. Newfang isn't like most teachers. She's young and tough. She has biceps and everything. She must work out a lot. Kickboxing or something. We're about the same size, but I seriously think she could kick my ass if necessary.

"Yes," I say. I always say yes. I don't know what she'd say if I ever said no, but I don't want to know.

"What's your plan for being successful today?"

She wants me to list some strategies. Three is enough to get me out of here. She thinks that by saying the strategies out loud to her, I'll somehow be more likely to use them. I have no idea if this is true. I don't think so, but I also know that I'm the subject of this behavioral experiment, so I'm not in a good position to know for sure. But the three minutes that I spend with Mrs. Newfang mean three fewer minutes in homeroom, which is always good.

"If I get angry, I'm going to try to count to ten," I say. "And do nothing at all if possible. Just give it time."

"Good," she says. "Is anything making you angry today?"

My answer is always no, even though it's never no. Lots of things make me angry every day. Glen. Homework. Mr. Morin. Mr. Lancaster. Monday. Vocal music class. Payday.

Max Kramer and his douchebag friends on the soccer team. Spaghetti day in the cafeteria. Charlie on a lot of days. Changing into gym clothes in the locker room. The way the bell rings so loud in the art wing that it scares the hell out of me every time.

But Mrs. Newfang isn't looking for me to talk about the things I'm always angry about. She wants to know if there's anything new that's making me angry. There are new things, of course. There almost always are. Too much homework. A substitute teacher acting like an asshole. Today there are huge things making me angry. Scared, too. This happens a lot. Fear and anger are like Siamese twins. I said that once to Mrs. Newfang, and she acted like I had said the most important thing ever. She even wrote it down. Then she told me that "Siamese twins" is offensive. The correct term is "conjoined twins."

Even though there are new things for me to be angry about—the biggest things ever in my life today—I say no almost every time because if I say yes, we end up talking forever, and we already talk forever.

"Okay," she says. "What else?"

She wants more strategies.

"I'll ask questions if I don't understand something. And I'll eat in your office if I'm worried about sitting alone or getting angry at lunch."

"Great," she says. She writes my strategies on a chart. At the end of the day, she'll ask if I used any of these strategies. "Did you take your meds this morning?" she asks.

"Yes," I say. I take a pill every morning because I have attention deficit disorder. At least they think I do. I kind of think that if I wanted to, I could focus on my work, but the work that teachers assign sucks so I choose not to focus on it.

Even so, the pill actually works. It helps me focus on stuff that I don't want to focus on. At least it does now. It sucked for a long time. Made me sleepy or crazy and one time kept me up all night, but once we got the right dosage, it helped. Of course, I'm still growing, so every six months or so it stops working and we need to screw around with the dosage again, which sucks all over again. But when we get it right, I feel a little better. It's not a magic pill, but it helps. It helps me listen. It helps me think about one thing for longer than a minute or two. I don't know how, and I sometimes wonder if it's just a placebo, but either way, it works.

"Okay," Mrs. Newfang says. "I think you're ready for your day."

I always find it amazing how much more excited Mrs. Newfang is for my day than I am. And her excitement is real. Some teachers fake excitement or pretend to like you, but Mrs. Newfang is the real deal. It's a little corny, but it's amazing, too. I wouldn't trade it for anything.

"Thanks," I say. "I appreciate the help."

Mrs. Newfang stares at me for a moment, her mouth half open. She's not sure what to say. I've never said anything like this to her before. I'm not sure why I said it. It just sort of popped out. Maybe when your life is in real danger, you want to tell people like Mrs. Newfang how you feel just in case. I don't think the other mother is going to kill me, but I also don't know why she is in my house. I don't know if she's killed my mother. This is the most dangerous thing that's ever happened to me.

"Thanks, Michael," she says. She's not crying, but her eyes are a little watery. "That means a lot."

It's true. Her eyes say it all.

"Okay," I say. I want to leave now. This is starting to feel weird, even though I'm the one making it weird.

"Are you sure everything is okay?" she asks. "Nothing you need to tell me?"

She's smart. So smart. Somehow she knows what my words mean, or she suspects that she knows. She knows something's up. I'd love to tell her about Sarah and the other mother, so she could save me and Julia and Charlie and even Glen, but I don't think she would. She wouldn't believe me, and I wouldn't blame her.

Sarah doesn't believe me. She thinks I'm crazy. Mrs. Newfang already knows that I'm crazy. This would just make it worse.

Besides, I need to deal with Brian first. One big problem before one gigantic problem.

sixteen

Brian Marcotte needs me. That's why he pretends to be my friend. It feels good to be liked, even if it's not real, and even if I don't like Brian all that much. Brian's in three of my classes. He talks to me, lends me pencils, and makes me laugh. When no one talks to you or even looks in your direction, it's easy to feel invisible. You start feeling like you don't belong. Like no one even knows that you exist.

Brian makes me look and feel like a part of the world.

I know Brian's not a real friend because I'm not friends with his other friends. They're all serious gamers. Guys who hang out in basements and play the latest version of games that Julia calls "Shoot Blood Kill Stupid." Brian's never invited me to play, even though he knows that I play the same games at home. He sort of keeps me on the side. It's like he's built a wall between his real life and me.

But a fake friend is better than no friend at all. I know most people would say this is stupid, but that's because most people have friends. They don't understand how humiliating it is to be alone while surrounded by so many people. They don't know what it's like to walk from class to class every day without a single person to talk to. Or to never have anyone save you a seat in the auditorium or the cafeteria. Sometimes I pretend to be texting on my phone rather than sitting alone before class with no one to talk to. Having people think that someone like Brian Marcotte is your friend—even when you know he really isn't—is a very good thing for someone like me. It makes me feel real.

I have Jeff, too, but Jeff is in seventh grade. He's fourteen months younger than me. If I was twenty-five and he was twenty-four, fourteen months wouldn't matter. But in middle school, fourteen months makes Jeff a seventh-grade loser, which means I'm supposed to ignore him.

But I don't.

I don't see Jeff much during the school day. He eats lunch before me. Most of his classes are downstairs. His locker is downstairs. We only see each other in study hall a couple times a week and every morning in band.

Jeff and I play the flute, which is a bullshit instrument for a boy to play. Mom made me play it because the trumpet and drums are too loud. Jeff's older sister played the flute before she quit in high school, so he was forced to play the hand-me-down. That's how we became friends. We both got stuck playing the stupid flute. It's me and Jeff and about eight girls who all can play better than us because they're girls so they actually practice. We sit in the back row together, pretending to play half the time.

Next year, Jeff will still be in middle school, and I'll be alone in high school.

I haven't told Jeff about my plan with Brian. He wouldn't like it. He's never had Mr. Morin for a teacher, but even if he did, he would try to stop me. That's why he's a real friend. There's already a big part of me that wants to stop, so I don't want to make it any harder than it already is to go through with it.

This plan felt a lot better last week. Before my mother disappeared and the other mother appeared. Before I met Sarah (even though she's mad at me now and will probably never speak to me again). Things are different. Mr. Morin doesn't seem nearly as bad anymore. He doesn't seem so important. And what we plan on doing seems a lot worse.

I avoided seeing Brian this morning. Our lockers are close to each other, and sometimes we talk in the hallway, but this morning, I grabbed my books and walked as fast as I could to homeroom. I'm going to see him in science, but I'm hoping that things don't fall into place. That today isn't the day. I'm hoping that he will change his mind like I'm changing my mind. I'm sitting at my seat in the back corner of homeroom, waiting for the first bell. It's a science lab with sinks and Bunsen burners along the back wall. A periodic table hangs in the front of the room. Shelves with beakers and test tubes and microscopes line the walls. Everything is dusty and old because we barely touch the equipment. We read from a textbook and listen to lectures and take notes. I haven't touched a Bunsen burner in almost two years. Haven't looked through a single microscope. It's like this stuff is here for show. Like we're on a movie set, and all the science equipment is just pretend props.

Mr. Beane is my homeroom teacher. He's one of those

teachers who sits at his desk and lets you do whatever you want as long as you leave him alone.

My classmates love this time of day. It's what Mrs. New-fang calls "unstructured time." This is the time when kids who know how to act around other kids get to talk and laugh and relax. It's when kids with friends talk to their friends. It's even a time when guys will sometimes hit on girls and girls will pretend it's not happening.

I am not good during unstructured time. I don't have anyone to talk to, and even if I did, I wouldn't know what to say. I would rather be sitting in math class, listening to Mr. Offen lecture about the quadratic formula because at least then, no one would expect me to be cracking jokes or talking about stuff that I can't even think of talking about. I can sit in math class and raise my hand once or twice every period to keep Mr. Offen off my back and otherwise look just like everyone else. It's so good to look like everyone else.

I almost never look like everyone else.

I didn't do my math homework over the weekend. I didn't do it on purpose so I would have something to do now. If I'm sitting at my desk doing nothing, with no one to talk to and nothing to say, I feel stupid. I look stupid. I stand out. If I'm trying to get my homework done, at least I have a reason to be sitting alone. I have a reason to say nothing. It's structured.

I do this a lot.

I also get to listen to everyone while I solve equations, because solving equations is easy. It's talking to people that's hard. I listen to the way other people talk. I listen to what they say. Shane Carter is talking today. He's got almost everyone's attention. He's making everyone laugh. He's telling a story about how he was eating dinner at his girlfriend's house this past weekend. It was his first time eating dinner with her parents. In the middle of the meal, he had to pee. The bathroom was right off the dining room. When he started to pee, he realized that everyone at the table could probably hear his pee splashing into the bowl, which made him think that everyone at the table was thinking about his penis. So he tried to aim for the back of the bowl. He calls it the porcelain backboard. Everyone cracks up laughing. Even me. It's a funny story.

I can't imagine having dinner with Sarah's parents. They would think I'm a mute. I would probably choke on my food and die.

The bell finally rings. Shane Carter takes a bow. A few kids clap. I can't imagine what it must be like to be Shane Carter.

Mr. Beane tells us to get out. "Beat the street! Get to class!"

I leave homeroom and head for first period. Brian is waiting for me by the door to French class. We don't have French together. He's going to be late for class by waiting for me. He doesn't seem to care.

"You ready?" he asks.

"Yeah," I say. "But today?"

"We said today."

"I know."

Brian sighs. "What's the problem?"

"Nothing," I say. "I just hate Mondays."

"You're not bailing on me, are you?"

"No."

"You understand how big this is, right?" Brian leans close and whispers. "This isn't just some bullshit prank. This is real-world stuff. This is going to be huge."

I want to tell Brian that this is anything but huge. I want to tell him that this is nothing compared to my problems. Who cares if Mr. Morin is a dick? Who cares if he has favorites? We spend forty-two minutes a day with him, five days a week. Big deal.

I don't say any of that. I just nod and say, "Yes. I know this is big. I just don't want to get caught."

"Relax," Brian says. He reaches in his jacket pocket and pulls out a flash drive. He waves it in front of my face. "Everything is ready to go."

"Did you decide who?" I ask.

"No," he says. "I was thinking last night that we could send it to more than one girl. Double his trouble."

"That's stupid."

"Why's it stupid?" he asks. I can see that he really likes this stupid idea. He was hoping for a better response.

"Do you really think he would be stupid enough to send it to more than one girl? That isn't a funny cat video on your flash drive. This is supposed to be a real thing for him."

"Yeah," he says. He says the word slowly, stretching it out, as if he's still trying to find some way to be right. "I guess sending it to more than one girl would be unrealistic."

"And stupid," I add.

"All right," he says. "Who then?"

"I don't know. That was your job." I've decided to be as unhelpful as possible. If I slow him down enough, maybe he'll have time to reconsider.

"Let me think," he says. "One of his pets, for sure. I just don't know which one."

"If we had more time," I say, "we could ask about their parents. Find someone with a serious helicopter mother. You know?"

"Yeah, but you should see what I have on this," he says, holding up the flash drive again. "Her parents could be meth-heads and they'd still go crazy when they see this."

I don't want to see what Brian has on the flash drive. I don't want to do any of this anymore. It's a lot easier to plan something terrible than to actually do it. "All talk and no action" is usually an insult, but not this time. This just doesn't seem right anymore.

"Besides," he says, "we got to do it today. This was the day we said."

I want to point out to him that this date was set by us. No one is holding us to it except ourselves, and in reality, it's just him. If we want to change the date, we can just change it. But it's all too much for me to say. Too much to explain, and I'm afraid that I will sound afraid if I do.

The bell rings. Mrs. Winn shouts at me to get moving. "French waits for no man!"

"Okay," Brian says. "I'll see you at fourth period then?"

"I'll be there," I say. I will, too. I feel like I got on the wrong train but there's no getting off now.

seventeen

Every other Monday, Mrs. Newfang pulls me out of Mr. Drake's health class to meet with her. Mr. Drake isn't my favorite teacher, so I don't mind one bit. He's not a total asshole like Mr. Morin, but he's not the nicest guy in the world either.

There are teachers like Mr. Maroney who don't really teach much but make you laugh every time you're in their class. There are teachers like Mr. Platt who teach like hell but can't remember your name. Then there are teachers who talk to you like a human being, like the time Mrs. Allen saw me coming out of the principal's office and whispered to me, "He's such a dick." Those are the teachers I like the best. The ones that are kind of like kids trapped in old, pudgy bodies.

I'm not sure if Mr. Drake ever knew what it was like to be a kid. One time Tim Maloney called Dan Baker a douchebag in class—just as a joke—and Mr. Drake stopped everything and asked Tim if he knew what a douchebag was. Then he spent the next half hour explaining feminine hygiene. He said it fit perfectly into the health curriculum, but we all knew his real intention was to just make Tim look like a dumbass and make the rest of us uncomfortable.

It worked. I hate Tim Maloney. He's a prick, but on that day, I felt bad for him.

Mr. Drake is one of those know-it-all bullies. He finds something that you don't know and makes you feel stupid for not knowing it. I want to stand up in class sometimes and say, "Hey, Drake, you're twice as old as anyone in the room. No shit you know more stuff than we do. Big fucking deal."

After I threw my book through the window in the office, I told Mrs. Newfang all about Mr. Drake and how much I wanted to tell him to fuck off, hoping she would be impressed with my self-control in health class and be less mad about the window, which I didn't mean to break.

She wasn't.

Mr. Drake is my PE teacher, too, and he's even more of a dick in gym. When we're playing volleyball, he calls the kids who can't hit the ball "idiot zones." Even the girls. He says, "Good strategy demands that you hit the ball to the weakest link. Find the idiot zone and punish it."

I don't know if he thinks he's funny or is trying to toughen us up, but he's not doing either of those things. He's basically a middle-aged bully who was probably the quarterback for his high school team a million years ago but hasn't been popular since.

I'm not a good volleyball player, but I'm better than a lot of the girls in my class who don't even try, so I've managed to avoid being labeled an idiot zone. It's weird. Three years ago the girls were throwing their bodies on the gym floor in elementary school, diving for the ball. Most of them were better athletes than the boys. They wanted to win. They would do anything to hit the ball or score a point. When we picked teams, girls got picked first all the time. But now they act like they've never even seen a volleyball before. They scream when the ball is hit in their direction and cover their heads with their hands. Mr. Drake is a prick for calling them idiot zones, but it's also not a bad description at times.

Sometimes I think Mrs. Newfang chose this time because she knew I wouldn't mind skipping out on Mr. Drake's class.

I like Mrs. Newfang's office. It's got big windows, so it's always sunny and warm. She has a pile of board games and a Nerf basketball net hanging on the back of the door. She also has couches with stuffed animals on them, which is kind of strange for a middle school. I asked her about them once, and she said that holding a stuffed animal can make a person feel better. Even kids my age. I never touch them, but she holds one sometimes. And I don't think she's doing it to be funny or to get me to do it. I think they make her feel better, too.

For the first time in my life, I kind of want to hold one of Mrs. Newfang's stuffed animals. I feel like I have "stuffed animal level" problems. But if I grabbed one of her bears or that crooked-necked giraffe, she would know something was wrong. She's a smart person. She might be the smartest person I know. I need to be so careful around her. I feel like she could discover all my secrets.

"You want to play a game?" she asks. Usually I like to play. Stratego. Parcheesi. Backgammon. Old-people games from before the internet. Mrs. Newfang asks me to play games because when I focus on the game I can't focus on what I say and she's hoping that something might slip out. She's right. It might. Maybe it does and I don't even realize it.

But I can't take that chance today. I have too many secrets. Part of me wants to tell her about the other mother. I feel like she might be the only person I can trust with this, but she's a psychologist. If I tell her that my mother has been replaced by an exact duplicate, she will definitely think I'm crazy. I'm sure that's something she learned in psychologist school. There's probably a sentence in one of her books that says:

> If a person thinks his mother—or any other relative or friend or anyone—has been replaced by a duplicate, that person is crazy and you should call the police immediately.

I could ask her to promise not to tell anyone, but I feel like either she would refuse or she would tell me that it's not a promise she can keep. She's like Sarah. She's a problem solver. It's her job. She's the president of problem solving.

So I say no to board games. She's surprised. She raises her eyebrows as if this little thing counts as saying something. She's good at this, too. She tries to say as little as possible. She thinks that if she doesn't talk, I'll have to talk, which is true. I can't stand it.

This should be in a psychologist book:

If a person can just sit there and stare at you without saying a single word, that person is crazy and you should call the police immediately, even if that person is a school psychologist.

"What?" I say to her eyebrows. "I'm just not in the mood to play today."

"First for everything."

"I guess."

She leans back on the couch. Mrs. Newfang is one of those ladies who always dresses like she's going somewhere fancy. Sweaters and dresses and shoes and everything else. It's like she walks out of a catalog every morning. Most of my teachers are a mess. They can get paint and food on their shirts and no one would notice. If Mrs. Newfang had even a crumb of food on her sweater, I would assume the world was coming to an end.

Or at least her world.

Even the way she leans back on the couch is perfect. Slowly. Easily. It's like she's practiced leaning back on that couch for hours in preparation for this moment. Everything she does seems just right. After a moment, she smiles. "So how was your weekend?"

Here's the other problem with Mrs. Newfang. Even though I know she cares about me, I also know that she is going to have this same conversation with about a dozen other kids today. She's going to ask them to play games and ask them about their weekend, too. So am I special? Does she really care about me? Does she really want to know about my weekend or is it just something that psychologists say? I'm never sure.

"It was good," I say.

"Really?" she says. "Another first."

"I've had good weekends before."

"If you do," she says, "you don't tell me about them."

"Well, I do. I did. It was good."

"What made it good?"

I pause. It's only a second or two, but I make an enormous decision in that second. I'm going to tell her. I don't know why, but it feels right. This is the moment. I'm telling her.

"I went fishing with Sarah Flaherty."

"Who's Sarah Flaherty?"

"A girl," I say.

"What school does she go to?"

"*This school*," I say. "What? Do you think I'm making her up?"

She laughs. "No. I just don't know the name."

"You wouldn't know her. She's not like me."

"What do you mean?"

"She doesn't have any problems," I say.

"Everyone has problems," Mrs. Newfang says. "Even Sarah Flaherty."

I don't tell her that I made this same argument to Sarah a couple hours ago.

"You know what I mean," I say. "She's not the kind of kid who has to talk to you. You're like the island of misfit toys. Sarah's not a misfit toy."

"I don't think of you as a misfit toy."

I cross my arms. I say nothing. It's a Newfang move. She does it all the time. Payback.

"But yes," she finally says, "I know what you mean. There's a reason I don't know Sarah yet. So how did it happen? How'd you meet?"

I tell Mrs. Newfang about the fishing trip to Barracuda Island. How Julia invited Sarah, but Sarah and I spent most of the time together. How we sat on the rock together. How I taught her to tie a lure and cast. Julia and Charlie's fishing contest.

And then I tell her about visiting Sarah's house later that day. How we sat in her bedroom eating popcorn and talking. Mrs. Newfang's eyes widen a bit when I mention Sarah's bedroom, but I ignore it. I want her to think that this huge thing was a small thing. That's the secret to being cool. Or at least one of the secrets. When everyone else thinks something is a big deal, you act like it's nothing.

I'm terrible at this, of course. When something's a big deal, I yell and punch and flip desks and throw books at windows. But not today. Not now. Today I play it cool and it works.

Then I tell her about the bus ride this morning. How Sarah was waiting at the bus stop even though she's never taken the bus before. How she sat with me and we talked.

Things I don't tell Mrs. Newfang
1. The way the universe grew larger when Sarah took her shirt off before getting in the canoe.
2. The fight between the other mother and Asshole Glen that got me invited to Sarah's house.
3. They way Sarah and I sat on her bed, leg to leg.
4. The little bit of sadness I saw behind Sarah's eyes.

5. How I could've kissed Sarah when I left her house. How she wanted me to kiss her, as crazy as that sounds. Maybe even crazier than the other mother sounds.
6. Our middle-of-the-night talk.
7. Sarah's asshole father.
8. I'm in love with Sarah Flaherty.
9. I've ruined everything with Sarah Flaherty.

I wish I could ask Mrs. Newfang about kissing Sarah. I could be wrong about her wanting me to kiss her. Trying to kiss her could've ruined everything. But there's no way for me to know for sure. Jeff isn't going to know. He'll just say that I should've kissed her when I had the chance. "Fortune favors the bold," he'll say, even though he's never been bold in his life.

But Mrs. Newfang would know. She's not exactly a teenager, but she's not that old, either. She has two kids, but they're still little. And she looks young. Younger than most of the other teachers. She would know. I wish I could ask her about the kiss and how to go back in time and unsay the terrible thing that I said to Sarah.

There's so much I wish I could tell her.

"It sounds like you two are becoming fast friends," Mrs. Newfang says.

"What are fast friends?" I ask.

"It means that the two of you are becoming friends quickly," she says. "Like friendship at first sight. It can happen when two people discover they have a lot in common."

"I don't think we have anything in common."

"It's not always things like having the same hobbies or

listening to the same music. Sometimes it's just the way two people think about the world. Their temperament. The way they fit together."

I don't know what *temperament* is, but she might be right about the way Sarah and I fit together. Before I fucked it all up, at least. It's easy to be with her. I've never been able to sit quietly with a person before and feel so okay.

I wonder if Sarah thinks we fit together, too. Before the bus, I mean.

"I'm happy that you've found a new friend," she says. "And a girl, too. Even better."

"Yeah?"

"Of course," she says. "A female perspective can be helpful. There are going to be times when you're going to want a girl's opinion."

"I guess."

"Trust me," she says. "You will. And it sounds like Sarah might be someone you can trust."

"You think so?"

"She hasn't given you any reason to think otherwise. Right?"

I wish I knew for sure.

eighteen

I should know that it's Sarah when I am grabbed by the wrist as I make my way through the hallway. She's grabbed my wrist at least twice in the past two days, but still, I pull away, assuming it's some asshole messing with me.

"Mike, stop."

I turn. When our eyes meet, all the anger I felt on the bus falls away. It was never real to begin with. I know this now. Too late, but at least I know.

"I'm sorry," I say. "I was . . . awful. I'm sorry."

"It's okay," Sarah says. She means it, too. Her eyes are wide and open. She's not angry. She's . . . I don't know. Worried? Excited?

"No," I say. "I really mean it."

"I know you do. It's okay. I promise. But you need to listen to me."

"What's wrong?" I ask, because now I can see that there's

definitely something wrong. She's shaking. Just a little. Trembling, really.

"I know what's wrong." She holds her phone up to me. The screen is glowing white with black text. She's still trembling, so much that I can't make out the words.

"What's wrong with what?"

"With you," she says. "I know what's wrong with you."

Anger flashes through my body again. Fast and hot. "What do you mean?"

"Your mother. I know what happened."

"What are you talking about?" My anger is washed away by a flood of excitement. We're standing in the middle of the hallway. People are passing around us. Bumping into us. Skirting our shoulders and hips. Rushing to get to class. Anxious to beat the bell that rings four minutes after the one that just released us from class. It's loud. People talking and shouting. Laughing. I don't notice any of them. My world is Sarah's face.

"Mike, your mother hasn't been replaced."

Just like that, the excitement rushing through my body falters. Dissipates. "Sarah, she has," I say. I try to explain but she stops me before I can speak.

"She hasn't," she says. "I know it."

"Listen," I say. "I lied to you on the bus. I'm not undecided. I know for sure. My mother has been replaced by another mother. The woman in my house is not my mother—"

"Mike," she interrupts, "She's your mother. It's not your fault. You have a thing."

"What do you mean I have a thing?"

"I looked it up," she says. "I Googled you."

"What?"

"I Googled this thing you have. After I got off the bus. You want to know what I searched exactly? It was *He thinks his mom is an impostor.* It was the first hit. It's a thing. A condition. You're not alone, Mike."

I want to tell her that she's wrong. I'm all alone. I've always been alone. I want to tell her I've felt alone for longer than she could ever imagine, but as we stand in this river of humanity, I realize that she may be right. I might not be alone for the first time in my life. This girl who keeps saying my name feels as close to me as I have ever felt.

"I have a thing?" I ask.

"Yes," she says. "Capgras delusion." She struggles to say the first word. She's not sure how to pronounce it. "It happens to people. You suddenly think your mom or dad or husband is an impostor. A duplicate. It's a thing."

"What is it?" I ask.

She holds her phone to me again, steady this time, so I can read the screen. "Capgras delusion," she says again, more slowly this time. "People suddenly think that their loved one is a duplicate. Your brain tricks you into thinking your mom isn't your mom."

"But she's not my mom," I say. "I can see it."

"Here," Sarah says. She's holding out her phone. "Read it for yourself. It's a thing, Mike. It's not your fault. You're not crazy. It's just a thing." There are tears in her eyes now. She's pleading. She's worried about me.

I take the phone in my hand. Now I'm shaking. My whole body is shaking. I look at the screen. It's a Wikipedia page.

Capgras delusion (or Capgras syndrome) is a psychiatric disorder in which a person holds a delusion that a friend, spouse, parent or other close family member (or pet) has been replaced by an identical impostor.

"A delusion?" I ask.

"Yes," she says. "It makes sense. Right?"

"No," I say. "I'm not crazy."

"I didn't say you were crazy."

"You think I'm having delusions. Or one delusion. One constant delusion."

"Mike," Sarah says, sounding a little bit like a parent or a teacher, "it's a thing. I don't know why this happened to you, but it's a thing. Your mom never went anywhere."

"Bullshit," I say, pushing the phone back into her hands. "This isn't just a delusion. It's everything. The way she talks to me. The things she says. She doesn't even look like my mother."

"Mike."

"Stop saying that! I'm Michael."

She's stopped in her tracks for a minute, her mouth still open, about to say a word that will never be said.

"Listen," I say. "I'm happy you're not mad at me. I was an asshole on the bus, and I'm sorry. But I'm not . . . deluded. Something is going on, and it's not happening in my mind. It's a real thing."

"That doesn't make any sense. This . . ." And as she says the word, she holds up the phone to me. The Capgras delusion Wikipedia page is staring back at me again. "This makes sense."

"I know it makes sense to you, but it doesn't make sense to me. I know it's not this. I know it in my heart, Sarah."

"But Mike, read this. It's exactly what you're saying."

"Listen, I understand why you're saying what you're saying. I really do. But this isn't me. Something has happened. I can't explain it, but it's real. This isn't the first time something unbelievable or unexplainable has happened to a human being. I'm just one of those people now. Someone who has something happening to him that no one believes, because it's never happened before, or when it does happen, it doesn't make the news. But I don't blame you for not believing me." I point to her phone. "For believing this."

"Mike, you just need help."

"Fuck you!" I shout, loud enough that the river of people around us, which has dissolved from river to stream, bends around me like I've tripled in size. I hate that I've said this. Hate where this whole thing went. I feel like I've just set fire to a garden. Flowers are burning, and there's no stopping the flames. I turn. "I have to get to class."

"Michael!" she calls.

I move quickly. She calls my name again. I keep moving. I miss Mike already.

nineteen

Brian is waiting for me outside Mr. Morin's classroom. He's shuffling from one foot to the other. It's the first time I've seen him look nervous. Mrs. Newfang is right. There is a first time for everything.

"You're late," he says.

"I'm sorry."

"Here," he says. He pushes the flash drive into my hand.

"What are you doing?" I say, pushing it back.

"Change of plan. You're going to send. I'll distract."

"No way. That's not the plan. That's not what we agreed to."

"What's the difference?" Brian says, a little too loud. "I thought we were in this together?"

"We are."

"Then who cares who sends the email?" he asks. "Either it works or it doesn't."

"If it doesn't matter who sends the email, why don't you send it?"

"Are you afraid?"

"No," I say, though I am. "I just want to stick to the plan."

"We're either doing this as a team or not at all. Either we win or we're fucked. It doesn't matter who does what. We win or lose together. Right?"

"Fine," I say. He's right, but something about this scares me even more than before. "But why the change in plan?"

"Me and Joey can make a better distraction."

"You told Joey?"

"No," he says. "But it won't take much to get him going. And two people causing trouble is better than just one."

This makes sense. Plus, now that I think of it, I hadn't come up with a plan to distract Mr. Morin. I hadn't gotten that far. A part of me never expected to make it this far. This whole thing was fun to think about, but I'm not so sure anymore.

The bell rings. The hallway starts to clear. Brian steps aside to let three girls through the doorway. He waits until they pass and then asks, "Is there someone in class who you can fool around with? Someone other than me to help you cause a distraction?"

"No," I say. Brian's not stupid. He knows the answer is no. He's just saying this to stick me in a corner.

"Okay, then," he says. "Me and Joey get thrown out and you send the email. Deal?"

I try to think of an out. A way to make this go away. I have nothing. "Sure," I say. I don't mean it, but I say it because I'm on this train, and I can't get off now. "Who am I sending it to?"

Brian smiles. "I was thinking Angie Padilla."

"Do you have her email address?" I ask.

"What do you mean? Just type her name and it'll come up."

"Her school email will come up," I say. "We need a home email address. He wouldn't be stupid enough to send it on the school email. That would look like a fake for sure."

"Fuck," Brian says. "You're right. Do you know anyone's personal email? A girl, I mean?"

"Not anyone in his class," I say.

"Not anyone in his class?" Brian asks. "What do you mean?"

"I mean I don't have the email address for any of the girls in our class."

"Whose email do you have?"

"Sarah Flaherty." I feel something close to pride when I say her name. Sarah Flaherty gave me her personal email address. I kind of want to tell it to the world.

"You mean that girl who lives on your street?"

"Yeah," I say. "But she doesn't have Mr. Morin for science."

"She's perfect," Brian says. His eyes are wide. "How did you get her email address?"

"She gave it to me," I say, still feeling pride. "And no, she's not perfect for this."

"Yes, she is." Brian's excited now. He looks like he could jump right out of his skin. "That girl's hot. I can totally see Mr. Morin going after her."

I can, too, but that doesn't matter. It can't be Sarah. As

angry as I am at her, I'm not going to involve her. "We'll find someone else," I say. "Someone in his class. Someone who makes sense."

"Why does she need to be in his class? I stare at girls who aren't in my class all the time. Besides, she could've been in his class last year. It actually looks better if she isn't in his class this year. Less suspicious."

"Less suspicious?"

"Exactly!" he says. He makes it sound as if he's just cured cancer.

I want to tell Brian that this doesn't make any sense. The chances of our plan working are infinitesimal (a word he wouldn't understand). I want to admit to him that I never expected to even get this far. Just pie in the sky (Charlie calls it "pie and the sky") fun. There's still time to end this. Call it all off. But this is what Mrs. Newfang would call a losing battle.

She says to avoid fighting them whenever possible.

"I don't care if it makes sense," I say. "We're not using Sarah's email address."

"What? Do you have a crush on her?"

"No," I say. I answer too fast. My no sounds more like a yes. Sometimes the speed of your answer is more important than the words you say.

"Why not?" Brian asks. "You should."

"We're not using her email address." I try to make my voice like a wall. Something hard and final. The same voice I used on the bus that day with Eddie Raymond. "I'll find someone else."

"It's not like she's going to get into any trouble," Brian says, plowing right through my bricks and mortar. "She'll just receive the email and report him. That's it. She won't even know it was you."

He's not wrong. I still don't like the idea, but it makes sense. Sarah won't get hurt. Not really.

"Don't you have an email address of someone?"

"What's your problem? This isn't a big deal. We're about to do something huge and you're worried about some girl's email address? Nothing's going to happen to her."

I want to keep fighting, but fighting with words is hard for me. I flip desks and break things when I get mad. Fighting like this is exhausting. I keep finding myself in these sharp corners with no way out.

"Fine," I say. "I guess it'll work. When will you do it?"

"I don't know. Whenever it makes sense. Just don't fall asleep on me."

"I won't," I say.

"Or chicken out."

"I said I won't."

But already I want to. Maybe not chicken out but just bail on this completely. Maybe because of Sarah's email, but I think it's more than that. It doesn't feel right anymore. It never did, but I felt like I needed it. Now I'm not sure.

No, I'm sure. This is the last thing I need in my life right now.

"Good luck," Brian says. He pats me on the back. Smiles. It's a real smile. Just like that, I decide that I'm back in. He may not be my friend, but I am a part of this thing. We're in this together. For better or worse.

I turn and walk into class. "Are the bells not loud enough for you, Mr. Parsons?" A second later, "And you, Mr. Marcotte?"

"Sorry," I say. I keep my head down and walk fast. I try not to be noticed any more than necessary.

Brian mumbles something and heads to his seat.

Mr. Morin makes us sit alphabetically, just like in my dad and Mrs. Foley's day. He's the only teacher who does this. Everyone hates assigned seats except for me. When we can sit wherever we want, kids clump in bunches. Friends sit with friends. I don't have a bunch, so I always feel like I'm on the outside of some circle, looking like an idiot.

Free seating is like unstructured time.

Mr. Morin is teaching about rocks today. Igneous. Metamorphic. Sedimentary. He has somehow managed to make the most boring topic in all of science even more boring. I watch the clock. The red second hand crawls around the clock like a one-legged dog.

I turn to a new page in my notebook and start a new list. I write down every idea that pops into my head, even if it's a stupid one.

Solutions to the Other Mother
1. Call the police and ask for help. Hope they believe me.
2. Tell Glen. Pray that he sees what I see.
3. Tell Mrs. Newfang.
4. Tell Julia. Pray that she sees what I see.
5. Confront the other mother when Glen is in the room.
6. Confront her alone.
7. Find a way to force her to admit the truth and tell me where Mom is.

8. Tell Jeff. Pray that he has a better idea than any
    of mine.
9. Find a way to prove that she is the other
    mother.
10. Pelt her with igneous rocks until she
    confesses.

Most of the ideas are dumb. Calling the police or asking someone like Glen or even Mrs. Newfang for help isn't
going to work. No one will believe me, and I'll just end
up like one of those characters in the movies who is either
locked up in the loony bin or running from the cops with
helicopters and spy satellites tracking him.

I would love to tell Julia because of all the people in the
world, she's the one most likely to see the other mother if
she looks closely, even though I don't have to look closely at
all. The other mother is like a neon sign to me. It's impossible to miss her otherness. But maybe if I asked Julia to look
a little harder, she would see it, too. But that wouldn't help
much. It wouldn't bring Mom back, but it would be nice to
have someone on my side. Someone who believes me.

Charlie might see her, too, if I asked him to look, but I
can't trust that nimrod with anything.

Confronting the other mother won't change anything,
and she'd probably just deny it. I'm also afraid that if she
knows that I know, she might try to hurt me and maybe
Charlie or Julia.

My best chance is to get her to confess or at least tell
me where Mom is. Mom's been gone for two days now. It's
hard to hide an adult. They're a lot smarter and stronger

than kids. They can be loud. They need food and water. Kids get kidnapped all the time. They're weak. They fit into small places. They can be tricked. They can eat cookies and be happy. Not adults. They almost never get kidnapped.

But getting her to confess isn't going to be easy. She's strong and smart. I can't exactly tie her to a chair and shine a flashlight in her eyes. I don't own a gun that I can point at her and demand the truth. I don't have a trapdoor with alligators underneath. Pelting her with igneous rocks isn't realistic.

Here's my best idea so far, even though it would only work in a movie: I feed the other mother some kind of slow-acting poison. Maybe slip it into her iced tea or her soup. Something that will kill her in twenty-four hours unless she takes the antidote. And I have the antidote, which I refuse to hand over until she hands over my mother.

In a movie, that would work.

I should really tell Jeff, but I know he's going to either laugh at me or give me some dumbass idea like tying her up to railroad tracks.

"Idiot!" Brian whispers to me from his seat. He's four seats down, one row over. "Are you even paying attention?"

I nod. I wasn't, but it's not like I'm going to miss any distraction big enough to get Mr. Morin out of the room. I reach into my pocket to make sure that the flash drive is still there.

It feels like a loaded gun in my pocket.

Brian turns to get Joey's attention. He sits about three rows over. He whispers Joey's name, but Joey doesn't hear him. He whispers it again, but Joey is looking to the front of the room. He looks mesmerized. I turn to follow his gaze, and that is when I realize that Mr. Morin is shouting. He doesn't raise his voice when he shouts, but it's loud just the same. Commanding. It wouldn't surprise me to learn that Mr. Morin was an asshole drill sergeant before he became a teacher.

I'm suddenly certain of this. It explains everything. Fits perfectly. Just like Capgras delusion would make sense if the other mother wasn't the other mother.

It takes me a second to figure out who Mr. Morin is not-shouting at. I've been lost in my list and my thoughts of slow-acting poisons. At first I'm worried that it's me, but no. It's not. It's Rachel Yousman, which is strange because I don't think Rachel has ever done anything wrong in her entire life. He has something in his hand. A folded square of paper. It's the kind of complicated fold that girls use when passing notes. He's holding it up. He's telling Rachel that this classroom isn't the place for nonsense like this.

Rachel looks scared.

I lean across the aisle and whisper to the boy sitting across from me. "What's going on?"

"What?" he asks. "Did you fall asleep?"

"Sort of," I say. The boy's name is Adrian. We've never spoken before, even though we've been sitting side by side all year. He's never been mean to me, but he's never been friendly, either.

"Rachel got caught with a note," he says.

"Did she write it, or did someone pass it to her?"

This makes a difference. Getting caught with a note can

be embarrassing either way, but if Rachel wrote the note, then she owns the words. If she wrote something mean about Mr. Morin or one of her friends or wrote a love poem to a boy who she secretly likes, and Mr. Morin decides to read it, she could get in trouble. He might even pass the note on to the principal or her parents.

If she didn't write it and was just the recipient, it might still be embarrassing for her. Mr. Morin might find out about some boy who likes her or some other deep dark secret, but at least she can't get in trouble for just taking a piece of paper from someone else.

"Don't know who wrote it," Adrian whispers. "But from the look on her face, I'm betting she did."

Mr. Morin is still holding the paper in his hand. He's holding it up for everyone to see. "This is how people end up believing that the Earth is five thousand years old," he says. He's speaking as if there are ten thousand people in the room who care about this shit. He thinks he's making some grand speech. "I'm standing here, teaching you the history of our planet, teaching you how to understand how everything came to be, and you're doing *this*." He shakes the paper. It's still folded into a small square.

Rachel is shrinking. It's almost as if she's pulling her head into her torso. If this were elementary school, she'd be crying already. She's holding back the tears, but it looks like she could crack at any moment.

Crying in front of people is the worst. In elementary school no one cares. Kids cry for all kinds of reasons. Lots of them are stupid reasons. I lost my mitten. I forgot my lunch money. Tony said I eat boogers for breakfast. But in middle school, when you cry, it becomes a part of your history. Your permanent record. It's like an invisible tattoo that everyone can see forever.

Mr. Morin moves from the center of the room toward the far side of the room, where Rachel sits. "You have no idea how much we have to learn and how little time we have," he says. Then he begins unfolding the square of paper.

He's going to read it. He's going to find out what this note says. Then—if it's embarrassing but not offensive—he's going to read it to the class. I know it. I've never seen him do this before, but this is exactly the kind of thing he would do. I know it. We all know it. Rachel knows it. I look to her again. It looks like she's holding her breath now. Like she can't breathe. She looks like a little girl who has lost both mittens and her hat and boots and lunch money and everything else she cared about. Mr. Morin is going to read that note out loud, and she is going to cry, and nothing will ever be the same for her again.

Kids should never look so afraid at school. That other voice in my head surprises me. The words pop into my mind and feel so true.

Brian turns. He's one row over, four seats down. He looks back at me, eyes wide. Half an hour ago he was a dick who wanted to do a terrible thing to a stupid teacher. Now I look to him, then to Rachel, and then back to him, and I see a hero. A genius. Brian wants to ruin Mr. Morin's life. He wants to take this asshole down, and suddenly his terrible plan doesn't seem so terrible anymore. Maybe Mr. Morin deserves to be destroyed. It seems so right now. Like Brian is Batman and I'm Robin, but we're a little too late to save the day.

Mr. Morin is reading the note to himself now. He's standing front and center again, in position to read aloud. He wants to read it aloud. It's clear as day. It takes him just a few seconds to read the whole thing to himself. He shakes his head in disappointment, but beneath that wrinkled brow and his downcast eyes, I can see his smile. His asshole smile. He likes this. He's getting off on this.

Finally he looks up. He takes a deep breath. He's going to read it now.

My hand goes up. Shoots up. I can't believe it.

"Mr. Parsons?" Mr. Morin says, except now he's Little Napoleon through and through. He is a squat little dictator about to rule this classroom like never before.

"I don't want to hear what they note says." I say it loud and true. I can't believe what I've just said when the next words come, even more surprising. "No one does."

Little Napoleon stares at me. If I were standing outside of myself, I'd be staring at me, too. I can't believe what's happening. It's unbelievable for so many reasons.

When Little Napoleon doesn't say anything right away, I keep talking. *Digging your own grave*, my other voice says, but I shove it to the back of my mind. *"If* you even planned on reading it out loud, I don't know if you were. If not, sorry."

Mr. Morin takes two steps to the left so that he's even with my row and staring directly at me. He puts his hand on his hip and leans in a little. "Since when did you start speaking for the whole class?"

I feel pride swell inside. I've found something to say to slow him down. I can see it. He was plowing ahead like a bull a second ago, ready to read, but now he's thinking things over. Considering his options. No matter what happens next, I've forced him to pause. He asked me a question instead of firing an order or an insult or an ultimatum.

"I don't speak for the whole class," I say.

"Good," Mr. Morin starts. He has more to say. I see it coming.

"Except for right now," I say, stepping on whatever words were about to come out of his mouth. "Right now, I speak for everyone. No one wants to hear it. I promise."

People are looking at me. Staring at me. Staring through me, it seems. Mrs. Newfang says I have a hard time reading people, and it's true, but today, I can read everyone just fine. I know exactly what those looks mean. I know exactly what they are thinking: *What the fuck are you doing?*

Every single one of them.

Little Napoleon, too. He is thinking the exact same thing.

Only Brian's expression is different. The look on his face is unlike any other. He's still staring at me, just as hard as everyone else, but he's smiling. I know what he's thinking. I can see it as clear as day. *You badass son of a bitch.*

"Did I ask if you or anyone else in this classroom wanted to hear the contents of this letter?" Little Napoleon asks. He's on the move now, walking up the aisle toward me. It's that slow, bloated walk that teachers do to intimidate kids. It works on lots of kids, but it's never worked on me. When you flip desks and shove bus drivers and throw cash registers to the floor, half-assed attempts to scare me by walking like some cartoon bad guy are ridiculous.

Mr. Morin repeats himself, louder this time. "Did I ask

if you or anyone else wanted to hear the contents of this letter?" He holds the letter high in the air over my head and shakes it.

"No," I say. Then something happens to me. I'm suddenly angry. I've gone from nervous and surprised to angry in exactly one second. It's the anger that makes me keep speaking. Keeps this particular boulder rolling down the mountain. But it is not red anger. For the first time in my life, my anger feels cold instead of hot. It's blue. Icy blue anger. I wonder where it's been all my life. "But you already knew that," I say. The words come out cold, too. Slow and sharp. "You already knew the answer to that question."

One of the girls near the windows gasps. A couple boys near the front of the classroom giggle. Otherwise the room somehow gets even quieter than before. It is like all sound has been banished from the room save for Mr. Morin's breathing and my beating heart.

"Do you have some interest in this note that I should know about?" Little Napoleon asks. "Or in Miss Yousman over there?" He points in Rachel's direction, so I look. She's stopped shrinking. She's sitting up. She looks angry now, too. If I had to guess, her anger is red. She is a volcano now, ready to explode.

"No," I say. "I just don't want Rachel to be embarrassed."

"Then maybe she shouldn't have written the note in the first place."

"Maybe not," I say. "But she never gets in trouble, so I don't think you need to go all nuclear on her. That's all. A little common sense would be nice."

Little Napoleon is standing beside my desk now. Looking down at me. I want to stand up. Or maybe ask him if I should stand up so I don't have to stare at his crotch. I wish I could say something like that, but as angry as I am, I can't get clever words like that out.

"Very chivalrous of you," he says, but I know he doesn't mean it. This is sarcasm. The weapon of every coward. He turns and heads back to the front of the room. "But you don't get to tell me what to do, Mr. Parsons."

He's right. I can't win here. It's just like Glen in the garage yesterday. No possible victory for me. But still, I feel like I've changed things a bit. At least Rachel won't feel so alone. Maybe she won't cry. I've said something to let her know that I'm on her side. Other people, too. No one has said a word, but I can feel them just the same. The class is standing with me. I know it. I'm hoping she can feel it, too. We are standing together in our stupid seats, even though I'm the only one who has spoken. I still can't believe I did this. I don't say smart things. I'm not quick or clever. My good comebacks always come two days too late. I'm angry, which isn't new, but it's a different kind of anger this time. It's so cold.

Suddenly I know why.

Rachel has a secret, and Little Napoleon is going to reveal it to the class. I can't stand for that. I am the king of secrets. I know how dangerous they are. How hard it is to keep them safe. The idea that a teacher might tell a bunch of kids one of my secrets is terrifying. I'm terrified for Rachel. I'm angry—but not for me, this time. I'm angry for Rachel.

Mr. Morin is front and center again. He's staring at

Rachel's note again. He looks over at Rachel. He looks back at me. He looks at the paper. He starts to read. "Dear—"

That's all I hear. I jam my fingers into my ears and start to hum. Charlie does this to me all the time when he's sick of listening to me. It drowns out all sound of Mr. Morin's voice and everything else in the classroom. All I hear is a hum.

Mr. Morin stops reading. He lowers the paper and stares at me. He says something. His lips are moving but I can't hear a sound.

He says something else. Louder, I suspect. Still, all I hear is a hum. I hum louder.

Then something amazing happens.

Ben Lemieux, sitting three seats over, sticks his fingers in his ears. Then Jackson Klenk. Gigi Baratta. Caroline Cronin. Index fingers all around the room press into ears. I pull my fingers out of my ears for a second to check. They are humming, too. I look to my right. Adrian has his fingers in his ears. He's humming, too. I scan the room. I can't find someone whose fingers aren't in their ears. The whole damn room is filled with humming.

Little Napoleon is red faced. He points at me and screams, "Get out!" I hear this so he must have shouted it at the top of his lungs.

I don't waste a second. I stand. I take one look around the room. I still can't find a single person who doesn't have fingers in ears. I can't believe it. They are standing with me. Beside me. I have never felt so much like I belonged before. I want to stay here forever.

Instead, I turn and walk out. The room is still humming as I yank open the door. I turn back to get a final look at the classroom. The humming is so loud. A few of the kids are looking back at me. Most are still facing forward. I look to Rachel. She's sitting there, looking around the room and smiling. I see tears in her eyes, but she is not crying.

"Out!" Little Napoleon screams.

I slam the door. I have never felt better about anything in my entire life.

twenty

It's funny. Of all the trouble I've ever been in, I've never been thrown out of a classroom before. I've been escorted from the room by the principal and the vice-principal and the security guard, and once in fourth grade the teacher made everyone else leave the room when I was throwing a tantrum, but I've never walked out of a classroom by myself.

This is new for me.

Mr. Morin didn't tell me where to go. He just told me to get out, which turns out to be worse than telling me to go to the principal's or vice-principal's office. I slam the door and stand for a second in the hallway, not sure what to do. Another unstructured environment. Even though I don't want to go to the principal's office, it would be easier if Mr. Morin had sent me somewhere instead of nowhere at all. I feel like a balloon without a string, just floating in space.

Then I decide. In an instant, I know exactly where to go.

I turn left and start walking. Two minutes later, I'm knocking on the door. I've been to this room a million times, but the door has never been closed before unless I'm inside. I knock again.

The door opens. Mrs. Newfang sees me. She looks confused. "Michael? What are you doing here?"

"Mr. Morin just told me to get out."

"You were thrown out of class?"

"Yeah."

"Okay," she says. "Come in."

I sit on a couch beside a stuffed alligator. I still have just as many problems as I had when I checked in earlier today, but it somehow doesn't feel like a stuffed animal problem kind of day anymore. I feel happy.

I never feel just happy, but in this minute, I really do.

Mrs. Newfang is sitting at her desk, talking on the phone, telling the secretary that I'm in her office. She hangs up. She sits on the couch across from me. Crosses her legs. Picks up the teddy bear and puts it in her lap. "So what happened?"

I decide to tell her everything that happened in Mr. Morin's classroom, but part of me wants to tell her about the other mother. I feel like she is somehow the real beginning of all of this, even though she just appeared yesterday and has nothing to do with Mr. Morin.

I speak slowly. I want to get it right. I describe the note and the look on Rachel Yousman's face when Mr. Morin started reading it to himself. I tell her how angry I was with Mr. Morin for even thinking about sharing one of Rachel's secrets with the class. "But it wasn't the same kind of mad that I usually feel. It wasn't hot anger. It was like ice. I didn't feel like flipping a desk or punching Mr. Morin in the face. I just wanted to stop him from ruining Rachel's life."

"Ruining her life?" Mrs. Newfang asks. She looks incredulous. This is the look you give when you think someone is full of shit but you want to say so silently and slightly more politely.

"Secrets can ruin lives," I say. I'm shocked that someone like Mrs. Newfang doesn't know this. She should know this better than anyone.

"So what did you do to get thrown out?" she asks.

I tell her. "It's not like I planned it," I explain. "I was kind of surprised that my hand went up in the first place. But I wasn't rude. I just told him that no one wanted to hear what was in that note. So when he told me that I couldn't stop him from reading it and then started reading it out loud, I stuffed my fingers in my ears and started humming. Then other people did, too."

Mrs. Newfang eyes widen. She smiles. This is not her "You used that strategy well" smile or even her "You said something funny" smile. This is the kind of smile you have when the bad guy in a movie gets tossed into the blades of a helicopter.

"Other people, too?" she says. "Other people hummed? How many?"

"A lot. Everyone, I think. I saw people putting their fingers in their ears, so I stopped humming to listen. There was *a lot* of humming. That's when he threw me out."

Mrs. Newfang is still smiling. She shakes her head in that "I can't believe what I just heard" way.

I don't blame her. Saying it aloud, I can't believe it happened either.

"I was just so mad because of the secret thing," I say. "Secrets really are dangerous. But I think I was also mad because Mr. Morin was trying to use me and everyone else in that class to punish Rachel. It wasn't his reading the note out loud that was bad for Rachel. It was our listening. So I just refused to listen."

Mrs. Newfang nods. "Are you friends with Rachel?"

"No," I say. "But you don't have to be someone's friend to help. Right?"

Mrs. Newfang doesn't say anything. She sits there, staring at me. Still holding that bear.

"What?" I say.

"I'm just really happy with the way you handled that situation."

"So you think I was right?"

It takes her a second to answer, but when the words come, they are soft and true. "Yeah, I do," she says. "I remember what it's like to be humiliated by a teacher. It hurts. And you know what? Sometimes that hurt never goes away. My third-grade teacher once said to me, 'Are you as stupid as you look?' She was probably having a bad day, but more than thirty years later, I still think about that terrible thing she said to me. I remember it like it was yesterday. But I can't remember a kid ever acting as bravely as you did today. There are so few heroes in the world, Michael. You were a hero today. Rachel will never forget it. No one in that class will."

It's been a long, long time since I felt like I had an adult on my side. Probably since before Dad died. I sometimes think that Mrs. Newfang might be on my side, and I know that Mom and even Glen are supposed to be on my side, but none of that has mattered much. I've felt so alone for so long. For the first time in forever, I feel like an adult is standing beside me.

I don't want this next thing to happen, but I can't stop it. I start to cry. Not disgusting snotty crying but tears, rolling down my cheeks, and a couple sniffles.

"It's okay, Michael," Mrs. Newfang says, leaning forward. "I don't think you did anything wrong."

I open my mouth to speak but then close it. I can't talk and hold back the sobs at the same time.

"Seriously," she says. "It's going to be fine. I promise."

I wipe my face with my sleeve. "I know," I say. These aren't sad or frightened or angry tears, but I can't tell her that.

"I'm so proud of you," she says.

Tears again, rolling down my cheeks in a river this time. I'm so annoyed. I feel so stupid.

The phone rings. Mrs. Newfang stands up, giving me a chance to wipe my nose and my eyes. It's the principal. I listen as she explains that I'm meeting with her.

I like this. We're "meeting." Like two regular people.

"I'll explain everything later today," she says to the principal. She listens for a few seconds, says goodbye, hangs up, and turns back to me. "Don't worry. I'll talk to him."

I pick up the stuffed alligator. Hold it on my lap. It's softer than I expected. "I need your help," I say.

"It's going to be fine," she says.

"No," I say. "It's something else. A secret. Something I need to tell you."

She comes back around to the couch and sits down. If she sees the alligator in my lap, she pretends not to notice. I'm sure she does, though. This is Mrs. Newfang. She sees everything. She sees things that I don't know I'm doing. She picks up the teddy bear again.

"Okay," she says.

"But you can't act like a crazy person when I tell you this. Okay?"

"What do you mean?" she asks. She leans forward a little. She sounds worried.

"I have something I want to tell you, and I need your help, but can you try not to make a big deal out of it? I know it might not be possible, but can you also try to keep other people out of it? If possible?"

"I can promise to try, but not knowing what it is, I can't guarantee anything."

"I know," I say.

"So?"

I squeeze the alligator. I can't believe I'm going to tell her. So much could go wrong.

"Michael?"

"Okay," I say. "Here goes." I take one more deep breath. I almost change my mind, but then I plunge forward before I have a chance to stop myself. "We had a plan. Brian and me. Brian Marcotte. We were going to send pictures of naked girls from Mr. Morin's email to a girl in our class. To get him in trouble." I look down at the alligator. "To get him fired."

Mrs. Newfang doesn't flinch. I know that inside her head, alarms must be going off. And not fire alarms, but those Klaxon horns you hear in movies when nuclear weapons become unstable or the secret underground lair is about to detonate. She must be thinking a million things, but on the outside, her expression barely changes. "Okay," she says. "How were you going to do this?"

"Brian has a flash drive with the photos. He got them off the internet. Mr. Morin uses one of the laptops in the classroom. He doesn't have his own machine. I was going to make a distraction. Actually, Brian was going to make the distraction. We changed the plan today. So Brian was going to make a distraction. Get kicked out of class or something. And while Mr. Morin was dealing with him I was going to swap laptops. Put the one I use in class on his table and grab his. He keeps his email open most of the time. We've seen it. So I would load the pictures from the flash drive into an email, write a message to the girl—something creepy—and send it. Then swap the laptops back. Or just put it back on the counter next to the one I swapped."

"When were you planning to do this?" she asks. She still hasn't flinched. She's acting like she hears this kind of stuff all the time.

"Today. Before the Rachel thing happened."

"Who were you going to send the pictures to?" she asks.

I don't want to say the name. I feel ashamed for even thinking about using it. But I've gotten this far into the secret. I feel like once you tell, you tell the whole thing.

"Sarah Flaherty," I say. I squeeze the alligator.

"Did she know the plan, too?"

"No. We just decided to use her email address a little while ago."

"Funny way to treat your new friend," Mrs. Newfang says.

"We had a fight. Two fights, really. I didn't tell you about the first one, and the second one happened in the hallway between classes. I was mad, so I acted like an asshole. Sorry. It's just the right word."

"It's okay," she says.

"I know. You think I'm terrible now."

"No, you're not. Still a hero. Just a flawed one. Those are the best kinds."

I'm not sure what she means, but I don't want to ask.

Mrs. Newfang smiles. I don't know if it's real or pretend, but I like it. It makes me feel a little better. "And you're telling me all this because?"

"I'm afraid Brian will still want to do it. I'm not sure, but it's possible."

"And you don't want to anymore?" she asks.

"No. I never wanted to do it. Not really. I thought Brian was all talk. I thought I was all talk. I didn't think today would ever come."

"Then why did you agree to do it?"

I just told her a big thing, but it was an outside thing. Not an inside thing. Inside things are a lot harder to tell. But if I'm going to tell anyone anything going on inside, maybe Mrs. Newfang is the right person. At least for this.

"It felt good," I say. "To have a friend."

"Do you think he's really your friend?"

"No," I snap. I feel like she should know this. She should already understand what I'm trying to say. "But sometimes it's just nice for other people to think that you have a friend. I'd rather have a thousand terrible friends than one great friend who no one can see."

"Really?" she asks. "How come?"

I'm annoyed that she doesn't get it. I'm annoyed that

she's even asking this question. Even if she was popular in high school and had lots of friends, she's a school psychologist. She should know why. "Because being alone sucks," I say, too loud. Too hard. "And it's embarrassing. Okay?"

I take a moment to calm down. I count to ten in my head. I'm using one of her strategies right in front of her. I wonder if she can tell. When I talk again, it's almost a whisper. "I sit in class every day and switch from being completely invisible to everyone around me to being the loser who sits on the edge of every group or alone at every lunch table. So when someone comes along and pays attention to me—even if he's not a real friend, and even if he's using me—I accept it. Not being alone is worth it. Sometimes the day is more important than the week or the month. Sometimes just looking normal for one second is the best thing that happens to me all day. If I can have a pretend friend for a day, that sounds pretty good to me."

She understands now. I can see it on her face. I can see it in the way she's squeezing her teddy bear a little tighter than before. She learned something new about me.

"I didn't know you felt so alone," she says. She sounds so sad.

I feel bad for making her sad. It's hard to believe that all I felt was happiness just a few minutes ago. It seems like a century ago. "It's nothing new," I say. "I've been alone for a long time."

"That doesn't make it okay," she says. She's still squeezing the bear.

"No, but it makes it a little easier. It was hard when all the times that I was alone or feeling embarrassed about being alone were piling up. One after another after another.

But now it's just a one gigantic pile. An infinite pile of awfulness. It really can't get any bigger."

"We should probably talk about that."

"Not today," I say. "Okay?"

"Okay," she says. She waits a second to see if I'll say anything else. I feel like I've said more in the last three minutes than I've ever said to anyone. I'm talked out. Finally, she asks, "So what do you want me to do about Brian?"

"Maybe nothing," I say. "But I thought it would be good for you to know, in case I need someone to do something."

"Makes sense," she says. She means it, too.

Suddenly everything is different. I can feel it. We've taken a step closer together. She's still a school psychologist, and I'm still sitting here because I have problems, but we're closer. Not friends but something in-between.

"Anything else?" she asks.

Yes, I want to say. A lot. But those problems are all too big for this small office. Too big for stuffed alligators and teddy bears. They aren't just Mr. Morin or Brian Marcotte level problems. They are life and death stuff.

Mrs. Newfang is good, and I love her more today than yesterday, but she's only a school psychologist. I need Batman.

There's no such thing as Batman.

twenty-one

When the bell rings, I drop the alligator and leave. The hallway is crowded. Kids moving in both directions, trying to get to class on time. The river of humanity is flowing again. Clumps of girls blocking traffic, trying to catch up on the latest gossip. There are way too many people for these hallways. If there were ever a fire, kids would burn. Lots of them. The slow and the polite first. We'd never all get out in time.

The air smells of sour milk. It makes no sense. The cafeteria is on the other side of the school, but this hallway always smells like sour milk. It's the worst place in the school to have a locker.

I take about ten steps before realizing that something is wrong. It sounds like the hallway is filled with bees. The voices and laughter and occasional screams from girls pretending to be excited about things that aren't that exciting are gone. Instead, it's just a buzzing. Like bees. Like static

on the intercom. Maybe some new secretary doesn't know
how to use the microphone.

I stop and look up, expecting to see I-don't-know-what.

Then I look around. I see. It takes me a second. Then I
realize what's happening.

People are humming. The hallway is filled with the sound
of kids humming. Loudly. As they hum, they make eye contact with me and smile. Nod. Some of them have their fingers stuffed in their ears. Not all of them, but a lot. Kids I
don't know are giving me the thumbs-up. Someone slaps
me on the back. Someone shouts my name.

"Michael!"

Then another. "Bravo, Michael!"

"Fucking-A, man!"

I stop for a moment, blocking the hall. For a moment,
it's almost as if I leave my body. It sounds crazy, but for a
second, I see myself from above, surrounded by kids weav-
ing around me, smiling at me, and humming. Someone
bumps into me. I nearly drop the book in my hand. Just
like that I'm back in my body and moving again. Halfway
down the hall, with the humming still all around me, I
turn into the boys' bathroom. I duck into the first stall.
There are tears in my eyes. I have goose bumps. I can barely
breathe.

It was the greatest walk of my life. I have never felt so
known before. I've never felt so appreciated. Even when
everyone was talking about me hitting the bus driver or
breaking the window in the office or throwing the cash register on the floor, they never looked me in the eye. They
never acknowledged my existence. I was just a thing to be

observed. Something to point at while whispering. A bomb waiting to go off.

This was different. It was amazing. It was like a scene from a movie, except in the movie, the character wouldn't need to hide in the bathroom because he can't stop crying, but I don't care. It was close enough. It was my movie moment.

I still can't believe it.

It takes me a couple minutes to pull myself together. I'm going to be late for band now. I'll use Mrs. Newfang as an excuse. She'll cover for me.

I push open the door to the band room. Everyone is already seated. They're talking. Playing scales and riffs. Waiting for Mr. Arnold to take his spot at the front of the room. I grab my flute from the cubby and take my seat in the back row.

"You're late," Jeff says as I plop down beside him. Jeff may hate the flute as much as I do, but he looks like he was made to play the flute. He's about six inches shorter than me and skinny. Not just skinny around his waist but skinny all over. Wrists. Neck. Thighs. He's just a small person. A tiny person. It's lousy to say, but it makes it even harder for me to be his friend. He's already younger than me, but he looks like he belongs in elementary school. When we're at the park or the bowling alley, people think I'm hanging out with a third grader. People ask if he's my little brother, and when they say little, they mean *little*.

"I know I'm late," I say. "I got held up."

"I heard," Jeff says.

"What did you hear?"

Jeff begins to hum. A second later the girl to his left begins to hum, too. The two girls in front of us turn and do the same. They're all smiling.

"Okay," I say. "Knock it off."

But it feels amazing. Even telling them to knock it off feels amazing.

Mr. Arnold walks from his small office in the corner of the room to the podium. He's a tall, balding man who walks as though he's stepping through a minefield. Every step is long and slow and deliberate. He lifts the white baton from the podium and raises both hands, signaling that instruments should be brought to the ready. He taps his baton on the music stand in front of him. The room gets quiet. Lips cover mouthpieces. Mr. Arnold wears jeans and a baseball cap almost every day unless it's a concert day. He's one of those teachers who lets you call him by his first name, but I haven't been able to yet.

I'm not sure if I ever will.

He raises his baton but leaves it hanging in the air for a second longer than usual. A clarinet squeaks, the owner expecting his hand to drop as it always does, our cue to begin playing our first scale. Instead, he points his baton directly at me, and then touches it to the brim of his cap.

He's tipping his cap to me.

Jeff elbows me. "Did you see that?"

"I'm not blind," I whisper.

Jeff laughs a little. "That was awesome."

"I guess," I say. But Jeff is right. It was awesome.

"I just wish I could've been there," Jeff says, poised to begin playing.

Me, too, I think as I play a concert B flat scale. I wish everyone in the world could've been there.

I wish my father could've been there.

Dad worked a lot. Constantly. He told me that there are only two ways to pay the bills: you work a lot of hours or you make a lot of money per hour.

He told me to find a job that pays a lot per hour so I don't have to work sixty or seventy or eighty hours a week to make ends meet like he did. Dad was busy or tired all the time. I understood, but it didn't make it easy. He was never able to help out with Boy Scouts or teach us to swim, and in the three years I played in Little League, I could probably count the number of games he watched on one hand.

In fairness, I was an awful baseball player. I can't catch or hit, so I only played the required one inning per game, always in right field, where no one ever hits the ball. I hit one homerun in three years and caught exactly four fly balls, but Dad wasn't there to see any of those moments. In his mind, I was probably a waste of a player. A boy taking the spot of someone more deserving.

Dad never saw me do anything well. My report cards were never good. I was a terrible soccer player. He tried to teach me to play chess, but I couldn't learn anything beyond how the pieces moved. I'm not sure why making him proud meant so much to me. Maybe it's because I never did. Maybe the things we want most in life are the things we can never get.

That sounds awful but also true.

If Dad had been in that classroom when I raised my hand and fought back, he would've been proud. I know it. Had he seen me beat Mr. Morin on his own turf, it might've made up for all the times I struck out at the plate or kicked the soccer ball out of bounds or came home with straight Cs.

Maybe this is why people believe in heaven.

It's why I wish there was a heaven. If only Dad could've seen me today.

I'm also a terrible flautist. I only play the third flute part. A fifth grader could play this part without much trouble. It makes sense, though. Since I hate the flute, I barely practice. But since my part is so easy, mostly whole notes and rests, it also gives me time to think. Time to chill. I just had the best walk of my life. Maybe the best moment in my life ever. The best meeting with Mrs. Newfang—or any other teacher—ever. I should be the happiest guy on the planet right now, and I am. I really am.

But I shouldn't be.

My mother is missing. Some impossible impostor has everyone fooled but me. She's even fooled Sarah, who thinks she's found an answer to my impossible puzzle. I'm still trapped in a real-life science-fiction movie. This Mr. Morin stuff would've been amazing a week ago, but I can't let myself get excited about it now. My life is still a disaster. I'm still facing the biggest problem of my life. I feel like a guy who just discovered the cure to cancer three days before an asteroid will kill every person on the planet.

Great job. Too bad the world is about to end.

I need to be focused. I can't let Mr. Morin or all this humming or even Sarah distract me, as good as they all may seem. This should be the best day of my life, but a person shouldn't feel happiness when his mother is missing and might be dead.

I can't believe you just let that word into your head, my other voice whispers.

If Mom is dead, that means she died not knowing the truth about Dad, and that would be my fault.

She's not dead. If she were dead, I would know it.

We finish our scales and it's time to begin the actual rehearsal. We're working on *Candide* today. Mr. Arnold says it's an opera almost always performed by an orchestra, but we're going to be playing it without any strings as part of our halftime show.

That's our band director's philosophy in a nutshell. Nothing is good enough for us. Everything must be nearly impossible.

I'm holding a C for five bars when I notice that Tricia Roberts, who plays the bass clarinet, is looking over at me, trying to get my attention. She smiles through her mouthpiece. I'm so surprised that I stop playing for a second. I turn around to see if she's smiling at someone behind me.

There's no one behind me. I turn back and she's still smiling.

Jeff elbows me, and I pick up the note.

Tricia Roberts is the eighth-grade class president. Not exactly the coolest kid in school but popular enough to get elected. And popular enough to beat Danny O'Sullivan, who everyone loves even though he's a complete douchebag.

Tricia Roberts is smiling at me.

Mr. Arnold waves us off halfway through the second movement, flapping his arms as if he's being attacked by a swarm of mosquitoes. The snares and toms have missed their entrance again. Drummers are the worst. All they need to do is count and bang, and yet they can't count to save their lives.

Mr. Arnold rolls his eyes, smacks his baton on the music stand, and runs the drum line through the last few bars while we wait. Jeff elbows me again and points to the back of the room. Rowan Sierra and Richie Aponte are waving their trumpets in my direction and smiling. When I look, they both give me the thumbs-up. Rowan and Richie are football players. Big guys with bruises and crew cuts and dirt under their fingernails at all times. Guys who have never said a word to me ever. Guys who I didn't think knew my name.

Rowan puts his trumpet down and starts flipping through the pages on his music stand. As he does, Richie empties his spit valve on Rowan's sneaker and laughs. He points to the Rowan's foot then looks back at me. He laughs.

He's letting me in on the joke.

Maybe this really is a movie.

I've stayed in the band even though I hate the flute mostly because I can disappear in band rehearsal. I never need to raise my hand to answer a question. I never get called on unexpectedly. I'm never asked to play alone. And when I play a wrong note or miss an entrance, no one really notices. There are twelve other flute players. My wrong note gets swallowed up by everyone around me.

But I've also never really felt like a member of the band before. I've always felt like some bit part clamped on to the side of something bigger. If I quit tomorrow, I don't think anyone other than Jeff would even notice.

Maybe I was wrong.

Or maybe people would notice if I quit today, and if they would notice today, maybe they would notice tomorrow, too. I wonder if this is the start of something new.

Suddenly I want to practice. I want to play this stupid flute better.

Mr. Arnold tells us to pack up a couple minutes before the bell rings. I put my head down and walk to my cubby. I don't wait for Jeff. I just need to get through this day and get home.

I close my flute case and push it into the cubby when I feel a hand tug on my wrist. It's Bethany Glenn. First chair flute. She sits in the second row in Mr. Morin's class. Three seats across from Rachel.

"I just wanted to say thank you," she says. "That was great."

"Thanks," I say. She's still holding my wrist. Everyone's holding my wrist these days, it seems.

"I know it meant a lot to Rachel."

"I'm glad," I say. Mrs. Newfang strategies at work. Accept a compliment by saying thank you or telling the person how you feel.

"He didn't read the note," she says. "You stopped him. Did you know that?"

"No," I say. "Really?" I can't believe it. I didn't think I had actually stopped him. Maybe delayed him. Made him look momentarily stupid. But prevented him from reading the note? "What did he do?"

"After he threw you out of class, he tossed the note on to his desk and started teaching like nothing ever happened. It was bizarre."

"Yeah," I say. She's right. Bizarre.

Bethany pulls me closer. For a second I think she's going to kiss me, which is an insane thought and proof that I have no clue about anything. She lowers her voice. "I don't know if Rachel will ever say anything to you, but things haven't been easy for her. At home, I mean. She had a lot of stuff going on. She needed someone to stand up for her today. It was a big deal for her."

These words hit me like a punch in the gut. Tears spill out of my eyes for the third time today.

Bethany smiles as I pull my wrist from her grip to wipe my eyes with my sleeve.

"I'm sorry," I say.

"It's okay," she says. She starts to say more, but I turn and walk away. I pull open the door to the band room just as the bell rings. Doors open down the hall. People are spilling out of classrooms. *Fuck.* I duck into the first empty room I see. Mrs. Walker's classroom. The lights are off. I sit down in the back against the wall. I feel like something has broken inside of me. Like my walls have been knocked down.

I can't go through the whole day crying like this.

It's crazy. When my dad died, I barely cried at all. My mom disappears and I don't cry one bit. But I do something good for a girl I barely know, and now I'm a mess.

It's not what I did. I know that. It's that I did *something.* Bethany said it perfectly. Rachel needed someone to stand up for her today, and I was the one who did it. I've spent my whole life waiting for someone to stand up for me. Waiting for someone to come to my defense. Save me. I've waited so long for someone to do something for me. Something like what I did for Rachel today.

I've needed help for as long as I can remember. I've been

lost and alone and so tired for so long. Overwhelmed. Angry. Guilty. I've prayed for help that has never come.

In the back of Mrs. Walker's classroom, when I'm supposed to be sitting alone in the cafeteria eating my free lunch, I sit in the dark and cry. I cry like I have never cried before.

twenty-two

I cut my last four classes. I skip detention. I don't talk to Mrs. Newfang before I leave, so I have no idea what the principal said about Mr. Morin. This will be a big problem for me tomorrow, but that giant asteroid could destroy the world before the day is over. Sometimes the now is more important than the later.

I don't know if that's a thing. I just made it up. A new rule. But it feels right.

I leave through the back doors by the gym and walk quickly across the parking lot and into the woods behind the school. I've never cut class before. I've never had a reason to cut class before.

There's a trail at the edge of the woods that leads up the hill, across Lincoln Street, and close to home. It's a long walk, and the trail is overgrown, but it's the fastest way home. I don't mind the time alone. I need to think about what to do next. My list of problems has gotten a lot shorter, mostly because only the big problems matter now.

My Problems
1. My mom is still missing.
2. The other mother has replaced her.

That's it. All that other stuff about Asshole Glen and Charlie being an idiot and Sarah and the yellow envelope don't mean a thing. They would be important if an asteroid wasn't about to destroy my world, but the other mother is an asteroid, so nothing else matters. I can worry about trying to make Sarah not hate me once I have my mother back.

Once this other mother is gone for good.

I'll be home around 12:30. Asshole Glen is driving to New Hampshire today to pick up an old stove that he bought on the internet. He says he can restore it and "make a fortune."

Glen's idea of a fortune—as far as I can tell—is any amount of money greater than what he had one minute before.

Last month it was a rocking chair in Rhode Island and an enormous gas station sign from forever ago that he picked up in a place called Soho. Both are sitting in the garage, untouched. I don't expect either one of them to ever move. The thing about Glen is that he doesn't want to be an asshole. He's just a dreamer. He thinks that all his ideas are big and bright and brilliant. It's probably a great way to be if you have a wife willing to work double shifts while you chase your dreams, but when your ideas suck and you don't follow through on anything, you end up as an asshole, whether you mean to or not.

If the other mother is keeping the same hours as Mom, she won't be back until dinnertime. I don't know if she's going to the hospital like Mom, but she's been leaving the house and coming home at the same times, which means I'll have a few hours in the house by myself.

Plenty of time.

I cross Lincoln Street and step on to the path. I love this space between school and home. A swath of forest where nothing is ever hard or stupid or sad. As far as I know, I'm the only one who uses the path, which is probably why it's so overgrown. Bushes and shrubs reach across the matted grass. I need to be careful not to trip ass-over-teakettle (one of my father's favorite expressions) in spots. It doesn't matter. This is my place. My time.

I try to remember the last thing I said to my mother before she disappeared. Maybe there's a clue in her words. It was Saturday night. Glen was out with his two asshole friends, Gary and Shep. He says they're starting some internet business together. Something like eBay but better. But they seem to do most of their work at the bowling alley, so I don't know if he's lying or just delusional. Either way, Glen was out.

Sarah thinks I'm delusional. She thinks that the other mother is my mother, but she didn't hear the way we talked this morning. She didn't hear the way she asked me questions and listened to my answers. My mother and I never talk like that.

I made macaroni and cheese for dinner on the night

before my mother disappeared. Peas, too. I hate peas. So does Charlie. Mom makes me eat as many peas as I am old, which doesn't sound like a lot of peas, but when you hate them as much as I do, fourteen peas is a lot of peas.

The pea rule also makes no sense. I have no curfew. No one has ever checked my homework. I sign my mother's name to every permission slip. I had to teach Charlie to stop peeing on the seat when he was little because Mom was too busy to help. I live with barely any rules, but when it comes to peas, Mom is a nutrition Nazi.

This is the hill she chooses to die on, my father would've said.

If I were making dinner for myself, I would never make peas. They're the last thing I would ever make. But I was making dinner for Charlie and Julia, so I made peas and pretended to like them.

I had left the pan with the macaroni and cheese on the burner while we ate, so the leftovers burned to the bottom. I was scrubbing the pan with a sponge when Mom walked in.

I was mad as I stood over the sink. Julia and Charlie were watching TV and eating Popsicles. I was still cleaning up. This was after making dinner and after eating peas so Charlie would. Actually, this was after watching them all day. Taking them to the park. Making lunch. Applying a homemade bandage made of a folded napkin and duct tape on Julia's knee after she fell off her bike. Screaming at Charlie for riding across Summer Street without looking.

Mom came into the kitchen and said something like, "Hey."

I didn't turn or say anything. I wanted her to know how mad I was.

She saw me scrubbing. She asked me if I let the pan soak first. I said yes, but that was a lie. I never let anything soak. Soaking is an excuse for people who don't want to work hard. I hate leaving dirty dishes behind. Dirty dishes in a sink is for heathens and cretins.

She walked over to the sink and stared for a second. Then she reached across and took a white piece of plastic from the flower pot that we used as a sponge holder. "Here," she said. "Scrape it with this."

I stared at this piece of plastic. Sharp on one end and round on the other. "Is this new?" I asked.

"Nope." She said she'd scrubbed a thousand pots and pans with it. "And there's a thousand more waiting in my future," she said. Or something like that.

She sat down at the table. She asked me if there was any left, and I told her that it was burned on the bottom of the pan.

She sighed and put her head down on the table. "That's okay," she said. "I'm more tired than hungry."

I can't remember saying anything after that.

I finished the pan and went upstairs to my room. That white thing worked like magic. Mom had gone to check on Charlie and Julia. I was still angry. I was tired, too. I went upstairs, took the yellow envelope out from under my mattress, and held it for a while. Turned it over and over again in my hands.

I didn't open it. Sometimes I do, but not on Saturday night. I was too tired. It didn't matter anyway. I know what's inside. I've read it a million times. I can't not know it, even if I wanted to.

I played video games for a while. Jeff and I played online. Charlie came in and we played a game together. I beat him. He acted like a jerk. He made me check the weather on my phone before he went to bed. He insists that I check for tornado and flood warnings before he goes to sleep, even though we've never had either.

In hurricane season, I need to check for them, too.

Julia popped her head in to say goodnight.

I don't think I even saw Mom again that night. She probably found something to eat and went to bed.

The last thing I said to her was something about leftovers.

The last thing she said to me was that she was more tired than hungry.

These can't be the last things we say to each other.

twenty-three

It's a lot harder to dig than I thought. The dirt floor isn't loose at all. It's compacted. And it only gets more compacted the deeper I dig.

I thought I would find some loose dirt or signs of recent digging in one of the corners of the basement and know for sure, but there's no evidence that someone has been buried down here except for the mystery shovel behind the water heater that I'm using to dig now.

This is good. When I decided to start in the basement, I knew I had given up hope. When you're trying to find your mother's body under the dirt floor of your basement, you don't expect to find her alive.

Another new rule. This one feels right, too. Awful but right. Almost like wanting two things at the same time. I don't want to find my mother buried in my basement, but if she's dead, I want to find my mother's body in the basement.

I thought the digging would take an hour, but it's been almost two and I'm not close to being halfway done. I'm digging holes every three feet or so, going down about eighteen inches at the most. I figure that if I can't break through the dirt, the other mother couldn't either. She's impossible, but she doesn't have super strength.

At least I don't think she does.

I spent some time reading the Wikipedia page on Capgras delusion, just so I could prove Sarah wrong when I see her again. It's definitely not my thing. It says that Capgras delusion is caused by brain injuries and occurs in paranoid schizophrenics and patients who take certain medications. I don't have any of those things. My brain is fine and the only medication I take are my ADD pills every morning. But I've been taking them for years.

I read about a nutjob in New Zealand who killed his wife and blamed it on Capgras. At least his lawyer said it was Capgras. I'm not sure what he believed. But I guess if you're crazy, it might be hard to see that you're crazy. Another one of those can't see the forest through the trees thing.

So who knows? Maybe he really had Capgras, but here's the thing: why would you kill someone even if you thought she was a duplicate of your wife? You're still murdering someone. Maybe it was his wife and maybe it wasn't, but even if it wasn't, why kill her? How does that help? It only causes more problems, and what if you're wrong?

It makes no sense.

If I'm going to be honest, it was also clear that nobody really knows what causes Capgras delusion for sure. It's sort of a mystery disease. Still, I can't have it. The patients who

I read about on the internet sound nothing like me. They were all bat-shit crazy.

I just see Mrs. Newfang a couple times a week.

A door slams shut upstairs. The front door. I freeze— the shovel just about to break through a new section of the floor. I hold my breath even though there's no way any-one can hear me breathing upstairs. I have goose bumps up and down my arms. It's my house. It's not as though some burglar just walked through the front door like he owns the place. I shouldn't be afraid. It's either Glen or the other mother.

Still, I am.

It's her. She's moving through the living room toward the kitchen. I can trace her footsteps on the floor above. She's talking to someone. Walking and talking. I start to put the shovel down but decide to hold on to it. It's hard and sharp and not too long. It might be the best weapon in the house except for the knives in the kitchen and the base-ball bat in the garage. I grip the handle tighter and move slowly toward the stairs. I barely breathe. I want to hear what is being said upstairs. I want to know who else is in the house.

I have a thought. What if it's not the other mother up-stairs? What if it's Mom? The other mother's voice doesn't sound anything like Mom's voice, but it sounds the same, too. Similar enough to fool Julia and Charlie and Glen and everyone else but me. The voice I hear upstairs is muffled by floor and door. I can tell that it's one of them, but I can't say for sure which one.

It could be Mom. She might be back. My problem might be solved. Disaster averted. Asteroid deflected.

I don't believe this, but knowing that it's at least possible—that it could still happen—feels good. It might not be happening now. It might not happen today. But someday this may all come to an end. This is what hope is, I guess. Believing that everything could be okay even when you think it will never be okay again. I cling to the possibility.

She stops speaking. I freeze. I hold my breath again. I wait for another voice that doesn't come. Silence above. Is she whispering to whoever else is in the house? Does she know I'm down here? Has she seen light under the crack of the door?

I wait. A minute later, she starts speaking again. She's still somewhere in the living room. It sounds like she's answering questions. She's saying yes and no. She's giving numbers and dates. Then she's moving again. She walks from the living room through the kitchen to the den. She passes by the basement door. She's just a few feet above me. I watch the shadow of her feet pass in the space beneath the basement door. For a couple seconds, I can hear her clearly.

It's her. The other mother.

Then I realize what's happening. She's on the phone. She's talking to someone on her cellphone. She was on the phone when she walked through the front door. Going back and forth with whoever is on the other end of the call. She sounds annoyed. Frustrated.

She's the only person in the house except for me. We're alone, and we'll be alone for at least another hour. Probably more. I wasn't expecting this. It's not what I was planning. At least not yet. But it might be the best chance I have. The only one I get.

I tighten my grip on the shovel.

I start to climb the stairs. The third step creaks as I place my foot on it. It's probably creaked every time I've ever stepped on it—hundreds of creaks before this one—but this time the creak is enormous. It's deafening. I pull my foot back and wait to see if it was heard. She's still talking. She's in the office down the hall. After a moment, I continue. I skip the third step. I keep climbing. Thirteen steps become twelve with the skip.

A much better number.

I'm two steps from the top when the other mother moves from the office back to the kitchen. I can hear her clearly again.

"No," she says. "My husband works part time. He delivers newspapers." A pause. Then, "I told the other person this already. That's my late husband." Another pause. "Yes. Thank you."

She answers yes and no to a bunch of questions. She says some numbers. Some are dollars and others are just digits. I hear her pull out a chair from beneath the kitchen table. It scrapes across the floor. She's sitting down. Sitting in the same spot where Mom was sitting two nights ago when she was more tired than hungry.

"There has to be something we can do," she says. "Listen, I have three kids. They lost their father not that long ago. I can't let them lose their home, too." She sounds angry and sad. It's strange. She doesn't sound like an impostor. She sounds like a real mother. Not my real mother, though. My mother doesn't fight like this.

"I'm not saying that I don't want to pay," she says. "I just need my payments lowered. Not forever, but at least for a while. We're still getting back on our feet. His death was unexpected, and there was no life insurance. There has to be something you can do."

I'm on the top step now. I'm holding the shovel in my right hand. If I push the door open, I'll be a dozen steps from where she's sitting. Maybe less. But she'll see me coming. The basement door opens into the kitchen. Still, I'd have surprise on my side.

"That's not good enough," she says. She's almost shouting now. "Is there a manager who I can speak to?" Another pause and then, "Fine, but you must have a manager. Right?" She's moved from angry to something else. She sounds rude now. And there's something else in her voice, too. Worry? Panic, even?

"Please do," she says. "Yes." A pause. "Yes." Another pause. "Thank you."

It's quiet for a moment. I hear the clatter of the phone as she puts it down on the table. She's still sitting. She's so close. Just a few feet away. I reach for the doorknob with my left hand. I grab hold and get ready to turn. I try to picture what I'll do in my mind. I'll push the door open and move quickly. I can cover the distance in five or six steps at most. I'm not going to hurt her unless I have to. I'll hold the shovel high over her head and force her to stay seated. I'll threaten to hit her if she moves. I'll be as loud and scary as possible. I'll take her cellphone. I'll see if it's her phone or Mom's phone.

Then I'll make her talk. I'll make her tell me where my mother is.

I take a deep breath. I turn the doorknob.

Then I hear her begin to cry.

I stop. I wait.

Her crying starts as a whimper but gets louder and louder. I hear a bang. She's hit the table with her hand. I can see it in my mind's eye. Then another bang. "Fuck!" she shouts. "Fuck!"

She weeps. Heaving sobs. I'm holding my breath again. Bracing myself for what might come next. Expecting her to shout again. Swear. Throw something. Break something.

She just sits there and cries.

I let go of the doorknob. I lower the shovel. I can't do it. Not because I don't want my mother back, and not because her crying has made me feel sorry for her. I stop because her crying makes no sense to me. It sounds like we're running out of money, but why is she crying? Why does she care if we lose the house? It's not her house. It's not her kids. Maybe her plan is to just replace my mother forever. Nothing more. My mother's life becomes her life. My mother's problems become her problems. But of all the people to replace in this world, why would anyone choose my mother?

Maybe she really thinks that she's my mother. Maybe she believes that she's been my mother all along. If that's true, then threatening to bash in her skull with a shovel isn't going to change anything. She might really believe that I'm her son. She might not even know where Mom is.

I don't really believe this, but I have to admit that it's possible.

I stand at the door, listening to her cry. I'm trapped. I can't keep digging into the basement floor while she's home. Besides, I stopped believing that Mom is buried in the basement a while ago. Wherever my mother is, she's not under the basement floor.

Her crying is getting to me. Worming its way past my

defenses, the same way you can hate Darth Vader all the way until the end of *Return of the Jedi* when you can't help but love the guy. I try to push back against it, just like I did with Vader. The guy destroyed an entire planet. Murdered millions of people. How can you find yourself rooting for him in the end?

And yet I do. Just like right now with this other mother. I remind myself that she's the bad guy. She may have killed my mother. She could be an alien. Probably not, but nothing about this situation is a probably. No matter how much I remind myself about who she is and what she's probably done to Mom, I feel sympathy creeping its way into my heart. My mother never cried like this. Not this kind of crying. She cried when Dad died. At the wake. At the funeral. Lots of other times, too. She cried in the principal's office after I threw the book through the office window and got suspended. She cried when Charlie shut the car door on his thumb and had to go to the hospital. She cried when I held Julia in the hospital room for the first time in that big chair. But this is different. This isn't crying because she's happy or sad or scared. This is hopeless crying. Helpless crying. End-of-the-world crying.

I know this kind of crying. I've done it a lot. Never in front of people. I'm good at holding it in until I'm alone, but I'm alone a lot. I cry when I think about how afraid Charlie is of the world, and how I can't make him feel safe enough to give up the canned food and life jacket. I cry when I think about how much Julia misses Mom when she's working double shifts. I cry when I think about how alone Auntie Carole must feel and how much she must miss Uncle Norman. I cry when I open that box in my brain labeled *Dad* and think about him in almost any way, but especially how he must have felt before he died.

It's the kind of crying that makes me wish I could save her, even though she's not my mother and might be something much worse. It's a ridiculous feeling. It's the last thing I should be feeling.

I press my hand against the basement door. I close my eyes. I know it's stupid, but I try to imagine her sitting there at the table, as tired as my mother was on Saturday night. I try to imagine a part of me reaching out to her. Letting her know it will be okay.

It's like some stupid movie moment. Something that means nothing. I do it anyway. It's all I can do. When nothing is all that you can do, you do nothing and try to make it feel right.

My heart breaks listening to her weep at that table.

Things may change very quickly. I know they will. My broken heart will have to mend fast if I'm going to find Mom. It will have to become something else. But in this moment, I don't hate the other mother.

I feel close to her. Like we are the same.

I tighten my grip on the shovel again. I remind myself about what I may have to do much sooner than I want.

twenty-four

The phone rings. Not her cellphone this time. The landline.

The other mother doesn't move. She's letting the answering machine pick up. A few seconds later, a voice begins speaking. "Hello, this is Mr. Nicastro at Kennedy School. Michael has skipped his last three classes today and appears to have left the school. If you could—"

The chair scrapes across the floor. Footsteps. Fuck. I never thought they would call home. I thought I would have until tomorrow to deal with this. A second later, I hear the clatter of the phone being picked up. "Hello," the other mother says. "This is Mrs. Steele."

I hold my breath. Mr. Nicastro doesn't like me.

"No," she says after a moment. "He's not here. At least I don't think he is. I haven't checked his room. Have you tried his cellphone?" A pause. "Right. Sorry. I can call him. Do you know why he might've left school? Did something happen?"

She walks across the kitchen into the living room. Then she climbs the stairs to the second floor. She's checking my bedroom. And she's listening. Mr. Nicastro is telling her what I did today. I try to imagine what he's saying. Something like Michael instigated a rebellion in science class. He spoke to the school psychologist, who is always way too easy on him, and then he ran away before I could punish him.

He's such a prick.

She's coming down the stairs when I hear her voice again. "Do you know when he left?" she asks. A pause, and then, "I'll call him and see if he answers."

A yes. A no. Then, "I'm supposed to be at work in a couple hours, but I can stay here and wait for him until then. And I can see about getting my shift covered. I'm a nurse. My husband is out of state. He's supposed to be back tonight."

Supposed to be back tonight. Even the other mother knows that Glen is an unreliable asshole.

"No," she says. "I understand. I'll call him now. She'll call me soon?"

A pause. I double-check my phone to make sure the ringer is turned off.

"Yes," she says. "I'll let you know as soon as I know something."

The phone clatters in the base. She walks across the kitchen back to the table. Then back again. She's pacing. Crisscrossing the kitchen. A second later my phone vibrates in my pocket.

"C'mon, Michael," she whispers. "Pick up."

It's so strange. It feels as if she knows I'm here. Like she's speaking directly to me. Telling me to pick up.

"Please, honey. Pick up." My phone stops vibrating. Voicemail.

"Fuck," she says. Silence for more than a minute. She has no reason to go into the basement, but she suddenly feels so close to me. Too close. A cough or a sneeze would give me away.

My phone vibrates again. I pull it from my pocket. It's a text message. It's from Stepwife. The other mother has my mother's phone.

I heard what happened today. Please let me know that you're okay.

I stare at the phone. No reply seems like the safest thing to do, but if I don't reply, she may send the cavalry. Call the police. Call Auntie Carole. If I say something, maybe she'll leave the house and go to work. I type a reply.

I'm fine. It was a bad day. I just needed a break. Don't worry. I'll be home for dinner.

A chair scrapes the floor again. She's sitting down at the table again. This wasn't my plan. I'm trapped in the basement.

My phone vibrates again. I expected a reply, but still, I'm so surprised by the vibration that I nearly drop it, and then I nearly drop the shovel, which is cradled in my arms.

Where are you?

I need her to leave so I can leave. Otherwise I'll be stuck in the basement all day. I need to get out. I have things to do. I need to write something that will get her out of the house.

Fishing. Thinking.

She sighs. I'm not sure if she's tired or annoyed or relieved. It's impossible to tell without being able to see her.

Another message.

Can we talk?

This is not my mother. If ever there was doubt—and I never doubted for a second—this is all the proof I need. My mother has never asked me a question like this before. She has never offered to talk. I get in trouble at school, and it's a week or two of silence at home. No questions about why I did what I did. Not a peep about anything I need to know about growing up. No talk about high school or college or girls. She's never even told me about sex. She just assumed that I knew everything I needed to know, and since I'm probably years away from having sex, I guess that's true, but still. When the guys in the locker room are talking about rubbers and blowjobs and you think they're talking about super balls and leaf blowing in the fall, it's a problem. It's like sending a soldier onto the battlefield without a gun. That's me. Forever unarmed.

I think carefully before responding. I want my answer to be perfect.

Later.

She responds immediately.

Are you sure?

Yes, I say. Then: *Later. Dinner. Please.*

I wait. A few seconds later she stands and walks across the house to the staircase. She's going upstairs. Maybe to change or shower. She has another shift in a couple hours. She should be home around 11:00, but she didn't say anything about work when I said that I'd see her at dinner.

Maybe she plans to come home early and eat dinner with us.

Or she's not going into work at all.

Or she lied to me.

The hot-water heater starts to hum. Water rushes through the pipes that weave their way through the ceiling. She's probably taking a shower or running hot water in the sink. Washing her face? Either way, it's my chance to leave. I look at my phone. 2:23. Time enough to get my bike and go before Charlie or Julia get home. They will wonder why I wasn't on the bus. It will make them nervous. They'll wonder how they will get in the house. I hope the other mother knows to stay here long enough to let them in. I can text her once I'm on the road and tell her to leave the door unlocked.

I move fast. I push the basement door open and walk quickly through the kitchen. I stop for a second in the middle of the kitchen and think about taking the knives. Emptying the house of possible weapons. I decide against it. Just as easy to kill someone with a frying pan as it is with a cleaver.

I can't take everything.

I go out through the side door. I still have the shovel. I'm taking it with me. It feels right to get it out of the house.

My bike is in the garage. Julia must've put it away last night. The garage doors are closed, and I can't risk opening them. They're too loud and too slow. I'll have to go through the side door. The garage will be dark and cold and claustrophobic, even with the lights on. Even in the middle of the day.

I wish Julia wasn't so damn responsible. The garage is the last place I want to go.

I push open the side door. I flip on the light switch. The shovel feels good in my hands now. I scan the garage. My bike is leaning against the back wall. I stand at the doorway. I don't want to enter this place. Not alone. Not ever. We shouldn't even live here anymore. This shouldn't be my garage.

The other mother was wrong when she was on the phone. We lost our dad, but we should lose our home, too. Leave it all behind. I should never have to set foot in this fucking garage again.

The bike is still leaning against the back wall. I still haven't budged from the doorway. Maybe I don't need it. I don't know where to go anyway. I have no place to go. I just don't want to be here right now, but getting away from here means I need my bike, and that means going into the last place on earth I want to go.

I'll walk fast. I'll keep my head down. It'll be like racing up the basement stairs when you think something is going to reach up and pull you back down. I'll just be fast. I won't look at anything except my bike. Only the bike.

Focus on the bike.

I go.

I'm halfway across the garage when I look up. I can't help it. Without thinking, I've stopped. I see my father's tool bench in the shadows to my left. I can't not see it. Glen can't fix a thing, so it's barely been touched since Dad died. His tools are still hanging on the board above the bench, gathering dust. His baby food jars of screws and nails are still hanging on the walls. His circular saw is still standing beside the bench. It's the thing that I see in my nightmares. I freeze and stare. I remember that day. I will always remember it. It makes the rest of my life seem impossible. I used to wonder if you can forget what you want to forget. What you need to forget.

Now I know.

The things you want to forget the most are the things you can't forget the most. It's life's dirty little trick. Bad stuff sticks to the brain like tree sap. There's no getting rid of it. Sunless days stretch into the future like a river without an end. I already know what is coming. I can see it as plain as day.

Suddenly I know where I want to go. It's perfect.

I move again. Fast. I grab my bike by the handlebars and drag it out of the shadows and into the sunshine. I climb aboard. I pedal hard. It feels good.

Sunless days ahead for sure. But maybe not today. At least not this afternoon.

twenty-five

I sometimes hear people say that their dad is the best dad in the world.

I never thought that about my father. Not for a second.

He wasn't an assistant scoutmaster. He never came to a parent-teacher conference. Never helped me with my homework. He didn't teach me to ride a bike. He didn't like to hug and never kissed me. If there was a Father of the Year contest, he might have come in dead last every single year.

He wasn't the best dad by a long shot. But he was the best dad for me. And I liked that. I didn't need to share him with the world. I didn't need him by my side all the time. Our tiny moments together became so important for me. Almost enough for me.

I have tried to remember the last words my father and I spoke to each other, but I can't remember. I'm not even sure when I saw him alive for the last time. Probably the morning before his death, but I have no recollection of that

morning. A week before he died, we had our last real moment together. My last memory of him. Dad was mowing
the lawn. It was late afternoon. The sunlight was sliding
from gold to orange. The first peepers had begun peeping.

"Brave or stupid," Dad always said about those first peep
frogs. "Probably a mixture of both."

The garage was still stifling from the day's heat, so rather
than taking up my usual position in the loft, I climbed the
willow tree in the backyard and watched as Dad finished
mowing the last bit of tall grass. Dad didn't believe in self-
powered lawn mowers. "If you're going to mow a lawn, might
as well get some exercise at the same time. Two birds. One
rock," he liked to say. So when he pushed that mower, he had
to really lean in and push. Dad was a short, thick guy. Sort
of shaped like a fire hydrant. A strong guy, too, but if you
didn't know him or looked from afar, you might think he
was chubby and out of shape. Not so.

Dad sweated a lot when he worked in the sun. Mom
called him a human sponge. His T-shirt was soaked through
as he paced back and forth across the rows of uncut grass.
He always kept a handkerchief in his back pocket to wipe
the sweat from his face. When he finished the final row and
shut the mower off, I called down to him. "Nice job, old
man."

"Old man, huh?" He walked over to the tree like a man
on a mission and then climbed straight up without missing
a beat, following the same path I took, until he was sitting
beside me on a branch, about ten feet off the ground.

I couldn't believe it. "I didn't know you could climb," I
said.

He laughed. "Neither did I."

We sat quietly for a while, watching the sun disappear between the trees. The breeze picked up, cooling us off. I felt so good that night, sitting next to him on that overhanging branch.

"You okay?" he asked after a while.

"Yup," I said. "Why?"

"You're not always okay."

"I'm fine," I said.

"Good. I know how hard things can get sometimes."

"I'm good," I said. I meant it. Life can get hard, but at that moment, in that place, I was fine. Right as rain, Dad would say.

"You're probably old enough to start mowing the lawn," he said.

"Yeah?"

"I thought you'd be excited. You've wanted to mow the lawn forever."

"It's funny," I said. "Things always seem like so much fun when you can't do them, but as soon as you can, the fun disappears. It becomes work."

"Truer words have never been spoken," Dad said.

"I assume that's why you don't eat ice cream for breakfast," I said.

"What do you mean?"

"I plan on eating ice cream for breakfast as soon I have the chance," I said. "But I assume that as soon as I'm old enough to actually do it, I won't want to anymore."

"I don't know," Dad said. "Ice cream for breakfast sounds pretty good. I think you might just be smarter than the rest of us."

"Yeah?"

"Every dog has its day," he said.

I smiled. "Woof."

He laughed.

We sat there for a while longer until the sun disappeared behind the trees altogether. Stars appeared in the sky. The moon peaked above the horizon, climbing slowly. We climbed down. Dad put the mower away while I went inside and did God-knows-what.

Two days later, there was a pint of chocolate ice cream on the kitchen table when I came down for breakfast. There was a yellow sticky note attached to the top with a single word written on it:

Woof.

I don't think about Dad much anymore. In fact, I've become an expert at not thinking about my father.

I especially avoid thinking about the good stuff. I push away all the happy memories. If I don't think about all the things he did to make me laugh or smile, then I don't miss him so much. It's easier to be mad at Glen or disappointed in Mom than it is to miss my father, so that's what I choose. I focus on other things.

Sometimes—no matter how hard I try—they still creep in.

The moments I remember best are the ones from before I became a dick. Somewhere around the end of elementary school or the beginning of middle school, I stopped playing with Dad. I decided that I was too old to hang out and play games with him. I started playing video games online. I watched a lot of TV. I read comic books. I tried to do all the things that I thought were cool, even if I was doing most of them alone. I was worried that if I played games with Dad and Charlie and Julia, I would never be normal.

We had so much fun together before I became a dick.

Dad was a serious guy when it came to games. We played Monopoly the real way, with auctions for every property and none of the stupid homemade rules that other people use. Our games would sometimes go on for hours, and you weren't allowed to quit until you either won or went bankrupt.

I loved it.

We played Risk, chess, checkers, backgammon, Stratego, darts, Twister, and "Don't Touch the Floor." We played tic-tac-toe, and for years—until I figured out his strategy—Dad would actually win. My father wasn't the kind of parent who ever allowed his kids to win so they could feel good about themselves. Every game was a competition. Every contest was a war. He won most of them, but when one of us managed to win, it was the best feeling in the world.

Dad also hated games that relied on luck instead of strategy. Card games like War and Gin Rummy annoyed him. He threw away Life after playing it once with Julia. He used to say that Chutes and Ladders was "an atrocity to all that is holy and good."

Of all the games that we played with Dad, my favorite was Monster.

We only played Monster at night and only when it was dark outside. Cloudy nights. No full moons. All the lights in the house were turned off except for the bulb over the kitchen sink. One tiny, yellow pool of light that served as home base.

Dad would hide somewhere in the house. Our job was to make our way through the house, from the living room to the dining room to the kitchen, then down the hallway past the office and the bathroom and my parents' bedroom, through the TV room, past the porch, and then back through the living room and into the kitchen and home base.

Sometimes all three of us made the circuit together. Sometimes just two of us at a time. Every now and then, Dad made us go one by one.

Julia loved going alone. Charlie hated it.

I did, too.

Monster was terrifying. I was afraid at every second. Even though it was only my father lying in wait for us, those walks through that pitch-black house were some of the most frightening moments of my life. My father was the master of hiding. It seemed as if every time we played, he would have a new spot to lie in wait. And since the house was so dark, especially in the back hall and the TV room, he would sometimes hide in plain sight, standing just inches from our faces. I would feel his breath on my cheek and scream.

My father seemed to fit in places no adult should fit. He would wedge his body into the top of door frames and let us walk beneath him again and again, not suspecting a thing. He used patience as a weapon. With every trip around the house, we became more and more frightened. Every minute that he remained hidden convinced us that he was about to strike. He would wait so long that we would sometimes wonder if he had fallen asleep in his hiding place or left the house completely. Just when I started to feel hope that I would make it around the circuit without being caught, he would strike, creeping up behind one of us, wrapping his hands around our mouths so we couldn't speak, and whispering something like, "If you make a sound, we'll skip your next birthday. And maybe the one after that."

Then he would take us away. Stuff us in a closet or cover us with a blanket behind a bed or shove us into the dryer. He would warn us not to move or speak until we had all been caught.

Charlie once made too much noise while he was in the dryer so Dad turned it on for a few seconds and gave him a little tumble.

Charlie laughed for an hour. I was so jealous that it hadn't been me.

I have never been more frightened than when I was playing Monster with my father. He was a roller coaster, a haunted house and a serial killer all rolled into one.

I've also never been as happy. Clinging to Charlie and Julia as we shuffled through the house. Feeling our way by poking our hands and feet into the dark. Trying to be silent so Dad wouldn't hear us coming. Waiting for this man who we all loved to snatch us away and hide us in some new and impossible place.

Then one day I decided that Monster and Monopoly and Twister and "Don't Touch the Floor" were too babyish for me. I was done being a little kid. My father was disappointed when I told him that I wasn't going to play. It didn't make sense to him. He was confused. But I guess he eventually figured it out. Either that or he just gave up on me. I couldn't blame him. Nobody likes to play with a dick. Charlie and Julia would still play Monster and Monopoly with him while I sat in my room and played *Call of Duty* or read comic books.

Part of me wanted to play with them, but I was just so worried that I would never have a friend that I gave up on the best friend I ever had. I decided that my father wasn't cool enough for me, so I tried to find someone cooler.

In the years since I first stopped playing with him, I haven't come close.

Then he died.

Mrs. Newfang told me that it's normal for kids my age to begin to separate from their parents. She said that I was starting to find my own way. Becoming my own person. Figuring out who I wanted to be. She says I was just doing what all kids my age were doing. Maybe that's true for kids, but maybe their parents are assholes who stare at their phones all day and constantly lecture to their kids. My dad never even owned a cellphone. All he wanted to do was play with me.

Even if Mrs. Newfang is right about everyone my age separating from our parents it doesn't make it right. It just means that we're all assholes.

Except they still have their fathers. They have time to fix things. My time is up.

Sometimes I forget that my father's dead. I'll see a commercial for a power tool or a new board game and I'll think, *I should tell Mom to get that for Dad for Christmas.* Or I'll be riding my bike home after catching a big-ass fish and think, *I can't wait to tell Dad about this one.* I woke up once and was so sure that Dad's death was just a bad dream that I made it all the way into the kitchen before I smelled the sausage that Mom was cooking and realized that he was dead.

Dad hated sausage.

I told this to Mrs. Newfang once, and she said that it was normal. She said that it meant that Dad was still "alive and well in my heart."

That was probably the dumbest thing Mrs. Newfang has ever said to me. Maybe the only dumb thing she's ever said to me. When you forget that your dead father is dead, there is nothing alive and well about it. It just means that you have to feel him die a little bit all over again.

I have so many questions about my father. So many things I want to know. So many things *I need to know.* When a person dies, it's like a hard drive crashing. All of their memories and information are erased forever. If you didn't ask that person a question, you can never ask that question again. You can never know the answer. You leave for school with a million questions that you've never asked and all the time in the world to get the answers, and then you step off the bus and discover that all the time in the world is gone.

Sometimes you don't ask the most important questions because they are the hardest to ask. You wait and wait and wait, and then you've waited too long. The answers are gone.

I don't know if I'm riding my bike in the direction of answers or not, but it might be the only place for answers. It might be my only chance to know the things that are unknowable.

twenty-six

I have only been to Mrs. Foley's house one time, and it already feels like a safe place for me. Maybe because it makes me think of my father.

I drop my bike on her front lawn and climb the steps of the porch two at a time, wondering what I will say. I feel like this is the right place for me at this very moment, but I don't really know why. I'm going with my gut. This was something Dad preached all the time. He'd say that when you're staring at a sixteen, listen to what your gut is telling you and don't hesitate.

A sixteen has something to do with blackjack, I think. I never had time to ask. He died before I could.

So here I am, standing at her door, listening to my gut. Listening to Dad. I don't hesitate. I ring the doorbell.

The door doesn't open nearly as fast this time. Mrs. Foley wasn't expecting me. It's the middle of the day. Last period. I should be sitting in Mr. Fedyzen's history class right now. I'm here to learn about history, so maybe Mr. Fedyzen won't mind me skipping class today.

The door swings open. Mrs. Foley is smiling. She's wearing a yellow apron. Her hair is pulled back into a ponytail. It takes her a second to realize who I am. "Michael?" Her eyes widen. She looks down at her watch. "What are you doing here?"

"You have flour on your nose."

She wipes her nose. Looks at her hand to see the flour on her fingertips. "I'm making cookies."

"You missed a spot." I point.

"Shouldn't you be in school?" she asks, wiping her nose again. "Are you collecting today?"

I don't like when people ask two questions at once. I know they don't mean it. At least that's what Mrs. Newfang has told me. She says it's just a bunch of ideas hitting a person at the same time and flying out of their mouth. Still, it's annoying.

"Yes, I'm supposed to be in school," I say. "And no, I'm not collecting money today."

"So why are you here?"

"I ditched."

She looks confused again.

"I left school early," I say.

"You're bunking?"

"Bunking?"

She laughs. "Bunking. That's what we called it when we skipped school."

"Oh." I wonder if Dad called it bunking. I wonder if Dad ever bunked.

"So what brings you here?" she asks.

"Something happened at school," I say. "I needed to leave."

Her smile disappears. "Does your mother know where you are?"

"No," I say. "But it's fine. She sort of knows."

"So why are you here then?" she asks, sounding confused and a little worried. "Are you in trouble?"

I want to tell Mrs. Foley that I've been in trouble for a long, long time. I've been in trouble since my father died and maybe even before that. I feel like I've been holding my breath for years—for most of my life—afraid of what I might say or do. Afraid of how I might make the wrong decision or no decision at all and hurt Julia or Charlie or myself. I want to tell her that I can't relax and don't know how to relax because nothing is easy and my problems just keep piling up.

I don't tell her any of these things. These are secrets, too. Not secrets like the other mother and the yellow envelope. You can't see them or touch them, but they are still big enough to keep. Big enough to hold inside and never let anyone see. "I'm not in trouble," I say. "Not real trouble. I just want to talk."

"Okay," she says. She sounds uncertain. Nervous, maybe. "You want to come in? Or sit out here on the porch?"

"The porch is fine," I say. I'd like to go inside the house, but she looks a little afraid of what's happening, and I think she'll feel better about this if I don't come inside.

"Let me put the cookies in the oven and I'll come right back. I'll get us something to drink."

She goes back into the house. I sit down in her porch swing. I lift my feet off the ground and exhale. It feels good to sit. Good to just rest for a moment. I'm so tired. I've been tired for most of my life.

I wonder if my mother is as tired as me.

The screen door opens. Mrs. Foley is back. She hands me a glass of lemonade.

"I love that swing," she says, pointing.

"Did you want to sit in it?" I ask.

"Don't be silly. I can sit there whenever I want."

"Okay," I say. "Thanks." I take a sip of the lemonade. I don't know where to start. I'm not even sure what I should say, so I'm relieved when Mrs. Foley continues to talk.

"To be honest," she says, "I don't sit in that swing much these days. Tom and I used to sit there every night in the summer. We'd watch the sunset and listen to the peepers start up. When I sit in the swing now, I can't help but think of him. That's not always easy."

The swing is Mrs. Foley's version of my garage. It probably doesn't feel haunted like my garage does, but it's "in the ballpark" as my father used to say.

"I have a hard time thinking about my dad, too," I say. "I even have a peepers memory, too. It hurts."

Just like that, I have told Mrs. Foley something that I have never told anyone before in my life. It feels great, but it's terrifying, too. Kind of like playing Monster with Dad.

Mrs. Foley nods. "It's good to forget sometimes, isn't it? Sometimes I wish that I could wake up and just have one day when I don't think of Tom. Did you ever see the movie *Eternal Sunshine of the Spotless Mind*?"

I shake my head.

"It's a movie about a man who wants to erase the memories

of his ex-girlfriend from his mind. Or maybe his ex-wife. I can't quite remember. Either way, she's dumped him, and now he wants to forget her, and there's a machine that can make it happen."

"Does he do it?" I ask. "Does he erase his memory?" The answer to this question suddenly feels so important to me.

"I think so," she says. "He starts to, at least. But her memory fights back, I think. I can't recall that either. See that? We forget the stuff we want to remember and remember the stuff we want to forget."

I want to tell Mrs. Foley that she just said one of the truest things I've ever heard.

"Either way," she says, "I think I'd like a machine like that. Not to permanently erase my memories, but to give me a break from them every now and then? You know?"

"I do," I say. I'm not sure if she can tell, but these words come out like a thousand pounds of truth.

"It must be hard to lose a parent when you're so young."

"What do you mean?" I panic. For a second—less than a second but it feels like a thousand seconds—I think she's talking about my mom and the other mother. How does she know?

"It must've been hard to lose your dad." She looks so sad when she says this. Like she feels the pain as much as I do. "It's never easy to lose a parent, but you were so young when it happened."

It occurs to me that I've lost both of my parents. I hadn't realized this until now. First Dad and now Mom. And if I don't get Mom back, I'm going to be left with Asshole Glen and an impostor. "You're right," I say. "It sucked."

"I'm so sorry," she says.

I take a sip of lemonade. Then I take another. I'm stalling. I'm not sure what to say. I'm still not sure how to begin.

Mrs. Foley shifts in her seat. She crosses her legs. It's something people do when they get nervous. When I don't keep up my end of the conversation. That's a Mrs. New-fang expression. She says that conversations are like a tennis match. It's never fun to play alone.

I hate tennis. I played it once and kept hitting the ball over the fence and into the woods.

After a long moment of silence, Mrs. Foley finally asks, "Was there something particular that you wanted to talk to me about?"

The answer is yes, but I don't want to ask. I wish I could just press a button and make Mrs. Foley spit out all the information I want without me having to say a word. I feel like I need to break through a wall to get to what I need. "I guess I'm just wondering about my dad," I say. "You knew him when he was young. I was wondering what he was like."

"You skipped school to hear about your dad?"

"Not really. There was other stuff, too. Other reasons for me to ditch. I didn't leave school to come here. But yes. I want to know."

"Okay," she says. "What do you want to know?"

I have to be careful. I have to sneak up on it. I can't be too specific. "Can you tell me what he was like when he was a kid?"

She smiles. She's thinking about my dad. Her smile lingers for a moment, and then it fades and she's back with me. "I guess you could call him an odd duck."

"How come?" I ask.

"Well, he didn't play sports, which was odd. All the boys played sports back then. But I don't think he wanted to. Or maybe he wasn't as athletic as he looked. I'm not sure. Either way, the boys played football on the back field or street hockey in the parking lot, but your dad would spend recess sitting on this crumbling stone wall under an oak tree, reading or drawing or whittling. Back then you could bring a pocketknife to school and not get in trouble. And sometimes he would just lie down in the grass and look up at the sky for the whole time we were outside." She stops looking at me for a moment. She's looking past me. She can see him now, sitting on that wall, reading a book, or lying in the grass, staring up at the clouds. I'm sure of it. I wish I could see through her eyes. I wish I could see what she's seeing.

"He didn't have many friends?" I ask.

"He wasn't the most popular kid in school, but he had friends. Kids liked your dad. I think they liked his confidence. It's why I liked him. He wasn't afraid to do things differently."

"But he spent recess alone?"

"Sometimes," she says. "But by choice."

"What were you doing during recess?"

"Back then boys and girls were separated at recess. The girls played on the upper field. The boys had the parking lot and the back field. Crazy, right?"

"Yeah," I say. "Pocketknives and separate recesses? It sounds like a thousand years ago."

"I know. Right? I would be jumping rope with my girlfriends or talking about boys. But I could always see your father down the hill, sitting on that wall. We would kind of keep track of each other. Make eye contact every now and then. Even wave."

"It must've been hard for him to be alone," I say.

"Maybe, but like I said, he had friends. He just didn't quite fit into the recess routines."

"Even if you have a million friends, it's hard to be alone. It's hard to be the kid who sits alone under a tree and stares at the sky."

"Sure," she says. "But that was your dad. And he really didn't care. Or at least I don't think he cared. And he wasn't always alone under that tree. Kids hung out with him sometimes. In fifth or sixth grade he brought *Helter Skelter* to school. Do you know that book?"

I shake my head.

"It's the story of Charles Manson. A serial killer in the 1960s. Your dad tore the cover off the book so the teachers wouldn't know what he was reading, and then he tore the book into four pieces. When he finished reading the first piece, he passed it on to a friend. And when that friend was finished, he passed it on to someone else. By the end of the year, the whole class had read that book without any of the teachers finding out. And you know what?"

I shake my head again.

"That was a great book." She smiles again. Nods her head a little. "Your dad had great taste."

"So he was happy then?" I ask.

"Happy?" She looks a little confused. I feel like I've asked the stupidest question in the history of the world. "I guess he was happy," she says. "I'm not really sure what you mean."

I try to find the words. Any words that make sense. I

wish I knew how to say the right thing at the right time. I don't think I've done that once in my life. I feel like I'm standing on thin ice. One wrong word and I could go crashing through. "I'm curious, I guess. Did he have any problems when he was young?"

She laughs a little. "Everyone has problems. Your dad wasn't any different in that regard. What kind of problems?"

"Anything," I say.

"Well . . ." she says, rubbing her hands together like they are cold. Mom does the same thing when she thinks. "He hated math. Couldn't multiply to save his life. And he couldn't dance. No rhythm. Stiff as a board on the dance floor." She smiles a little. Her eyes brighten. "I found that out at the freshman-senior dance. What a disaster. Oh, and he had the ugliest haircut I've ever seen. Sort of like a reverse mullet. And worst of all, he thought it looked good. No matter how much I begged him to get it changed, he refused. He was stubborn. Stubborn as a mule when he thought he was right." She can see him again. She's looking just past me at a memory that only she can see. She's staring at a young man who I can't begin to imagine. A kid about my age who will grow up to be my father. Her smile widens. Her eyes are bright. I think she probably loved him.

A part of her might still love him.

"And I know he didn't get along with his dad," she says, breaking from the memory. "Your grandfather. They fought a lot. Your grandfather thought that your father was a flake. Not serious enough about his future. He wanted your dad at home, in the shop, learning the family business. But that just wasn't what your father wanted to do."

"Grandpa was a plumber. Right?"

"I think so," she says. "But not toilets and sinks. Heating and air-conditioning, maybe? Something like that. Whatever it was, your dad wanted nothing to do with it."

"What did he want to be?"

"He didn't know for a long time. He used to say he wanted to be a thinker, but there isn't much money in thinking. Even he knew that."

"It's funny that he ended up as a mechanic."

"Not really," she says. "In high school your dad started building things from scratch. Sculptures from old car and bicycle parts at first. Then windmills and weather vanes, all made from bike tires and gears and appliances that he would steal from the junkyard. And then one day he started building actual bikes. Crazy designs, but they worked. You could ride them. They weren't fast, and they were almost impossible to steer, but they were beautiful. Weird but really lovely. Eventually he started working with motors and built his first motorcycle. That was it for him. It was impossible to get him out of the garage after that. He just started building and tinkering and never stopped. He was good at it."

"What about Grandma?" I ask. "Did he get along with her?"

"It's hard to say. I didn't know her all that well. But she wasn't entirely there all the time. Sort of an absentee parent. Is she still alive?"

"No," I say. "She died before I was born."

"I'm sorry. That's too bad." She takes a breath. She chews on her lip. She's thinking about what she wants to say next. Like she might be stepping on to thin ice now, too. "Do you want more lemonade?" she asks, reaching for my empty glass.

I do. My throat is dry. My stomach is tied in knots. My whole body feels like it's been wound like a spring. But I say no. I don't want her to stop speaking. I'm afraid that she might not get started again. "What do you mean that she wasn't there?" I ask.

"I don't like to speak ill of the dead, but I think your grandmother had a drinking problem. At least she did back then. She wasn't around much for your dad. But people change. Maybe it was a temporary thing. Or maybe I'm wrong. Maybe I was imagining it."

She wasn't. Mom once told me that Dad never drank because he watched his mother drink herself to death.

"But even without the drinking," she says, "your grandmother was just distant. Uninvolved, I guess. Never asking about homework. Never worrying about curfews."

"So Dad wasn't . . . I don't know. Weird?"

"What do you mean?"

I want to ask if Dad had to meet with the Mrs. Newfang of his middle school. Did he ever break a window or flip a desk? Did he have trouble talking to people and making friends? Did he get pulled from class two or three times a week to talk to the school psychologist? Did he have a letter in his file about his behavior? Did he spend time in the principal's office? But all that ice is way too thin. Way too close to the truth. "Did he have any learning disabilities?" I ask, hoping this is steadier ground. "Any trouble with his temper?"

"Not that I recall."

"Was he ever . . . ? I don't know." I don't want to say it, but if I don't, I know I'll come back here and ask it eventually. It's an answer I need to know. "Was he ever depressed?"

"I don't know." She pauses a moment to think. "Maybe. Aren't all middle-school kids depressed at some point?"

"Probably," I say, but that's a lie. Shane Carter has never been depressed a day in his life. Neither has Kayla Nguyen or Samuel Lee or every other popular kid in school. I'd like to think that Sarah has never been depressed, either, but I haven't forgotten about that flicker of a shadow I saw behind her eyes.

Mrs. Foley leans forward in her seat. "Why do you ask, Michael?"

I'm so lost in my thoughts that the question hits me like a brick.

She leans in closer. She somehow seems to block out everything except her face. "Why do you want to know if your dad had problems? If he was depressed?"

There is an acceptable answer to this question, and then there is the real answer to this question. An answer that I don't want to think about. A truth that I have pushed away for a long time.

I decide to tell Mrs. Foley the acceptable answer. An answer that's at least in the ballpark. "I know that Dad was depressed before he died. I guess I want to know if he was always depressed. If being depressed was always a part of him. Or if something suddenly made him depressed."

"That's not exactly how depression works," she says. "It's much more complicated than that. Anyone can become depressed, and lots of people suffer from depression at some point in their lives. More than you might suspect. And depression can be brought on by any number of things. Anxiety. Trauma. Illness. Aging. A big life change. The birth of a baby. The death of a loved one. So it's possible that your dad was depressed at times in his life, just like lots of other people. Like me. But if you're asking me if he was depressed when I knew him, I don't think so. Not the guy that I knew back in school."

"How do you know so much about depression?" I ask.

"My husband, Tom, battled depression for much of his life."

"Oh."

"It's okay," she says. "It's actually not that unusual. And it doesn't mean we weren't happy. We had a great life together."

I sit silently for a moment, thinking about what she has told me. Trying to imagine the boy that she has described. Wondering when my father's trouble started. When things began to change for him. When he stopped being that happy boy.

"Why is this so important to you?" she asks.

The question startles me. I'm supposed to be asking the questions. Not her. I speak without thinking. Without testing the ice. "I just want to know. I want to know if he was depressed for most of his life or just at the end."

"How do you know he was depressed at the end?"

The ice is suddenly thin. Really fucking thin. "I don't know," I say. "I thought he might be."

"He seemed sad to you?"

"I guess," I say. "Maybe. I don't know." I want to stop right here. I don't want to take one step farther. I should end this conversation and leave now. Get while the getting's good.

Something else my father used to say.

But I don't. I don't expect this, but I keep talking.

Words are tumbling out of me now. "Actually, no," I say. "Dad didn't seem depressed at all to me. He seemed perfectly fine. But maybe he was depressed for the whole time I knew him. Maybe he was full of stuff he never told anyone about. Maybe he was a mess inside. Maybe depressed was his normal. That's what's so confusing to me."

"But why do you think he was depressed?" she asks again. "At the end of his life, I mean. Why would you think he was depressed if he never seemed depressed to you?"

I don't move. I don't breathe. I don't have an answer. At least not an answer that I can tell her or anyone else. The ice has never been thinner beneath my feet. Part of me wants to say it. Wants to answer her question. Say the secret. Tell her the real reason I need to know if my father was depressed or angry when he was my age. It seems almost right to say it here. On this porch. In this swing. To this person. Like this might be the reason I'm here. To finally say my secret aloud.

I've wished for the day when I could tell a stranger all my secrets, just so I don't have to carry them on my own anymore. Mrs. Foley isn't a stranger, but she's close. As close to a stranger as I might get. And maybe I don't have to tell her all my secrets. Maybe getting rid of just one of them would be enough.

I look at Mrs. Foley. She's still leaning forward in her seat. Her hands are folded in her lap. She somehow knows that she's asked an important question. A question with an important answer.

"I want to tell you something," I say.

"Okay." Now she sounds like the one who knows she's

standing on thin ice. She knows how easily I could change my mind and end this conversation. She knows how badly I want to run.

"But I don't want you to tell anyone," I say.

She shifts in her chair. Leans back a little. I feel the distance. She's stepping away. "I'd like to make you that promise, Michael, but it may depend on what you say. Some things can't be kept secret."

I could argue with her. Try to convince her that what I'm about to say isn't going to send her running to my parents or the police. But it won't matter. She will hold my words in her heart or tell the world. She will keep the secret or she won't. No matter what she says, she will do the right thing because that is who she is.

I think she'll keep my secret. I know she will.

Even if she doesn't, that might be okay, too. It's becoming too heavy for me to carry. Maybe it's time to put it down, as impossible as that may seem. "Okay," I say. "I understand."

"I'm sorry, Michael. I wish I could make that promise. But if you can't tell me, maybe there's someone else? Someone you trust?"

I want to tell her that I can't tell someone I trust, because I have no one to trust. My father is dead. My mother is gone. My brother and sister are too young. Jeff isn't ready for something like this. Mrs. Newfang wouldn't be able to keep my secret. There's no one else. I need a stranger, and she's the only stranger I know.

"No," I say. "I think I'll tell you."

"Oh," she says. She's surprised.

I am, too.

"All right," she says. She leans in. Closes the distance between us. Smiles. "Fire away."

I take a long, deep breath. I lean forward in the swing far enough that my feet plant flat on the porch. I look down at my sneakers. Maybe if I don't look at her, I can say it.

But that's not right. That's not the way to do it. You can't be a coward if you're going to give away your most important secret. I need to be brave. I look up. She's looking right at me. Her eyes are soft. Relaxed. She's waiting. Not rushing me. Not pressuring me. Giving me all the time in the world.

"Okay . . ." I say. It sounds like the start of a sentence, but I can't make the next words come out. I'm stuck before I even get started. That damn wall between me and the words.

Mrs. Foley doesn't move.

"My father . . ." I say, but I don't have the next words. I'm stuck again. I take another breath. "My father . . ." Again, I stop. I feel like I'm standing on the edge of a cliff. It's a place where I have been standing for a long time. I've dreamed of jumping off this cliff, but I know that if I do, I can never go back. Everything changes if I make this leap. It might be better after I jump, but it might not. It might be terrible, and standing on the edge of the cliff isn't terrible. It's hard and lonely and frightening and sad, but it's never been terrible.

I leap into better or worse. Or I stay here, trapped and alone.

"Michael?" she says.

I leap.

"My father . . ." I say. Then I force the next words out. Three impossible words. "He killed himself."

She tries not to act surprised, but she's not trained like Mrs. Newfang. She hasn't heard crazy kids say crazy shit for years and years. She blinks hard. She leans back a bit, as if my words have hit her like a strong wind. Her hands clench into fists. Her eyes widen ever so slightly. She's holding her breath. She doesn't realize any of it. She thinks she's playing it cool, but she's as uncool as a person can be.

I see all of it.

"I'm so sorry," she says.

I need to keep talking. She thinks that this is all I had to say. She doesn't know that it's just the beginning. The tip of a better-or-worse iceberg. I can't stop now or I'll stop for good. I'll keep the big, ugly part of the iceberg—the worst part—hidden under the ocean, and I've come too far for that. "No one knows," I say. "Everyone thinks it was a heart attack. Only I know."

"What?" Her eyes are saucers now. Enormous. Her jaw has dropped open. Her right foot is tapping nervously.

"Everyone thinks that he died of a heart attack," I say. "But it was suicide."

She leans forward. Closes the gap between us again. "I don't understand. How is that possible?"

"He left a note. Mom didn't find it. The paramedics didn't find it. No one did. It must've gotten knocked off the worktable. Maybe by the wind when they opened the garage doors. I found it under the circular saw a couple weeks later. Sort of jammed between the saw and the wall."

Her eyes widen again. Practically launch from her head this time. "Oh, Michael." She says my name the same way

Sarah said it last night in the gazebo when I told her my other secret. Secrets are falling like dominoes today. I'm almost out. She reaches across the space between us and takes my hands into hers. She grabs them like she owns them. She squeezes them like letting them go will mean letting go of me forever. "Your mom probably knows it was suicide. The doctors can usually tell these things, even without a note."

"No," I say. "They told everyone it was a heart attack."

Her eyes soften. She's still again. Her voice drops to a whisper. "I'm sure they know the truth. There are ways of telling if it was a heart attack or something else."

It's like another corner of the universe unfolds before my eyes. This enormous corner of unimagined possibility.

"Then why would they tell me it was a heart attack?"

I know the answer as soon as I ask the question. Before I ask the question. Thoughts pile up in my brain. Memories of what Mom said when she told us about the heart attack. How she stared at her feet when she spoke. How there was something other than sadness in her eyes. Something that seemed out of place. Anger, maybe? Confusion? Whispered conversations between relatives at the funeral and the wake. Phone calls taken in other rooms.

She must see me working things out in my mind. She just sits and waits.

"I can't believe it," I say. "I thought I was holding a secret all this time."

"Why didn't you tell your mother?" she asks. "About the note?" As soon as she asks the question, she knows, too. "Oh, Michael. You were doing the same thing. Your mother was trying to protect you, and you were trying to protect your mother."

"A heart attack is a lot easier than suicide," I say. I'm crying now. I think I've been crying for a little while, but I just realize it. "I thought I'd just make the note disappear. I stuffed it under my mattress. I'm the only one who knows about it."

"Was it written to your mom?" she asks.

"Yes."

"Then she has a right to see it." She squeezes my hands. "She needs to see it."

"I know," I say. I wipe away tears. "But it's been so long. *Years.* And every day that passes makes it worse. She's going to hate me for hiding it from her for so long."

"She won't hate you. She'll understand. She would want to know."

"Maybe," I say. I think she might be right. But I can't show it to my mother now. Maybe never. I may never see her again.

"Is this why you wanted to know about your dad?"

"What do you mean?"

"You asked me all those questions about him," she says. "Are you trying to figure out why he did it? Because sometimes there aren't any answers to that question. Sometimes there's no way of knowing what was going on in someone's mind."

"That's not why," I say. I don't want to tell her that I know why he did it. I know why my father killed himself. I won't ever understand completely, but I know well enough. Enough for me. But that would mean telling her what's in the letter. I feel like that is for my mother only.

"Then why all the questions?"

Another decision. To tell or not. It's strange. I thought

my father's letter—stuffed in that yellow envelope—was my biggest secret and would be the hardest to tell. Second only to the other mother. But now I think it was easier to tell her about the letter and dad's suicide than this other thing. The real reason I'm here today. Maybe it's easier to tell about secrets that you can see and touch than the ones you can't. The ones inside. The ones that no one can ever find unless you say them out loud.

I'm going to tell. I've come this far.

"I'm not an easy person," I say. I wait, hoping she'll say something. Ask something. Help me along.

She doesn't. She just sits there. She's a lot like Mrs. Newfang. She's a good listener, which most people think is a good thing. But when you're someone like me, who never knows what to say, good listeners suck. You'd rather have someone who can talk all day and night because that's easier than finding your own stuff to say.

"I have a lot of problems," I say. "I lose my temper sometimes. And I have a hard time talking to people." I stop again, hoping she'll say something. Anything. She just sits there, waiting. "I have a lot of stuff to do at home. I take care of my brother and sister. I worry a lot. I'm afraid a lot."

I look to my empty lemonade glass. If it wasn't empty, I could reach for it and drink. Stall. Make her say something. At least ask me a question. I sigh. "I'm just not an easy person."

"Okay," she says. She's still waiting. She knows I haven't answered her question yet. She's just sitting there, waiting for me to get to it. I already have a Mrs. Newfang in my life. I don't need this.

But I've come this far. I decide to finish. Mrs. Foley is

as close to a stranger as I am going to get. I've wanted to tell this to someone for so long. She will be the one. Maybe she'll say something that will save me.

"My dad never seemed sad or depressed or worried or messed up. He was just a normal guy. Then he killed himself. But maybe he was messed up inside." Another cliff. Another leap. I can stop here and keep my secret forever or leap into better or worse.

I leap again.

"Maybe my dad was like me. Maybe I'm just like my dad."

Mrs. Foley is crying now. Not sobbing but tears are spilling down her face. "Michael, are you worried that you might do the same thing your dad did?"

It's the question I wanted. I feel like she has reached across a thousand-mile canyon and taken my hand. I suddenly feel less alone than I have felt in a long time. "Not to-day," I say, and the words start to tumble out. "I'm not going to kill myself today or tomorrow or next week. But someday. I'm worried about someday. Maybe he had all the same stuff hiding in him that I have hiding in me. Maybe I'm just like him. Maybe I'm a ticking time bomb. Just like him. Maybe one day I will explode."

She squeezes my hands. I had forgotten that they were in hers. Everything has gone away except for her face and our hands. "Do you feel like you want to kill yourself?" she asks.

"No," I say. "God no. Even if I wanted to, I'm terrified of dying. But no. Not at all." I take my hands back to wipe away the tears on my cheeks. "But maybe Dad felt this way, too. Maybe he felt exactly the same way I do, and then one day everything changed. I'm afraid that someday every-thing will change for me, too. All the stuff inside me will change me, and I'll do the same thing my dad did and leave behind everyone I love. Just like he left me behind."

She stands up and moves across the space so she's sitting beside me on the swing. I feel a flicker of guilt. I've made her think of her dead husband. But then she puts her arms around me and pulls me in close. "We all have stuff inside us," she says. "Your burden may be heavier than most right now, but you're no different than the rest of us, Michael. I have no idea why your father took his life, but it was a choice he made. He made the decision to take his life. You have a choice, too. You always will. I promise. You're going to be fine, Michael. Better than fine."

I wish I believed her. Maybe a tiny part of me does. A speck of light. Maybe it will grow brighter someday.

I cry like I've never cried before.

twenty-seven

I'm in the house now. Sitting at the kitchen table. My glass is full of lemonade again. Mrs. Foley is taking cookies out of the oven. I can feel the heat pouring out. The room smells like my childhood. Lemon floor wax and chocolate chips. I'm suddenly starving.

"Will you keep my secret?" I ask.

Her back is turned to me. She's wearing oven mitts. She's reaching for the second sheet of cookies. She pauses, bent over in front of the oven. She's thinking about my question, I think. "I can keep your secret," she says. She sets the sheet on top of a cooling rack and turns. "But I don't think you should."

She's right. I'm going to tell Mom about the note. As crazy as it sounds, it feels even more important to get my mother back now. I can't bear the thought that she might never know what the note from my father says. His last words to her. I've kept them hidden for so long. She needs to know. I don't think my mother is dead, but part of me doesn't think I will ever see her again.

I can't let that happen.

"Not just the note," Mrs. Foley says, as if she's reading my mind. "The rest of it, too."

"What do you mean?"

"You can't go through life keeping all that stuff trapped inside you. You need to tell someone about your worries. Your fears. You can't just plow through life like none of it matters. You need someone to talk to."

"That's why I told you."

"I'm glad you told me," she says, passing me a plate with three cookies on it. "Be careful. They're hot." She hands me a napkin. "But someone else needs to know. Your mom. Your stepfather. Someone in your everyday life."

"Glen?" I say. I laugh. "I don't think so."

"You don't like your stepdad?"

"That's an understatement. I have no idea what my mother saw in that asshole."

Mrs. Foley removes her oven mitts. She sits down beside me. "Don't be too hard on your mother. She lost her husband. Suddenly and terribly. She was alone with three kids. Probably afraid. Probably worried out of her mind. Grieving for a husband. Confused about why he did what he did. Sad as sad can be, and yet, she had no time to take care of herself. She had three little people to worry about. Three mouths to feed. Three children to raise on her own. Sometimes we run to the first person we think can save us."

"Glen isn't exactly saving us."

"I know," she says. "But maybe your mom didn't know. Maybe she saw a man who was willing to take on the responsibility of a widow and her three kids and thought that was enough. Maybe she thought that was the best she'd ever get. Maybe she was shocked that anyone showed any interest in her at all. You have no idea how frightening the world can be when you feel like you have the lives of others in your hands."

I open my mouth to fire back, to tell her I know exactly how frightening the world can be when you feel like you had the lives of others in your hands. When you are forced to grow up faster than anyone around you. Take on responsibilities that you didn't want. I want to tell her I know exactly how it feels to worry about your brother and sister day and night. When all you think about is how much they need you and how sure you are that you will fail and ruin them forever.

I don't say any of that. It's not her fault that she doesn't know. She doesn't need to know.

"And you probably don't know this yet," Mrs. Foley says, "but love is a strange thing. There's no predicting it. No understanding why one person loves another. No one ever understood my marriage to Tom. They thought that we were doomed from the start. My brother predicted divorce in five years. My parents thought we would kill each other. The only thing that doomed us was the cancer. So maybe your mother loves Glen. Don't discount that. I don't doubt that Glen is a son of a bitch. I met him. Remember? He's not exactly Prince Charming. But maybe your mother sees something in him that you can't. Or won't. There's nothing wrong with thinking that your stepfather is an asshole. Just don't think that your mother should feel the same. And don't think less of her because she loves him."

"Okay," I say, and I mean it. Or at least I'm going to try to mean it. It makes sense. A little.

"But you need to be talking to someone, Michael. If not your mom or stepdad, a teacher maybe? A school counselor? Find someone. Okay? Promise me this, and I promise that I'll keep your secret."

I leave with a paper bag of cookies for Charlie and Julia. Mom and Glen, too, but I can't give any to Mom until I find her, and I'm sure as hell not giving cookies to the other mother or Glen. Mom may love Glen, or maybe she married him because she was afraid to be alone with three kids, or maybe she is still head over heels in love with him, and maybe I shouldn't be so angry about her marrying him, but that doesn't mean I'm sharing cookies with him.

That would be a bridge too far, as my father used to say.

I straddle my bike and thank Mrs. Foley one more time. I feel lighter than I did when I turned into this driveway an hour ago.

One hour just changed my life.

Or it will change my life if I can get my mother back. None of this will matter if I can't find her. Save her.

I don't know what the other mother knows. I don't know if she can tell me where my mother is or even if she knows that she isn't my mother. But it's time to find out.

No more fucking around.

twenty-eight

I know that the time is now. Mom's car is in the driveway, which means the other mother didn't go to work for her second shift. She must've found someone to fill in for her. Glen won't be back until later tonight with his dumbass stove, so he won't get in the way. But Charlie and Julia are home. Probably watching TV in the living room right now.

That's a problem.

Whatever I decide to do, it will mean confronting the other mother, and I can't have them in the house when I do. If she has done something to Mom or knows where she is, she may try to hurt me or worse. If she can't, she might threaten Charlie or Julia. I'm willing to take the chance, but I can't risk Julia or Charlie.

I need to get her alone.

I'm straddling my bike at the top of the driveway, thinking of a way to get the other mother out of the house—maybe into the garage, as much as that thought terrifies me—when Sarah's mother pulls into her driveway. Sarah is sitting in the back seat.

That's it. That's my solution. Maybe an impossible solution since Sarah probably hates my guts right now, but my only solution, too.

When the impossible is your only option, it suddenly becomes a lot more possible.

It's perfect, too. Sarah can watch Charlie and Julia. She can babysit while I do whatever I'm going to do. They would love to see Sarah again. They wouldn't even complain. Sarah may hate me and think I'm a crazy person, but all I need is fifteen minutes. Fifteen minutes and she never has to talk to me again if she doesn't want to.

"Hi, Mike," Sarah shouts as she climbs out of the car. Her voice surprises me. She sounds normal. Not pissed. Excited, even. I'm suddenly worried. She's supposed to be angry at me. Maybe not even talking to me. Something is wrong. Something must be terribly wrong.

I drop my bike in the grass and wave. Before I can decide if I should I walk over there or wait until I've had time to plan what to say, she's crossing the grass strip that separates our driveways. Her voice might've sounded normal, maybe for her mother's benefit, but her walking says something else. She's not walking over to me. She's storming over to me. Stomping on the grass as if she despises it.

"Hey," I say. I'm suddenly terrified of her.

"What the hell happened today?"

"I'm sorry," I say. So much for planning. So much for strategy. I blurt it out because it's what my whole body needs to say in this moment. It's what I've wanted to say since this morning. "I'm sorry for the bus, and I'm sorry for the hallway. I know you were just trying to help. I'm an idiot."

"No," she says. "Not an idiot. You were mean. You can be stupid all you want. I don't mind stupid. Stupid is normal. But you weren't nice. I don't want to be around someone who treats me like an asshole."

"You're right," I say. "I know."

"Why did you do it?" she asks. Some of her anger has fallen away. She sounds disappointed now. It's worse than anger, I think. "Why were you so mean to me?"

"I don't know," I say. It's not true, but how are you supposed to tell a girl who you like and maybe love that you were mean because you were afraid?

She just stares at me. Glares at me. Hands on her hips. She's breathing hard like she just finished a run. Her silence is worse than any words she could speak.

"I'm sorry," I say again. "You don't need to talk to me anymore. Ever again. I'll understand." I turn to leave, only remembering the other mother and how I need Sarah's help as she grabs me by the shoulder and turns me back toward her.

"Don't be stupid," she says. She sounds annoyed. I don't like this either, but it's a lot better than angry or disappointed. "It's okay. But you can't be an asshole like that to me ever again. You got it?"

"All right," I say. "I promise." Suddenly feeling the need to be honest, I add, "At least I'll try not to be. Sometimes I can be a real jerk. I know that."

She smiles. It's tiny and beautiful. The fire in her eyes is gone. Just like that. "I guess I can live with that," she says. She takes a step closer to me. Her voice drops almost to a whisper. "Now what happened today? Are you okay?"

"I'm fine," I say.

I'm not, of course, but I'm fine in the way that Sarah is asking. In the way that everyone has been asking since Dad died. When people ask if I'm okay, they aren't trying to find out if I feel broken or alone or lost inside. They don't want to hear how much I worry about Julia and Charlie and how hard it is to take care of them when I feel like I'm going to fall apart at any minute. They don't want to hear about how angry and disappointed and confused I am about my mother's decisions and my stepfather's laziness. They don't want to know how impossible every day feels sometimes. They just want to know if in this moment—in the moment that they are sharing with me—I'll be fine. They want to be sure that I won't make things awkward or scary by crying or flipping a desk or hitting someone. No one is interested in the long term. They just want to get through the next few minutes and escape before the bomb goes off.

"Don't tell me you're fine," Sarah says. She's annoyed again. Her words are like arrows. She fires them off at me. "Tell me what's going on."

Then the realization that this is Sarah Flaherty hits me. Hits me like an arrow to the heart. It's strange. A second ago I thought of this person as Sarah, the girl next door who might be my friend and who I need to watch my brother and sister. An instant later, it's like I have new eyes, and she's no longer just Sarah. She's *Sarah Flaherty*, the most beautiful girl in our school. A girl who shouldn't be speaking to me. A girl way too cool for me. The conversation shifts from casual and easy to terrifying and impossible in the span of a second.

"Nothing's going on," I say. "I'm fine. I'm just really sorry about today."

"Dummy, I know about what happened in Mr. Morin's class. But what about after that? They paged you three times on the intercom."

Mr. Morin. She's talking about school. It's incredible. I was in Mr. Morin's class just a few hours ago. Mrs. New-fang's office after that. Then I was running across the parking lot to the path in the woods. It all feels like a lifetime ago. I stood up to an asshole teacher and had one of the greatest moments in my life, but somehow it doesn't seem to matter anymore. It feels like ancient history. I spent two hours digging up my basement and an hour or so with Mrs. Foley, and now I'm somehow a different person. A new person. My protest in Mr. Morin's room. My talk with Mrs. Newfang. Even crying in the back of Mrs. Walker's classroom. It all seems so tiny and faraway now. Unimportant.

"Sorry," I say. "I didn't know what you meant. I left school early. I didn't hear any of the pages."

"You just took off?"

I nod. "I bunked."

"You what?"

"I ditched," I say. "Skipped my last three classes."

"Damn. You do that a lot?"

"My first time," I say. "I just had to get out of there. I knew that Mr. Powers was going to be pissed about what happened in Mr. Morin's room. I didn't want to deal with him today."

"If he wasn't pissed about the thing in Mr. Morin's

room, he's pissed for sure now. He paged you the third time himself. It sounded like his head was going to explode."

"I guess tomorrow's going to suck."

She smiles. "You don't look too worried."

She's right. I'm not. I don't care at all. I don't give a damn about Mr. Morin or the principal or anything else that might happen at school tomorrow. I've got an impostor living in my house, a missing mother who I may never see again, and a suicide note under my mattress, and all of them are a billion times bigger and more important than some stupid-ass teacher or some prick principal.

An asteroid is hurtling toward my planet. The last thing I should be worried about is detentions and suspensions.

"You're right," I say. "I guess I'm not all that worried."

"You're braver than me," she says. "I'd be scared out of my mind."

"Maybe tomorrow I'll feel differently."

"It won't be all bad tomorrow," she says. "You're like a hero in the school. People can't believe what you did. Everyone's talking about it. They loved it." She smiles. "I loved it."

"It wasn't just me," I say. "A lot of people were humming along with me."

"Yeah, but you started it. And from what I hear, you did more than hum. You let him have it. And you were the only one who got thrown out of class. You're the one people are talking about."

"Yeah?"

"Yeah," she says. "It was brilliant, Mike."

I look closely at Sarah's face and try to capture this moment in my memory forever. Trees and sky. The corner of

my house just above her head. A robin perched on the gut-
ter. Gravel under my feet. Sarah's smile. The way she said
my name. I want a mental picture of this moment in my
mind forever. One of the best moments of my life.

I'm having a lot of them today.

"Mike?" She looks confused. Like she wants to poke me
to see if I'm still alive.

"Sorry," I say. "Can I ask you a favor?"

"Sure."

"Can we go inside your place for a second? That's not the
favor, but I don't want to ask out here."

"Sure," she says. "Is anything wrong?"

"No," I say, looking back at my house. "I mean, yes,
there is. You know there is, but it's fine."

I don't want the other mother to see me standing out
here. If she does, she'll come out for sure, wanting to talk to
me about Mr. Morin and ditching school. Maybe for real or
maybe just pretending to be worried, but either way, if that
happens, I'll never get Charlie or Julia out of the house.

Sarah leads me through the front door of her house.
"Mom! Mike and I are going to my room for a few minutes."

"All right," her mom says. She sounds worried. Her
daughter is bringing a boy up to her bedroom again. I feel
like a criminal. I feel a little guilty even though I haven't
done anything wrong.

"Do you want something to drink?" her mom asks.

Sarah looks at me. I shake my head. "No thanks!" she
says. "We won't be long. Just some homework stuff."

"You guys are in the same classes?" Sarah's mom pops
her head out of the kitchen. She's got a glass bowl in her

hand. She's drying it with a towel. She's speaking to Sarah but looking at me. Sizing me up.

"No," Sarah says. "But Mike has to write an essay for English. Same one I wrote last year. I'm just going to read it and give him some ideas."

Her mom nods and disappears into the kitchen. We climb the stairs.

"That was fast," I say.

"What?"

"That story. You didn't even hesitate. You're a good liar. No offense."

"I want to write fiction someday," she says. "Novels. I'm good at making shit up."

"I guess so."

I avoid the wicker chair in the corner this time. I sit on the edge of her bed like I own the place. The idea that I'm about to confront the other mother makes everything else seem so easy now. Sarah sits beside me. Close enough that our thighs are touching again. Even with everything in my mind, this sends sparks through my body all over again.

"So listen," I say. "I need you to babysit for a little while. If you don't mind."

"Who?" she asks. Then she smiles. "You?"

"No, not me. Charlie and Julia. I need to do something, and I can't have them in the house when I do it, so I want to send them over here for a little while."

"What are you planning to do?" She leans in close when she asks. I can smell the soap on her skin. I can see the barely visible freckles on her neck. She's wearing a pink sweater. It looks itchy against her skin.

"I'll tell you when it's over."

"Mike, please listen to me."

"Stop," I say. "I read about Capgras syndrome. I don't have it. Okay? I appreciate you trying to help. I wish this was as simple as a disease. But this is the real thing."

"Mike, it can't be."

"It is. I know it sounds crazy, but it is."

Or not, the other voice says. My voice, I know, but it feels somehow alien to me this time.

"Mike, let's tell someone about your mother. My mother, maybe?"

"I'm going to tell someone," I say.

"Who?"

"The other mother. I'm going to tell her what I know."
I'm going to make her tell me where my mother is. I think this but don't say it.

"Your stepfather, too?"

"He's not home," I say. "He's in New Hampshire."

"Maybe you should wait until he's back."

"It'll be fine," I say. "Better this way."

Sarah opens her mouth to say something but pulls it back. She stares at me. Looks into my eyes. Maybe through them. "You planned it this way. You want to be alone with her."

"I can't control when my stepfather is going to be home. I didn't tell him to go to New Hampshire."

"You know what I mean."

I look at the clock on her nightstand. Almost five o'clock. The minutes are ticking away. Time that I might need if I'm going to save my mother. "What do you want me to tell you? You think I have a mental disease. I think my mother has been replaced. Your explanation makes sense in the real world, but somehow I'm not living in the real world anymore. I need to do this. Why can't you just let me go?"

"Because I like you," she says.

"So?"

"No," she says. "I mean I like like you. And I think that you like like me. And people who like like each other should share stuff like this." She tilts her head and smiles. It's like a giant wink. She knows what these words mean to me.

I can feel my face getting warm. This might be what it feels like to blush. My leg is doing that nervous shaking thing that my dad used to hate. The same nervous shaking Mrs. Foley was doing earlier today on her porch. I'm suddenly aware of my hands. I don't know where to put them. Don't know what to do with them. Then before I know it, one of them is in Sarah's hand. She has taken my hand and is holding it.

Sarah Flaherty is holding my hand.

"You okay?" she asks.

"Fine," I mumble and instantly hate myself.

Fine?

"Sarah!" It's her mother, calling from what sounds like the base of the stairs. I pull my hand back but she holds on tight. Doesn't let it go.

"Yeah?"

"Your father isn't coming home for dinner tonight, honey. I was thinking about ordering pizza. Pepperoni and mushroom?"

"Sure," she says. But the word sounds flat. Suddenly flat.

I look back to Sarah. Something has changed. Her light is gone. A second ago, she was a yellow balloon, floating beside me, bouncing on the air. Now she's deflated. Not completely but enough to have dragged her back to Earth. She's sagging. Lifeless.

"What's wrong?" I ask.

"Nothing." There's a fake bounce in her *nothing*. Like she's propping it up. Not the real bounce she had a second ago.

"I don't believe you," I say.

"I don't care." She pulls her hand back. She stands up and walks across the room to her dresser. She picks up a book and adds it to a pile on the corner. She drops a barrette in a bowl. She's tidying. Her back is to me, but I can see her in the mirror. I can see her face. Her light is completely gone.

"I'm sorry," I say. "I didn't mean anything by it."

"I know," she says. Her back is still turned to me. She's looking at her hands, I think. Looking down. "I'll babysit. It's fine. You can send them over whenever you're ready. Whatever you're doing, just be careful."

"Tell me what's wrong," I say.

"It's nothing. Just go. Please." Her voice shakes like it's on a wire. I think she's going to cry.

I stand up. "Are you sure?" I ask.

She nods her head. She can't speak.

"Okay. Thank you."

I leave. I take six steps down the hallways toward the stairs, and then I stop. I can't leave her. Not like this. I can't leave her standing there alone and lightless. I know what it's like to carry something heavy. I know how lonely and hopeless it can feel. I know what it's like to need to talk to someone about something but not be able to. I know how it might be one of the worst things in the world. I can't leave Sarah with this burden. I can't leave her like me.

I turn around. I step back into the room. "Sarah?"

She turns. "Go," she says. "Please, Mike. Go do what you need to do."

I don't know why, but hearing her say my name—the way only she says it—makes me want to tell her. Maybe hearing my secret will bring her light back. Allow her to tell me her secret. Besides, it's not a secret anymore. I've shared it with someone. I'm not ready to shout it from the rooftops of the world, but I feel like the black box is open. Saying the words seems so much easier now.

"My dad didn't die of a heart attack. He killed himself."

Sarah turns. She looks at me like she's trying to see inside me. "What are you talking about?"

I take a step closer so I'm in the room. "I found the suicide note two weeks after he died. I've kept it hidden since then, under my mattress. But I'm pretty sure my mom knows he committed suicide. At least I am now. I think she told me and Julia and Charlie that it was a heart attack to protect us. Heart attack is a lot easier than suicide. But she doesn't know about the note. No one does. I want to give it to her, but now she's been replaced by this other mother. So I need to confront her. Find out what she knows. I need to find my mother."

Sarah starts to cry a little. She's not crying for me, though. She's crying for something she's carrying.

"I told one other person about the suicide note. Told her today. Just a little while ago. But you're the only one who knows that my mother is missing." I take a deep breath. It felt like I was underwater as I said all those words.

Sarah's face is wet with tears. I want to take the three steps between us and hold her, but I can't. I don't do things like that. I don't know how.

I decide to go all the way. It's her tears that push me to speak. Force me to say the rest. I just can't stand the thought of Sarah being as sad as I have been for so long. I make the leap. "I'm also afraid that someday I might grow up and kill myself, too. That I might be too much like my father. Even though I don't think about it now, I'm worried that I might eventually think about it and do it. I'm a little less afraid of that now. Someone helped me today. It was a big day for me." I smile. I can't believe I said all that and can still smile. "There's other stuff, too. But those are the biggies."

Sarah wipes the tears from her eyes with her sleeve. She straightens. Looks me in the eye. I can feel it. She's getting ready to leap.

"I heard my father talking on the phone last night," she says. "After I came in from the gazebo. He didn't know that I was still awake."

I want to say something, but I don't. I can see she isn't finished. I know how important it is to keep going when you're on a roll.

"He was talking to that other woman," she says. She says these words like they are stones that weigh ten thousand pounds each. "I don't know why he would do it. It feels like he's cheating on me, too. On the family. He's going to ruin our lives. I know it. I know it, and I can't do anything to stop it."

"I'm so sorry."

She nods. She's still crying.

"It feels better to say it," I say. It's one of those annoying questions that isn't a question, but this time, it feels okay.

She nods again. "It does."

"I know. I didn't know it for a long time, but I do now."

We look at each other for a moment. There are tears in my eyes, too. Tears for Sarah. Tears for her secret and her fear.

"Mike?" she says. Almost whispers.

"What?"

"Your mom isn't missing. It doesn't make any sense. You just have a thing. It doesn't mean you're crazy. It just means that you need to talk to someone. Get some help."

"I know that Capgras makes sense," I say. "And I know that what I'm saying doesn't. Believe me. I've tried to find a way out of this. I don't want to believe it either, but it's true. That woman in my house is not my mother."

"That's not possible."

"I know," I say again. "But that's what everyone says when things seem impossible. Then somehow the impossible turns out to be possible. I don't know who she is or how she did it or even if she knows she did it, but that woman is not my mother. I'm going to find out how and why."

"You're going to talk to her?"

"Yes."

"And that's why you want me to watch Julia and Charlie."

"Yes," I say. "I don't want them to be there. I don't think she would hurt me or anyone else, but I don't want to take any chances."

"And Charlie and Julia don't think she's someone else? They still don't see what you see?"

"No," I say. "I'm the only one who sees it."

"Mike," she whispers again. "That's impossible."

"I know. I've been living in the impossible for two days now. I've tried to find a logical solution to the problem. I know you think Capgras is the solution, but it's just not. There just isn't one. Not one that I've found, at least. That's what I plan on doing. Find the solution. Find my mother. Don't worry. I'll be careful."

Sarah takes the three steps for us. She wraps her arms around me. I don't hug her back at first—not because I don't want to—but because I'm an idiot. When I finally wrap my arms around her, I feel not alone in a way I haven't felt in a long, long time.

"Why did you tell me all that?" She's whispering in my ear now.

"I knew you were carrying something heavy. I could tell. And I know how hard that can be. I wanted to help you carry it. Or at least let you put it down for a while."

I am so happy with these words. I feel like I just said the perfect thing to the perfect girl.

She pulls me closer. "Thank you."

We hold each other for a moment, and then she pulls away. Wipes her face with the sleeve of her sweater again. Then she kisses me on the cheek. "We'll probably have a better kiss someday, but not today. Today isn't the day for those kinds of kisses."

"Okay," I say.

She wraps her arms around me again. Whispers in my ear. "I don't know if you're right about your mother, but leave some room in your heart for the possibility that it's her. Promise me that, at least. Please?"

"I promise," I say.

I can't tell her that there's no room in my heart for doubt. I know that woman is not my mother, and I suspect that she knows exactly where my mother is.

twenty-nine

She's right back where I saw her the first time. Standing at the stove. This time she's stirring something in a pot. Macaroni and cheese, I think.

Charlie and Julia are next door with Sarah. Playing Monopoly. Julia is teaching Sarah the real rules. No one collects $400 for landing on Go in our family.

The other mother is making dinner. She expects us home in an hour.

She didn't flip out when I arrived home ten minutes ago to get Charlie and Julia. Didn't raise holy hell, as Dad loved to say, but that was because Sarah came over to the house with me. It's hard to yell at your kids in front of other people, and especially other kids. I could tell that Sarah was looking closely at the other mother, trying to see what I could see. I was hoping and praying that she could. That it didn't have to only be me.

I thought the other mother might make me stay behind

to talk to her while Charlie and Julia left with Sarah, but she let us all leave. She plans on talking to me later about ditching school, I'm sure.

Later is now.

"Hey," I say.

She jumps and almost knocks the pot off the stove. "Jesus!" she shouts. "You scared me half to death."

She turns. As she does, I try to look at her the way Sarah was looking at me in her bedroom. I try to look inside her. I try to dissect her with my eyes. I want this to be my mother. I want this to be over. But she's not my mother. As crazy as it sounds, she's just not. She's all wrong. She looks older than my mother. More worn out. Everything about her seems slanted. Everything is just a little bit off.

People thought it was impossible to break the sound barrier, and then someone did it. This is the same thing. It seems impossible for this woman to not be my mother, but she isn't. I'm just the first one to know it.

Except for maybe her.

"Sorry," I say.

"Why aren't you playing Monopoly?" She looks down at my hands. "And why did you bring a shovel in the house?"

"I found it in the basement." I watch for a reaction. A flash of fear in her eyes. A flicker of guilt. I don't see any.

"What's it doing up here?"

"I brought it outside," I say. "I'm returning it."

"Instead of playing Monopoly?"

"I guess," I say. I'm stuck. I thought I was going to charge in here and let her have it. Let her know what I know and watch her try to deny it. I thought I was going to take the lead. But now that I'm actually here, I'm stuck. There was no practicing this conversation. It's probably never happened before in the history of the universe.

"Are you okay?" she asks. She puts down her wooden spoon, then she pulls a paper towel and begins wiping her hands with it. I look at her hands. I want them to be my mother's hands, but they just aren't.

"I'm fine," I say.

"The fishing was good?"

"What fishing?" I ask.

"You said you went fishing this afternoon."

"I didn't."

"Oh," she says. "Where'd you go?"

This is not my mother. My mother would already be yelling at me for lying about where I was today. She would be asking me questions about ditching school. I would be grounded and probably sitting in my room by now. I just wish I knew for sure if she knows that she's the other mother.

"I just rode my bike around," I say.

"Since you're here," she says, "I wanted to tell you something. I've been waiting all day to tell you."

"Me, too," I say. "I have something I've been waiting to tell you, too."

"Yeah?"

"Yeah," I say. "But you go first."

"Rachel's mother called."

"Who?"

"Rachel's mother," she says again. "Rachel Yousman's mother. She's in science class with you."

"She called here?"

"Yes," she says. She's smiling. "She wanted to talk to you."

"Rachel Yousman's mother wanted to talk to me?"

The other mother laughs. "Yes. *You.* She told me about what happened. What you did for her daughter."

"She did?"

"Why is this so hard to believe? You did something amazing, Michael. And I spoke to Mrs. Newfang, too. She called. She filled me in on the rest."

She walks across the kitchen toward me. My grip on the shovel tightens. She reaches out with her hands, and for a second, I think she might choke me, but then she's hugging me. Hugging me hard.

"I'm so proud of you," she says.

For a second, I believe it's my mother, but only because I want to. I want this to be my mother more than anything else in the world.

She is your mother, my other voice says, but I can hear Sarah's voice mixing with it. The two are working against me now. They don't understand. They can't understand.

"You did such a good thing," she says, and for a second I wonder if I can just pretend that this is my mother because this is what I have always wanted from my mother. Then the thought of my mother—trapped somewhere or worse—replaces the thought. I push her away. "Who are you?" I want to sound angrier than I do.

"What?"

"I know you're not my mother," I say.

"What are you talking about?" She's smiling, either because she doesn't know that she's the other mother or because she's pretending not to know.

"I know you're not my mother, but I don't know if you know it."

"Knock it off," she says. "That's not funny." She turns back to the stove.

"No!" I shout. My voice rattles the glasses in the drying rack. "I need to see your face! I need to know if you know!"

She turns. She's startled. Scared a little. "I said this isn't funny. Stop it."

"No, it's not funny," I say. "But I don't know what to do. I want my mother back. My real mother."

"Michael, are you okay?" She starts to walk toward me again.

I lift the shovel. I hold it out between us. "Stop! Don't come any closer."

She freezes. She sees the shovel. She's afraid now. Not just a little. Her eyes widen. She's dissecting me with her eyes. "Michael, did you hurt yourself? Hit your head? What's wrong? Put down the shovel."

"Where have you been going when you say you go to the hospital? Where do you really go?"

"What do you mean?" She looks confused and afraid. Her hands might be shaking a bit. Maybe she doesn't know that she isn't my mother. Maybe she really believes it.

"Where do you go?" I scream. More rattling of glasses.

She takes a step back and then another. "To the hospital. To my job. What is wrong with you?"

"So you know how to be a nurse?"

She throws up her hands. "This is crazy." She's shaken away her fear. Now she's angry. I can hear it in her voice. I can see it in her eyes. "Sit down. I'm getting you some water. Maybe you're dehydrated."

"Don't move," I scream. I shake the shovel.

The fear returns. Fills her right up. But it's a different kind of fear now. She's not afraid because I shouted at her. She's afraid because she knows that this is something serious. No joke. No easy fix. I still can't tell if she's afraid because I know the truth or afraid because she doesn't know who she is and is confused. Afraid I may hurt her.

"Michael, let's just sit." She motions to a chair at the table.

"Don't move," I say. "I need to figure this out."

"Do you really believe I'm not your mother?"

"You're not my mother," I say. "I know that. I just don't know what you are."

"Something's wrong. It's okay. Maybe you hit your head?"

"I didn't hit my fucking head!" I say. "I've known for two days who you are."

She takes another step back. When she speaks again, it's softer. "Who am I then?"

"Not my mother," I say. "That's all I know."

"What can I do to prove to you that I'm your mom? Ask me a question. Something only your mother would know."

"You know what she knows. I don't know how, but I know you know." I sound crazy. I can hear myself sounding crazy. I know that nothing I say makes sense. Nothing except Sarah's Capgras delusion, but it can't be that because this is not my mother.

"You're saying that I'm not your mother, but I know everything your mother knows?"

"Yes," I say. "I know it sounds crazy, but it's true. You might even think that you're my mother. I don't know."

"Honey, listen to me. Something is wrong with you. It's not your fault. Sometimes a virus can make things seem like something they're not. Or maybe you're under a lot of stress. Whatever it is, I'm not going to hurt you. Put down the shovel and we'll fix this. I promise."

I almost do it. I almost put the shovel down. She nearly has me. But then I look into her eyes and know the truth. "I need to know if you know where my mother is. You need to tell me."

She takes a small step forward. Maybe she's hoping that I don't notice, but I do. "Your mother is standing right here in front of you. Let me prove it."

"You can't."

"Your name is Michael Patrick Parsons. You were born on March seventeenth just before midnight. That's why your middle name is Patrick. It was going to be Bartholomew, but I talked your father out of it at the last minute thanks to your St. Patrick's Day birthday. Your favorite food is chili from a can. Your favorite baseball team is the Rangers because you liked Alex Rodriguez before he got traded to the Yankees and turned out to be a steroid user. You hate him now but still love the Rangers, though honestly, you don't care all that much about baseball. You pretend to love it because your sister loves it. Your brother Charlie makes you crazy, but you would run through fire for him. You love your sister more than any brother ever has loved a sister, and I believe that with all my heart. You loved your father so much. You loved watching him build things in the garage. You loved getting grease on your hands so you would look just like him. I know you, Michael. I'm your mother, and you are my son."

This is not my mother. She thinks these words will convince me, but my mother doesn't say things like this. She never has. But I love them just the same. They are words I wish I could hear from my mom. Words I've wanted to hear for a long time.

"Do you believe me?" she asks.

"No." Then I have an idea. *The* idea. "Tell me how Dad died."

"What?" She's flustered. I can see it. It's like a neon sign.

"Tell me how he died."

"He had a heart attack in the garage. He'd been working so many—"

"No," I shout. "Tell me the truth."

She wavers. It's the first time she doesn't know the answer. She's nervous. She knows that she's the other mother.

"He had a heart attack," she repeats.

I take a step forward. Still holding the shovel out in front of me. She's done something with my mother. I know it. "My father didn't have a heart attack. Tell me how he died. Tell me the truth. If you're my mother, you'd know the truth."

Tears. Tears are spilling out of her eyes. Her hands fly up and cover her mouth. She's shaking. Her hands. Her whole body.

"Tell me the truth," I repeat.

"Oh, Michael," she says, sobbing. "I'm so sorry."

"No. Tell me. If you're really my mother, tell me. My real mother knows."

She takes another step toward me. I push the shovel out,

holding it with both hands. I almost hit her with it. "Stay back. If you're my mother, you'd know."

A river of tears pour from her eyes. Her lips are quivering. Her hands are shaking. "Michael," she says. "I'm so sorry."

"Tell me!"

"He killed himself, Michael. He closed all the doors and windows in the garage and turned on his car. Then he went to sleep." Then there's silence. The words seem to take up the whole room. They might be the heaviest words that anyone has ever had to say. "I'm so sorry," she says again. "So sorry, honey."

She's crying now. Real crying.

I am, too.

"I should've told you," she says. "This is my fault. You're okay. This is my fault. I'm so sorry, honey. Please . . . put the shovel down. This isn't your fault."

I look at her. I can't believe that someone could say all this to me and cry all these tears for me and not be my mother, but I still can't see her. I look so hard. I want to see my mother, but all I see is the other mother.

"No," I say. "You're not her. You might think you are, but you're not."

"Honey, please. This isn't your fault. You've done nothing wrong. I should've told you. Please, honey."

I look again. I want this woman to be my mother. I want this older, tired version of my mother to be real. The one who knows me like my mother has never known me. The one who said she still misses Dad even though she married Glen. The one who worried about where I was today when

I ditched school. The one who was proud of me for what I did for Rachel. I want the tears rolling from the eyes of this woman to be my mother's tears. I look again. I look through my own teary eyes. I still can't see her. I want to see her so badly now.

"How did you know?" she asks. "About Dad?"

I shake my head. I can't speak.

"Did you overhear something? Did someone tell you?"

I shake my head again.

"I'm so sorry, honey. I shouldn't have hidden it from you. But I thought it was better that you didn't know the truth."

I don't know what to do. I'm stuck in between two places. I know this person is not my mother. I know it as much as I've ever known anything in my life. But I want her to be my mother. She's like a better version of my mother. The mother I've always wanted.

But I can't just abandon my mom. I can't allow her to be replaced by this other mother. She can cry a million tears, but she's still not who she's pretending to be. Or who she believes she is.

"Where is my mother?" I demand. I steel myself. I make my words like arrows. "I need to know."

"Honey, please listen to me."

"No. I want my mother back. I need to know where she is. Tell me."

I don't want to hurt her. I don't think I can. Hitting her with this shovel is impossible, but I need her to tell me the truth. I take a step forward. I'll scare her. I'll make her think that I'm going to hurt her. I'll make her tell me the truth. I raise the shovel to my shoulders. I take a step forward. "Tell me where my mother is!"

"Mike."

This new voice isn't angry or frightened. It isn't rushed or loud and panicked. It's calm. Nonchalant. It's as if we are still sitting in her bedroom, talking about nothing important.

I turn. She's standing in the doorway to the kitchen. She's smiling.

"Sarah? Why are you here?"

"Mike," she says again, as calmly as the first time.

"I wasn't going to do anything," I tell her. "I was just going to scare her. I need her to tell me where my mother is."

"Mike," she says a third time, just as soft and casual as the last two. She's the only one who uses that name, and for some reason, it makes me feel so close to her. It makes me feel connected to her. "She's your mother."

"She's not," I say. I try to explain but she stops me before I can speak.

"It's your mom, Mike. It's not your fault."

"She's not my mom," I say. "I can see it."

"Michael," the other mother says. She's behind me now. She's closed the gap between us while I was talking to Sarah. Her hand reaches out. She doesn't grab for the shovel. She reaches for my forearm. She squeezes it. Holds on to it. "It's me, honey. I swear."

I look over my shoulder at the other mother. I look so hard. "You're not. I still don't see my mother."

"I know," Sarah says. "But it's not your fault."

I turn and face the other mother. I can't imagine how

this woman could be my mother. She looks nothing like my mother. She acts nothing like my mother.

"It's me, Michael. I swear."

I want it to be her. I want this impossible mother to be my mother. I want this tired version of my mother, with all the right words, who seems to love me more than my mother ever has, to be my mother. I want this to be over. I want my mother back. I just can't see my mother in this mother.

"You should tell her," Sarah says. "Tell her everything you told me."

"I already know," the other mother says. "This is my fault, Michael. I should've told you the truth."

"The note?" Sarah asks. "You told her about the note?"

"What note?" the other mother asks.

I want to tell Sarah that the note is not for the other mother. It's for my real mother. This is not my mother. But it's like she sees this coming.

"It's okay, Mike. You should show her."

"She's not my mother," I say.

"I am," the other mother says.

"She is," Sarah says. "Just show her the note. Nothing bad can come of it."

"I can't," I say.

"You can," she says. "I'll stay right here with you. I won't leave. I promise."

"No." But I've lost some of my fight. Most of it. I can feel it draining away. I'm pleading now. Begging to be believed.

"Yes," Sarah whispers. "Show her."

"Okay," I say. I agree because it's Sarah. The other mother might still try to hurt me, but Sarah never would.

She might be wrong, but she means right. I lean the shovel against the counter. Walk upstairs. I can barely feel my feet on the floor. I lift my mattress. The yellow envelope is there, just as it's been for almost two years.

She's going to hate me. If she's my mother, she will hate me for hiding this for so long. Maybe that can be my test. If she hates me, she's my mother.

Sarah and the other mother are sitting at the table when I walk back into the kitchen. The shovel is still leaning against the counter. I thought they might move it while I was gone. Hide it. They didn't. They're not afraid of me.

Sarah doesn't think I'm completely crazy.

Sarah's phone is in the other mother's hands. She's reading the screen. I know what she's reading.

She looks up. "Michael. This isn't your fault. It's going to be okay."

She's about to say something else when Sarah reaches out and grabs the other mother's forearm. She squeezes it. "Wait," she says. Sarah's suddenly the oldest person in the room.

I sit down opposite the other mother. I place the envelope on the table and slide it over. Her name is written on the front in my father's handwriting.

Pauline

She takes it in her hands. She holds it like it's fragile. Like a baby bird with broken wings. I guess it's all those things and more. "What is this?"

I look to Sarah first, and then back to the other mother. "I found it in the garage. A couple weeks after Dad died."

It takes her just a second to understand. "Oh, Michael," she says. "You've been holding it for all this time?"

"I thought you thought he had a heart attack," I say. "I didn't want you to know."

"Oh my God." She begins to cry.

"I'm sorry," I say.

"Shush," she says between sobs.

"You're not mad?"

"Mad?" she says. She wipes away tears with her sleeve. She doesn't want them to land on the envelope. She knows how precious it is. "You were trying to protect me. The same way I was trying to protect you. Of course I'm not mad."

I look at her so hard. I want to see my mother so badly.

"Maybe you should read it," Sarah says.

"Now?" the other mother asks.

"Mike has been carrying it for a long time," she says. "Maybe it would be better if he didn't have to carry it alone anymore."

I hear my own words in Sarah's voice. Echoing back to me what I have always needed. I don't think I was in love with Sarah Flaherty before this moment. Not real love. I don't think I knew real love like this before now. I didn't understand it.

Now I do.

I love Sarah Flaherty.

"Okay," the other mother says. "I'll read." She opens the envelope and removes a sheet of white-lined paper that I have held in my hands hundreds of times. She looks at the page at first, not reading it but just taking in the hand-writing. The signature. The smudges. She takes a deep breath. I know how she feels. I remember looking at it for the first time and thinking that these were my father's final words. My last chance to hear his voice. She is experiencing that now.

I watch her read. I don't need to see the paper. I know the words by heart.

Pauline,

I will always love you.

I will always love Michael and Charlie and Julia. Please tell them. Tell them as often as your heart can bear it.

This has nothing to do with you. This has been something inside me for a long, long time. I can't explain it. I wish I could. Some people weren't made for this world. I have always felt this way. You lifted me to a place I never dreamed possible. You gave me love beyond measure. You gave me three beautiful children. You do not deserve this. You deserve happiness. I want you to find it. Find someone more worthy than me of your love.

I will not ask you to forgive me. What I have done is unforgivable. I know. Please know that I fought for you and the kids. I truly did.

I lost.

This doesn't mean I didn't love you and will love you and my children forever.

Your loving husband,
Vin

She is sobbing by the time she has finished the letter. Tears like rivers pour from her brown eyes. There is something else, too. She seems . . . relaxed. It's like she's taken a breath. I can see it in her face. Her eyes. Her shoulders. It's like she's been holding her breath since the day he died, and at last, she has let it out. She has exhaled at last.

I know this feeling. I took one of those breaths earlier today. I'm taking one again now. The note in the yellow envelope is no longer hidden underneath my mattress. The words are no longer hidden away in my mind. She knows. She carries the burden, too. We carry it together.

In fact, it's no longer a burden. It's just my father's words. His last words. The words I will cling to for the rest of my life when I wonder if he loved me.

Then I know. My father's love carries me across some unseen chasm.

This is my mother.

I can't see her. When I look at her face, her hands, her eyes, her neck, I still see the other mother. I hear the other mother in her sobs. Everything about her is the other mother.

But this is my mother. My eyes and ears say one thing. They scream it. Nothing about this woman is my mother. But my heart says something else. My heart says that her tears and sobs and saddest smile I have ever seen can only be my mother. Everything tells me that this is not my mother, but it's my heart that I will listen to until the rest of me catches up.

"I can't see you," I say, stifling sobs of my own. "I don't see my mother. I wish I did, but I don't. I can't. But I believe you. It's you. Isn't it? It's you, Mom?"

"It's always been me," she says. "I'll never leave you."

I have found my mother. My impossible mother. The

mother I have always wanted. The mother I have needed more than I ever knew. She was here all along.

She turns to Sarah. "Thank you."

"It wasn't me," she says. "It was Mike. He had a hell of a day. He saved me today, too."

I smile. It was Sarah who saved me. Saved me in so many ways.

She turns to me—this other mother who I know is my mom. It's strange. It's like I'm seeing her with fresh eyes. Eyes that are free of all the anger and disappointment of the past. She isn't the mother I've always wanted, but she's also not the mother who I have resented for all these years either. These fresh eyes see my mother. Perfect and imperfect and all mine.

She's *my mother*. The mother who I have been seeking— for the last two days and for all my life. She's the mother who I thought I had lost forever and the one who I found when I needed her most.

My mother is home. She's always been here. I just needed to open my heart.

acknowledgments

Many thanks to the following people for making this book possible:

My wife, Elysha, who has always been my ideal reader, even when she's not reading on a timely basis.

My in-laws, Barbara and Gerry Green, for continuing to fill my life with their enthusiasm, excitement, and unsolicited counsel. About once a month, Gerry will say, "Tell me something exciting, Matt! Give me some news!" He has no idea how long I have waited for someone to ask me a question like that.

Matthew Shepard, who remains my first reader and the person who always sees what others do not.

Alison Tulett, my copy editor, who has undoubtedly spared me many literary embarrassments.

Becca Allen, the proofreader of the final text of this book. As a perfectionist, even the smallest error makes me lose my mind. Knowing that a professional perfectionist read every line of this book allows me to sleep well at night.

Lastly, thanks to Taryn Fagerness, my agent, friend, and partner in this creative life. She found me in the slush pile years ago and changed my life forever. She makes my sentences better, my stories better, and as a result, my life better. It's not often that another human being can make your dreams come true, but she did, and I am forever thankful.